(

MW01673923

Rambles Roundabout and Poems

Anatiposi

George De Wilde

Rambles Roundabout and Poems

Reprint of the original, first published in 1872.

1st Edition 2023 | ISBN: 978-3-38213-332-0

Anatiposi Verlag is an imprint of Outlook Verlagsgesellschaft mbH.

Verlag (Publisher): Outlook Verlag GmbH, Zeilweg 44, 60439 Frankfurt, Deutschland
Vertretungsberechtigt (Authorized to represent): E. Roepke, Zeilweg 44, 60439 Frankfurt, Deutschland
Druck (Print): Books on Demand GmbH, In de Tarpen 42, 22848 Norderstedt, Deutschland

RAMBLES ROUNDABOUT

AND

POEMS.

BY THE LATE

GEORGE JAMES DE WILDE,

EDITOR OF THE NORTHAMPTON MERCURY.

EDITED BY EDWARD DICEY.

Northampton:

PRINTED AND PUBLISHED BY DICEY & Co., MERCURY OFFICE, PARADE.

1872.

CONTENTS.

	Page.
"IN MEMORIAM" ...	iii.—vii.
BLISWORTH ...	1
FAREWELL TO SUMMER ...	7
KINGSTHORPE ...	9
BYEWAYS AND HIGHWAYS ...	21
DODFORD ...	22
LINES FOR THE FLY-LEAF OF A DIARY ...	29
ABOUT JOHN CLARE ...	30
BY THE CANAL ...	50
HOLDENBY ...	52
SONGS BY THE WAYSIDE ...	66
GAYTON ...	67
SIMON, THE PIPING CROW ...	74
ABINGTON ...	76
THE MONKS OF YORE: A BALLAD ...	88
ROTHERSTHORPE ...	90
AUTUMN IN KENT ...	95
COTTERSTOCK ...	97
BATH: EVENING FROM CLEVELAND BRIDGE ...	112
TOWCESTER ...	113
THE OLD MAN AND THE CONQUEROR (From Béranger)	129
GREEN'S NORTON ...	131
EYDON HALL ...	137
WELLINGBOROUGH ...	138
THE ADVENT OF SPRING ...	152
GREAT DODDINGTON ...	153
A LEGEND OF MONT DU CHAT ...	159

	Page.
WESTON FAVELL ...	163
THE WATER MILL ...	170
LAMPORT ...	171
THE TUN UNVISITED ...	177
NEWPORT PAGNELL...	181
TO H. P. P. ...	191
WEEDON BECK ...	193
A SUDDEN WINTER ...	197
BARNWELL ST. ANDREWS & BARNWELL ALL SAINTS (a fragment)	199
THE BURIAL PLACE OF BEETHOVEN ...	203
NORTHAMPTON—BRIDGE STREET ...	206
NOVEMBER ...	215
NORTHAMPTON—THE DRAPERY ...	216
A POET'S HOME ...	221
NORTHAMPTON—THE MAYORHOLD AND HORSEMARKET ...	223
A BALLAD ...	228
NORTHAMPTON—ST. THOMAS'S HOSPITAL...	229
THE HAVEN...	234
NORTHAMPTON A HUNDRED YEARS AGO ...	236
THE VISION OF DRY BONES ...	251
CANON'S ASHBY ...	253
CARISBROOK ...	254

"In Memoriam."

IF, according to the old proverb, those nations are the happiest which have no history, I think it may be stated with even greater truth that those lives are happiest whose records are least full of incidents. Each man seeks his own happiness after his own fashion. But to me, from such observation as I have made, it does not seem that to have been an actor in great events; to have experienced many vicissitudes of fortune; to have known many men and many cities, adds much to the sum of human happiness. Be this as it may, there were few lives more devoid of incident; more uneventful; more even in the tenor of their way, than that of the author of these "Rambles Roundabout." Yet, looking back upon long years of intimate acquaintance and constant intercourse, I may say that I have never known any one to whom the epithet "Happy" might be more truly given. Such, I deem, must have been the impression left on the minds of all who knew him; and this record, brief and meagre as it necessarily is, would yet be wanting in its first duty, should it fail to convey—if the metaphor may be pardoned me—a certain reflection of the sunniness of a life so barren of events, so placid in its outward course.

George James De Wilde was born in London in the year 1804. His family were of Dutch origin, his grandfather having emigrated from Holland during the troubles in the close of the last century. His father was a painter of considerable reputation in his own line. The stage in the reign of George III. and

George IV. occupied a very different position from what it does now. The portraiture of favourite actors in popular pieces formed an important department of the pictorial trade; and of this department Mr. De Wilde's father had an almost complete monopoly. In the dramatic gallery of the Garrick Club a very large portion of the paintings bear the signature of De Wilde. The pursuit, howéver, of a theatrical portrait painter was neither very sure nor very lucrative; nor was the society, into which the artist was inevitably thrown, one exactly calculated to develope the qualities required for family life. Mr. De Wilde was not much given to talk about his early years; indeed, I never knew any one less prone to make himself the subject of his own conversation. But I fancy his childhood and youth were chequered by the vicissitudes often accompanying the lives of men who bring up families on uncertain and irregular incomes. He has told me that as a boy he passed his time mainly behind the scenes of theatres; and it is possible he acquired there the strong artistic tastes which characterised him afterwards. Of regular classical schooling he could have had but little, but his love for letters—a love developed early, and which grew with each succeeding year—more than supplied the place of regular training. Mr. De Wilde was originally destined to be an artist; and his sketches and drawings give proof of a natural talent, which with more culture might have attained eminence. But somehow, like many men, with whom art is rather a taste than a ruling passion, Mr. De Wilde soon drifted into the by-paths of letters. With Leigh Hunt and his family, with the Cowden Clarkes, and other literary personages of note, Mr. De Wilde formed intimate acquaintance during the brief period of his life in London as a young man. About the time, however, of his coming of age, he obtained temporary employment in the Colonial Office. While there he attracted the notice of the late Sir James Stephen, then Assistant-Secretary for the Colonies, and was employed by him as amanuensis, after his engagement with the Colonial Office had come to a close.

In 1825, Mr. De Wilde married Mary Caroline Butterworth, and in 1830 he was recommended by Sir James Stephen to his brother, in-law, the late proprietor of this journal, for the Editorship of the *Northampton Mercury*, which was then vacant. For upwards of forty years, indeed to the very day of his death, Mr. De Wilde retained the post in question. Of his merits as Editor, it is not possible for the present writer to speak without touching upon personal considerations, nor can I do more than allude in passing to the long, close, and unbroken friendship which subsisted between the Editor and the Proprietors of the *Mercury*. But of his relations with the outer world I can speak more freely. He came here a very young man. He died at a ripe, though not an advanced age, and during forty and odd years he never wrote or said an unkind word, never lost a friend or made an enemy, never asked a favour or refused a service. His life here was of the quietest and most regular. With the exception of short holiday rambles in the summer, he never quitted Northampton for any time till the approach of his last illness. Except when he was engaged in editorial duties, he was seldom away from the *Mercury* office; and the moments not occupied by the cares of an engrossing business were spent in reading and study. During the intervals of leisure, he learnt French very thoroughly; he made himself a good Italian and Latin scholar; he attained to considerable proficiency as an antiquarian; while the amount of book lore he acquired in odd hours was something wonderful. He also contributed many papers to the *Gentleman's Magazine*, to *Notes and Queries*, the *Mirror*, and the *Casket*, chiefly under the *noms de plume* of Sylvan Southgate, Camden Somers, and Vandyke Brown. Indeed, if Mr. De Wilde could have fashioned out his life to please himself, he would have spent it, I fancy, amidst the books he loved so dearly. Yet there was about him nothing of the selfishness of the bookworm. Though not a man fond of public life, he was always ready to take part in any undertaking which he regarded as a public duty. As one of the chief promoters of the Mechanics' Institute in this town, and the Northampton Museum, and as a Governor of the General Infirmary, he did no small service to the town in which his lot was thrown, and which he had learnt to regard as his home.

So the years went by. The hair that had been full and brown

when he came first to Northampton became spare and gray, the step less active, the eye less bright than of old. But to the very last he preserved a freshness of look which most men lose before full manhood, and which was strangely characteristic of the man. There was something of "the boy in heart" about him. The cheerfulness of childhood, the true child-like appreciation of simple enjoyments, the child's faith in human nature, remained with him unchecked, in spite of the wear and tear, the sorrows, cares, anxieties, and disappointments of a busy life. His wife died in 1840, leaving him a widower with five children, the youngest of whom survived its birth but a few months. In 1845 he married Miss Packer, by whom he leaves one daughter. His family relations were regularly happy and affectionate, and though his children by his first marriage made homes of their own and went out to seek their fortunes away from Northampton, there was none of that separation which so often parts parents and grown-up sons and daughters. His children were the companions he loved best, and his society was the one most welcome to them.

A man of singularly temperate and regular, though not active habits, Mr. De Wilde enjoyed extremely good health till within a few months of his death. Towards the middle of last summer alarming symptoms set in, of whose existence he had himself been some time aware, but of which, according to his natural wont always to think of others before himself, he had made no mention. It was thought that rest from work was all that was required to remove the malady, and, for the first time in his life, he went away from Northampton, meaning to be absent for some weeks. The weeks went by, and his strength diminished gradually, while reluctance to remain away from his post seemed to tell upon his mind. He came back to Northampton after some two months' absence, sank rapidly, and died somewhat suddenly upon the 16th of last September. His last illness was a lingering and painful one; and to a man of singularly active mind, whose mental powers remained unimpaired to the close, it was rendered exceptionally harassing from the peculiar features of the malady. Yet his sweetness of disposition, his serenity of temper, never varied: his reluctance to let others do the work which was his by rights, increased, if that were possible, with his failing strength. Within a very few hours of his death he corrected the proof-sheets of the forthcoming number of the *Mercury*, and then went into a sleep from which he never woke.

Such is the scant outline of a life as worthy, blameless, and upright as, I think, has often been led in this world of ours. No human being, to the best of my belief, was ever the worse for having known George James De Wilde: there were few who were not better for the knowledge, and than this I know of no higher—and I can add—no truer epitaph.

These "Rambles Roundabout" were not written for publication as a complete work. They were published in the *Mercury*, at various intervals, over a period of many years; and the poems inserted between them are selected from the author's contributions to different periodicals. These "Rambles" must therefore be taken, not so much as a work representing the writer's powers, but rather as a memorial offered to those who knew him, and would gladly preserve some record of his memory.

EDWARD DICEY.

Mercury Office, Northampton,
Dec. 30th, 1871.

RAMBLES ROUNDABOUT.

Blisworth.

"Blisworth, Northampton, Peterborough—change here!"

THE traveller by the night mail starts from his uneasy nap as the cry of the railway porter runs along the lengthy train; and, peering out into the night, forms his idea of Blisworth as of a long enclosed platform, with a refreshment room at one end and bowery tea gardens on the other, with, perhaps, twinkling lights in the shrubberies, and the lingering sounds of music,

"And ladies' laughter coming through the shade."

In the old coaching days, a town or a village and its name were associated together; now you may hear the name of a place duly announced hundreds of times, yet never get an inkling of the place itself. Your mail coach penetrated the very heart of a town; you were familiar with its Guildhall, its market-place, its church, and its chief inn, though you never left your seat on the box. The mail train only skirts the places at which it professes to stop; the town itself may be a mile or two off, and even where you touch upon it the chances are that you are introduced only to its most squalid suburb. Great are the advantages of railways, but the advantage of seeing towns as you travel is not one of them. You run *by* them, not *through* them, and to read as you run is out of the question.

Blisworth is a good mile from the station. The walk thither by the canal side in the early morning is delightful, though the introduction of steam in the canal boats, and the repair of the towing path with cinders and clinkers, have not improved it. On the left the view is bounded by the railway embankment, covered with trees; on the right meadows slope to the water's edge; here and there a fringe of willows, reflected in the stream, tempts the sketcher to linger. Southward the church tower, with the lofty elms about, peopled in the early spring with busy rooks, makes a picturesque distance. As you approach the Blisworth Bridge, a red-brick wharf, toned with grey and yellow lichens, repeating in the water its rich and glowing tints, can be passed unheeded by nobody who appreciates colour. It is a remarkable instance of the way in which nature sets about correcting the unpicturesque works of man. Time, destroyer though he be, is a great artist, and converts the most unlovely forms into objects that arrest the passer-by, and compel his admiration. Blisworth itself looks like a place that has been more important than it now affects to be. It abounds in sixteenth and seventeenth century houses, substantially built of stone, with good Tudor windows, stone mullioned and square hooded. Mr. Gibbs's house is a good specimen, and retains, though somewhat mutilated in the heading, the original doorway. Some of the buildings present striking instances of the use of lines of dark coloured stone. Many houses, now occupied as cottages, were obviously built for tenants of a much higher class. One bears the date 1616; another 1631. A stone in a building, more decidedly of the cottage character, near the blacksmith's, is inscribed—NGIG 1613. The dead wall in the centre of the village, on the southern side of the highway, has the appearance of having been at some time an extensive building; it bears traces of doors and windows, which have been walled up, and the stone work is very substantial and well finished. Bridges makes no allusion to it. He speaks, indeed, of the Manor House near the church, and says, "The old seat which stood there was formerly the residence of the family of Wake. Here was antiently a park and a warren." The wall in question can scarcely be said to be near the church in the strict sense of the word, but "near" is a vague word, and part of the appurtenant buildings may have stood here.

The church, dedicated to St. John the Baptist, stands towards the western end of the village; it consists of a western tower, battlemented; nave, north and south aisles, and chancel. Within the last few years it has been restored, and is in substantial condition. The old high, square pews, in which our forefathers loved modestly to screen themselves from the curiosity of their neighbours, and upon the possession of which it is certain that very much dignity was supposed to depend, have given way to uniform low seats; the tower arch, which used to be blocked up by a gallery, has been opened; and the pillars of the nave have been cleaned of their many coats of paint. The interior presents no remains of an antiquity greater than the Decorated Period, unless we are to accept the font, a perfectly plain bowl on a bowl reversed, as Norman. The chancel is of ample dimensions, and has a handsome Perpendicular screen, and stalls and panelling of the same date. A small piscina remains in the south wall. Just without the chancel are the doorway and opening above to the Rood-loft. A stained window in the chancel represents the raising of Jairus' daughter, in memory of the son of the rector, the Rev. William Barry. In the south aisle is a canopy of rather peculiar form, over a founder's tomb, and nearly in front is a fine altar tomb, which Bridges thinks may have formerly stood beneath the arch. But they evidently belong to distinct periods, and we see no reason to suppose that the tomb has been removed from its original site. It is to the memory of Roger Wake; the sides are of the freestone of the neighbourhood, the upper slab of marble, into which are let several brasses. One of these represents a marble figure in complete armour with the hands in the attitude of prayer; another, a female figure in a similar attitude: beneath the former are three figures of children, and beneath the latter four similar figures. At each corner of the slab is a shield charged with the arms of Wake and Catesby, and similar shields connected with the Wake knot occur on the North front and West end of the monument. There appear to have been sculptures of a similar kind at the East end, but the work is too much defaced to be intelligible. Another brass of an ornamental form is missing from the centre of the upper part of the slab. A border of brass encloses the whole, part of which is missing, in part since Bridges' time. What remains is inscribed as follows:—"Here lyeth Roger Wake, Esquyer, lorde of Blysworth, in the counte of . . . . which Roger decessyd the xvith day of Marche, the yere of our Lorde God M.CCCCCIII., on whose soule jhu have mcy." Bridges partly supplies the gap with the words, after "counte of"—"Northampton, and Elizabeth, his." It is singular that the date of the wife's death is not given; nor is any mention made of the children; Bridges, in copying the legend, has given only four C's, making an error of a hundred years, and antedating the period of Roger Wake's death 1403 instead of 1503. This Roger Wake was descended from Baldwin Lord Wake, who derived the manor and advowson of Blisworth from William de Briwere, who received them as a grant from King John. He was a man of mark. Having married Elizabeth, the daughter of Sir William Catesby, of Ashby St. Ledgers, the favourite of Richard III., he espoused the cause of that monarch, with whose fortunes his own also succumbed. After the battle of Bosworth Field his lands became forfeited to the Crown, and in the third year of Henry VII. the manor of Blisworth was granted to Sir James Blounte. His attainder, however, was reversed in the same reign, and he was reinstated in his possessions, including Blisworth, where he founded a Free-school. His son, Thomas Wake, sold the manor to Sir Richard Knightley, of Fawsley, whose descendant, Sir Edmund Knightley, exchanged it for the manor of Badby and certain other of the dissolved Abbey Lands. It was then annexed to the Honour of Grafton, and his Grace the Duke of Grafton is its present possessor.

In the tower hangs a wooden tablet, recording an exploit of some of the forefathers of the village, when Blisworth seems to have cultivated bell-ringing:—"To the memory of the following ringers, John Gudgeon, Wm. Peach, Benjamin Goode, Thomas Carter, and Thomas Garner, Who on ye 31st December, 1790, Did Ring 45.6 scores in 3 hours and 40 minutes, which amounts to 5,000 changes. Written by R. Dunckly, clerk, May 12, 1791." Taking this inscription in its literal sense, one would be led to understand that those gentlemen all died of their exertions between December and May. We hope that was not so, and that the tablet was put up in memory of the exploit, not of the actors in it. On the north side of the chancel there is a confessional window; and in the churchyard, which is ascended from the road by a flight of steps, are the steps of a cross now carrying a sun-dial.

Blisworth, irregular, straggling, and covering a considerable area, is a pleasant and picturesque village, picturesque and pleasant in its very irregularity. Gardens and trees intervene between the houses; huge elder trees, roses in masses, brilliant tiger lilies, profuse wall-flowers, delight the eye, and fill the air with odour. Blisworth seems to have a special enjoyment in flowers. On the Stoke Bruerne turn Mr. Westley makes the entrance to his steam mills perfectly dazzling with geraniums and petunias, and other brilliant plants. A noble row of elms borders the churchyard, and the rectory is fairly hidden in trees. Almost from any point in the village, an artist may make a picture. At the North-East turn there is the tree which was once the indispensable feature in the scenery of our ancestral villages:

> "How often have I blest the coming day,
> When toil remitting lent its turn to play,
> And all the village train, from labour free,
> Led up their sports beneath the spreading tree."

Blisworth lies high, and a little distance North of this point you look down upon the railroad. Descending towards it, the arch which connects the embankment over the road has a noble appearance—noble in its severe simplicity and stately proportions. We have already noticed the pleasant effect of the plantations of firs which adorn the slopes of the embankment.

To write of Blisworth, and to say nothing about Blisworth Gardens, would be almost like playing Hamlet and leaving out the character of the Prince of Denmark. It is a pity that the access to them from the station is not easier, or rather that it is not more obvious, for it is really easy enough. The weary half-hour which one often has to spend oscillating up and down the platform would pass lightly enough if one might pass it instead, in wandering about those really charming grounds, brilliant with flowers, and refreshing with greenest turf and shady bowers. People are too apt, we suspect, to think of them only on those days when they are gay with groups of merry company, and to ignore the quiet charm of them at ordinary times, when they are comparatively deserted. But a pleasanter place to saunter in with a book at noon-day, or when you desire a "nest for evening weariness," you will not easily find. Among its other attractions, it has a lawn so beautifully embanked and so smooth shaven, that it seems impossible not to play at bowls there, or croquet, or archery, or any other of those good out-of-door games which ought to be encouraged for the sake of the ladies, and the health we desire them to possess.

Farewell to Summer.

ALAS, the pleasant time is going,
The pleasant summer time:
Farewell to noontides bright and glowing,
Sweet nights and balmiest prime.

Farewell, sweet time of meeting twilights
Of never ceasing song;
From morning's lark to night's lone warbler,
Singing all night long.

Farewell to sweet walks by the river
At sunny eventide;
Farewell to gay barks homeward going,
Faint through the gloom descried.

Farewell to serenades by moonlight;
To white hands putting by
The jasmine and the clustering roses,
Farewell the answering sigh.

Farewell when least the spirit waileth
The bonds that hold it in;
Farewell the time when least the vessel
Tainteth the wine within.

The last brown sheaf is cut and garner'd,
The gleaner's work is done;
And many a cloud of stormy purple
Barreth the setting sun.

Fierce winds are in the forest stirring;
Sear leaves come eddying down;
And from the eaves and from the river
The busy martlet's flown.

Ah! happy bird! that chasest summer
Where-e'er her footsteps flee,
Nor ever of the frozen winter
Knowest the misery.

Farewell, farewell, beloved season,
Till thou com'st back again
The memory of thy joyous sunshine
Shall round our hearths remain.

Sweet verse shall aid our happy dreamings,
And music, sweeter still:
And painting, with its deathless splendours
The outlined canvas fill.

Farewell, the pleasant time is going,
The pleasant summer time;
Farewell to noontides bright and glowing,
Sweet nights and balmiest prime.

Kingsthorpe.

THIRTY years ago somebody writing in Hone's Year Book pronounced Kingsthorpe one of the prettiest villages about Northampton, and he describes the way thither "by a rural route." Thirty years have wrought strange alteration, and it may be not unamusing to accompany that rural rambler of a remote period, and contrast the way to Kingsthorpe of 1831 with the way of 1863. The world has moved forward since then with mighty strides, and Northampton has moved with it, not *pari passu* perhaps, but still forward. It has put out a long arm northwards, and almost shakes hands with the pretty village beyond. In another thirty years it will probably have absorbed it. Thirty years ago Leicester Terrace (then unfinished) was the "*ultima Thule*" of Northampton. Beyond those three or four houses there was not a building, with the exception of the Roman Catholic Chapel and the Bishop's House, till just south of the toll-gate at Kingsthorpe; and these were considered so remote from the town that there was considerable difficulty in getting them tenanted. Beyond "The Bull," indeed, at North End, you had bidden adieu to the town, and were fairly in the country. St. Andrew's Terrace was not built, nor the streets westward of it; Royal Terrace was of nothing like its present extent, and there was a considerable interval between the last house and the Barracks. Beyond the Barracks again there was another interval of hedge and field before you came to Leicester Terrace. On the east side there were a few houses, and only a few, with like intervals of 'hedge-row and garden ground. On that side the last house northward was the pretty "Bell-

Alliance Cottage," at the corner of the Race-course, scarcely a cottage ornée, and conspicuous chiefly by its row of noble poplars. Just beyond the last house in Leicester Terrace there was a gate opening into a field, where the corn-crake might be heard on a summer's evening. Pushing open this gate, the rambler in Hone's book followed a path which took him into "Semilong" (he was out for a rural stroll, and so avoided the direct way along the road), which he describes as delightfully pleasant and picturesque. When he came again into the London road he probably met one of the Northern stage-coaches to London. Proceeding along the road only a few yards, he crossed a low stile on the left into a path running parallel with the road across a field. This path has been destroyed within the last twenty years; not without a fight for it on the part of the pedestrian public, who regularly demolished the obstructions at the stiles. They were defeated at last when the field became a brickyard. You might still assert your right to get over the stile, but you did it at the risk of being drowned or smothered in a clay-pit. This path led to another stile, crossing which you entered the park of Kingsthorpe House, and kept a path close to the road, but separated from it by a row of noble trees, still the pride of the Kingsthorpe road. A relic of this path still exists, in a forlorn and dilapidated condition, at its northern extremity. Here our rambler emerged again into the high road by the toll-gate, which was new then, and disconcerted his eye. It sinned against the picturesque cluster of primitive-looking cottages of stone and thatch, probably, he says, constructed out of the ruins of an hospital founded there about 1200. His sense of the proprieties would receive a severer shock if he were to wander this way now, and see the row of modern brick houses which have pushed his rural cottages and the ruins from their stools. The toll-gate, with the roses climbing up it, is now the more picturesque object of the two.

Strange that our friend in the "Year Book" should have omitted all mention of the two attractive inns which at that time met his view when he got through the toll gate. That unfortunate structure appears to have so disconcerted him that he hastened out of its presence as quickly as possible, and, turning down the lane to the left, sought the village proper, clustering about the church out of the way of toll gates, and secluded from stage-coaches. We shall take leave, however, to pause here awhile and ask the reader to enjoy with us a pleasant prospect—pleasant still, though one of the inns (The White Horse) is an inn no longer. When the coaches went off the road, it died, we suppose, of insufficient patronage, though one might have thought that the increasing population of Northampton would have kept alive so agreeable a place of summer resort; for it had very special attractions. Its situation in the wide open space facing the west, with a prospect of trees and undulating fields and rustic roofs in the distance; its ample grounds fenced in with noble trees; and its beautiful bowling-green ought, one would have thought, to have saved it. Then there was a porch, and the wide road, with the grassy plot between, made it possible and pleasant to have a cheesecake (it had a reputation for cheesecakes) and a glass of amber home-brewed, on a little round table outside, in the evening sunshine. It had had its day. Bowls was a courtly game once, and the White Horse was no doubt the aristocratic Inn, frequented by the rank, the fashion, and the beauty of the neighbourhood. For beauty in the gallant days of the second Charles played at bowls as well as the manly sex. Pepys, speaking of White-Hall Gardens, says—"Where lords and ladies are now at bowles, in brave condition." The White Horse is at least as old as the time of Charles II., and we may be sure that its Bowling Green presented a brilliant spectacle in the days when the dress of the gallants was as showy as the costume of the ladies. Silks, satins, ribbons of all gorgeous hues, feathers, flowing periwigs, glossy ringlets, bandeaux of pearls, all manner of "bravery," as it was called, must have gone nigh to put the very flowers out of countenance. Why ladies do not play at bowls now, when there is a disposition to revive old and graceful sports, we do not know. Bowls is a good and healthy game, and might supersede "Aunt Sally" to great advantage. "Aunt Sally," let Fashion patronize it as she will, is essentially a vulgar sport: how *can* there be anything graceful in a bevy of ladies shying sticks at a poor caricature of their own sex?

Kingsthorpe, it is certain, was no ordinary village. At every turn of its windings you find traces of stately mansions no longer existing. Baker says it was "traditionally reported that three coaches and six were formerly kept here," a tradition which we have little doubt was well founded. Coaches and six were luxuries two centuries ago no doubt, but they were also luxurious necessities in days when wealthy people travelled in their own equipages, and roads at some seasons of the year were next to impassable. "The White Horse" is now the residence of W. Tomalin, Esq., the Clerk to the County Magistrates, who has ornamented the front, covered it with clambering roses, and enclosed a piece of ground and planted it with evergreens. Very cheerful and agreeable it looks; answering exactly to the poet's desire:

> ——— "dressed with blooms
> Of honied green and quaint with straggling rooms,"

with rambling out-buildings about it, as if ground were "not an object."

But though "The White Horse" is out of commission, "The Cock" remains. "The Cock" is an Inn to glad the Rambler's eye; its front overspread with the vine; its ample bay windows with seats in them; its old-fashioned door with a through passage that affords a glimpse of the back yard with its trees and flowers; above all, its porch, with the seats and balcony over it, reminding one of the Inns in Hogarth's Pictures. We never see it without imagining a Captain Macheath exchanging courtesies with the landlady above as he takes his stirrup cup.

The lane down by "The Cock" is very tempting, shaded as it is by the noble trees in the Park of the Misses Boddington, and we are not surprised that our predecessor in the "Year Book" turned down the green and shadowy way. But we shall keep the high road a little further, and passing Mr. Tomalin's house go on to the Blacksmith's, which is worth looking at. A country Blacksmith's Shop is a pleasant place mostly :

> "And children coming home from school
> Look in at the open door;
> They love to see the flaming forge
> And hear the bellows roar;
> And catch the burning sparks that fly
> Like chaff from a thrashing floor."

And this one is specially pleasant. It has the counterpart of the tree which Longfellow has made immortal as an appanage to the craft, excepting that the tree is a sycamore instead of a chestnut :

> "Under the spreading chestnut tree
> The village smithy stands."

Nor will the archæologist pass it heedlessly by. One large arch and two small Decorated niches, one blocked up, tell of an origin more stately than its present occupation would indicate. It is singular that Baker makes no allusion to it. Bridges evidently points to it as the remains of the Hospital of the Holy Trinity, or as it is called in some records, the Hospital of St. David or St. Dewes. Baker puts the Hospital at "the east side of the entrance into the village from Northampton, where several small arches are still remaining in the cottage walls." When the Rambler in the Year Book wrote his description, these arches were still existing, but of late years the ruins have been greatly diminished. Mr. Pretty ("Wetton's Guide") says "the Hospital was no doubt at the spot now occupied by the Blacksmith's shop," and he speaks of the ruins to which Baker alludes, as "probably a relic of one of the chapels attached to the Hospital. At that time (1849) they consisted of a doorway, partly hid, and a window above, blocked up, apparently of Decorated architecture. This conjecture is borne out by Bridges, who says, "The ruins of this hospital *and of one of the chapels* are still remaining."

The story of the Hospital is well told by Baker. It was founded, he says, "in 1200 (2 John), by the prior and convent of St. Andrew's, Northampton, who, on the petition of Peter, the son of Adam de Northampton, and Henry, his son, gave a certain house near St. David's Chapel, within the limits of their parish of Thorpe, for the reception of travellers and poor persons, under the following conditions and regulations: that there should not for the future be any college of monks, canons, templars, hospitallers, or nuns in the place, or the said house be changed into a church; that Divine Service might be performed therein, but that there should be two altars only, one in the chapel of the holy Trinity, the other in the chapel of St. David, and one bell only should be allowed; that a burial ground should be provided for travellers, poor people, and others dwelling there, and that any of the parishioners might be buried there on proof of their having requested it in their life time, or expressed it in their will, but not otherwise; that in the body of the house adjoining the chapel of the holy Trinity there should be three rows of beds joined together in length, in which the poor and strangers and invalids may lie for the purpose of hearing mass, and attending to the prayers more easily and conveniently; that there should be provided one procurator, chaplain, or clerk or layman of good character, with the consent of the said prior and convent, or of the abbot of Sulby, and all irregularities to be corrected by them or the abbot, and any dispute arising between them as to the appointment of a procurator, to be settled by arbitration; the procurator to be elected by them and the abbot at the house in Thorp, and to take a prescribed oath; that there should be only two chaplains besides the procurator, who are to take the same oath; that there might be six novices to wait upon the poor, so that the whole number of officers in the house should not exceed nine; that the procurator and chaplains should have decent habits, becoming their stations, and the novices should have habits all alike, viz., capes and hoods and cloaks of black, without any mark or ornament; that it should not be united to any other house, nor to any private person, contrary to the said statutes; that the rents and profits should not be converted to any other uses, or diminished, but wholly applied to its benefit; and in augmentation thereof the said prior and convent grant all the land in Thorpe which Helias held of their fee of the church of Thorpe, viz., two virgates, a messuage and croft, and common of pasture, with consent of Henry, son of Peter (rector of St. Peter's), who now holds of us the church of Thorpe, free from tithe; but if the said house obtain any other land in Thorpe, or any other parish, where the said prior and convent are entitled to tithes, by gift, purchase, or otherwise, all tithes arising therefrom shall be paid to the church to which they are due, notwithstanding the aforesaid exemption."

The expressions, "*near* St. David's chapel," and "in the body of the house *adjoining* the chapel of the Holy Trinity," seem quite to confirm Mr. Pretty's view, that the ruins in the cottages near the toll gate belonged to St. David's chapel. In the list of persons presented as masters occurs the name of one William Richardson, who, on the 25th February, 1570, was presented, but not instituted, because he could not translate into English the two first lines of the 2nd Epistle of St. Paul to the Corinthians. In the fourth of Philip and Mary the hospital, with all its lands and other appurtenances, was granted by the King and Queen to Hugh Zulley, clerk. They were afterwards held in lease from the Crown by the family of the Morgans. In the State Paper Office is a grant (1616) to Francis Morgan, Francis Barnard, and others, of the fee farm of the town of Kingsthorpe, at suit of the tenants of Kingsthorpe, who were heretofore obliged to renew their lease every forty years on payment of increased rent.

Pursuing the road to its bifurcation, and taking the left or Welford road, we come at the extremity of the buildings to the "Court Farm." It asserts its title to this lordly appellation by an entrance gateway of stone and a side doorway of the transition period between the Gothic and the Renaissance. There used to be a ball of stone on each of the piers, but they have now fallen from their high estate. The farm buildings within have traces of the same period; but of the history of the place, so far as we are aware, there is no record.

You get into the heart of the village by many ways—by streets, so called, full of quaint cottages half lost in greenery, and old stone houses, that seem to tell of more prosperous times; by old, old walls, rich in ferns and lichens; by narrow lanes, running between low stone fences, which enclose gardens and orchards. When you emerge into the wide space occupied by the village Green, the scene is eminently rural, and when the writer in the Year Book visited it it was still more so. Bright, sparkling springs glittered in the sun; ducks paddled in the clear, cress-lined brook; a noble tree overspread the Green, and the "King's Well," never known to freeze or to fail, bubbled up its abundant waters; south-westward, on a rising ground, is the Church, which used to be neighboured by majestic elms. The tree on the Green is still there, but it has not its old amplitude, and the springs are less copious. One of them is but a mud pudding, and the brook is but a remembrance of its former self. On the Green, so lately as 1722, a Quintain was erected, on the marriage of two servants at Brington. The Quintain was originally a Roman exercise, and it became a popular sport in this country. On a high, upright post, was a cross piece or a swivel, broad at one end and pierced full of holes, and a bag of sand suspended at the other. A horseman, armed with a blunted spear, ran a-tilt at this board; he won the prize if he split the board with the sharpness and dexterity of his blow; if he struck it merely with sufficient force to swing the cross piece round, he stood a chance of being unhorsed with a heavy blow from the sand-bag swinging round upon his neck. On the occasion in question the reward of the victor was announced in the *Mercury* thus:—"A fine garland is a crown of victory, which is to be borne before him to the wedding house, and another to be put round the neck of his steed: the victor is also to have the honour of dancing with the bride, and to sit on her right hand at supper." In Bridges' time there was a town house, consisting of one long room, neatly built of stone, for the meeting of the feoffees, who had a common seal, inscribed, "Sigillum Commune de Kingsthorp," round a crowned head between two fleurs de lis. It was afterwards converted into a workhouse. A bailiff used formerly to be chosen by the freeholders, and he in Court used to appoint a Lord and Lady of the May-games on Easter Day after evensong. The custom had long been in disuse even in Bridges' time:

> "No, those days are gone away,
> And their hours are old and grey,
> And their minutes buried all
> Under the down-trodden pall
> Of the leaves of many years,"——

But it must have been a merry time once in Kingsthorpe, with their May-games, and quintains, and bowling-greens, and coaches-and-six.

In the Kingsthorpe Church there are traces of an earlier church (Saxon probably) than the oldest of the Norman work visible. It is the old old story of all our old churches most of which go back to a very early time, and record every stage of their transition. The Saxon rubble work in the head of the window over the chancel arcade is very distinguishable from the work which superseded it; it is of the character of herring-bone work, small stones set in mortar, a sort of conglomerate, stones and mortar of equal hardness; the latter work is in a great measure set with no better stuff than mere road scrapings. These windows were very deeply splayed, leaving an opening of but four inches, and bearing no traces of having been glazed. The crypt beneath the chancel has long been used as a charnel-house, and, until recently, was filled with ghastly evidences of the contempt which familiarity breeds for matters the most solemn. It was a mound of bones of all sorts. You slipped yourself in at a recently-opened doorway, and found yourself upon a heap of crunching skulls, and bones in various stages of decay, and miniature coffins of "chrysoms." You instinctively thought of Hamlet:—

"*Hamlet:* Has this fellow no feeling of his business? He sings at grave-making.

Horatio: Custom hath made it in him a property of easiness.

Hamlet: That skull had a tongue in it, and could sing once. How the knave jowls it to the ground, as if it were Cain's jawbone, that did the first murder. * * * Here's fine revolution, an we had the trick to see it. Did these bones cost no more the breeding but to play at loggats with them? Mine ache to think on't. * * * Why may not that be the skull of a lawyer? Where be his quiddits now, his quillets, his cases, his tenures, and his tricks? Why does he suffer this rude knave now to knock him about the sconce with a dirty shovel, and will not tell him of his action of battery?"

These dealings with the relics of mortality are not commendable.

"Blest be the man that spares these stones,
And curst be he that moves my bones,"

says Shakespeare's epitaph, and our instinct agrees with the anathema. Let these elements of our humanity mingle with the mother earth and perform their appointed part; there is nothing revolting or ungraceful in all that is mortal in our nature being reproduced in herb and plant, but this heaping together of multitudinous bones and skulls, some of them with the scalp and the hair scarcely gone from them, gives one an involuntary shudder. It was the custom, when a grave was opened, to shovel the bones of its previous occupier into this charnel house, through the window at the east end; and children used to peep in, "snatching a fearful joy," at the jumble of grim relics. Very grateful we are to those sanitary reformers who shut up the overgorged churchyards, and put an end to these desecrations. The crypt is now cleared, and the bones have been buried in a pit at the north-east end of the churchyard. The crypt is in excellent preservation, and is of the Decorated period. From a central pillar spring vaultings which rest upon eight responds in the wall. There is no trace of an entrance from the interior of the church, yet the work is certainly too good to have been originally intended for a charnel-house.

Our friend in the "Year-Book," having got down to the Green, set about sketching it and the church, and forgot to pursue his enquiries any further. So he says nothing about the Lanes, and the Morgans and the Barnards, and the Cookes, the local aristocracy of the traditionary coaches-and-six. Some of their residences are easily traceable. The mansion of the Morgans was situated east of the church where the stone casing of a door-way, with the pediment above, and an alcove on either side, may still be seen. It is described in an advertisement in the *Northampton Mercury* of 1721, as "a very handsome, large, pleasant house, with a very good close, gardens, stables, coach-house, dove-house, brew-house, and other outhouses and conveniences thereunto adjoining, being late the dwelling house of John Morgan, Esq., deceased." This John Morgan was the last of the name. He left a daughter, who was married to Sir John Robinson, of Cranford. She died at the early age of 24, in 1734. We first meet with the Morgans in the person of Judge Morgan, who died in 1558. There are remains of the residence of the Lanes in the close at the back of the Cock Inn. Sir Richard Lane was Lord Keeper of the Great Seal in the reign of Charles I. The Cookes had a mansion not far from the present residence of the Misses Boddington. On the right of the lane leading to the mill, the dove house and other buildings, indicative of an important structure, still remain. There is also an avenue of elms, leading direct to the Green, which no doubt was appurtenant to the mansion. The mansion of the Misses Boddington was built by James Fremeaux, Esq., who took the estates by his marriage with Margaret Cooke, and whose grand-daughter and heir was married to the late T. R. Thornton, Esq., of Brockhall. Mr. Fremeaux died in 1799, aged 95, and his wife in 1801, aged 82. The beautiful grounds of the Misses Boddington are well known to the many who avail themselves of the privilege of visiting them during the annual show of the Kingsthorpe Horticultural Society.

"The lane leading to the mill"—the words recall a truly beautiful lane, overarched with lofty elms, and leading to a mill which has often arrested the attention of the artist. The path continues over pleasant fields to Dallington.

We need not return to Northampton by the high road. There are other tracks; one across fields nearly the whole way. But we shall go by the beaten, yet pleasant, road, eastward, by Mr. Tomalin's grounds, and debouching into the Kettering-road or over the Race-course. This lane is very rural, bordered with untrimmed hedges, bright with marsh mallows, and overhung with trees, between which on either side are "long fields of barley and of rye;" and it is undulating and deviating enough to gladden the sketcher's heart with its frequent pictures. Down in its deepest dell a brook crosses it, and there is a foot-bridge by the side. We dare say the Rambler in the "Year Book" did not miss it, though he has said nothing about it. Rural as it now is, it was more rural then, being scarcely a bridle way. You might sit there a long summer's day with the birds alone for company. It is not greatly frequented now, but there are indications of building, and other tokens

"That dreadful guests will come and spoil the solitude."

Meanwhile we commend it to our brother ramblers.

Bye-ways and Highways.

"*Such puffs about highways!*"—LEIGH HUNT.

"*He loved heads with a diverting twist in them.*"—CHARLES LAMB.

I LOVE to turn into a pleasant bye-way,
Half-overgrown with wilding flowers and grass,
And sweet brier, here and there, an odorous mass
And quaint old roots, twisted in many a wry way.
Far better I love this than the smooth highway,
Level as bowling-green or looking-glass,
Where, though from Dan to Beersheba you pass,
'Tis hard and barren all; *this* is not *my* way.

So, too, I choose my friends and books; I like
Quaint men who love quaint authors; minds with roots
Knobbed and twisted; scrambling briery shoots
That catch you as you pass them by, yet strike
A wholesome fragrance out—something apart
From common place—a warm, yet rough and racy heart.

Dodford.

DODFORD is a village of surprises. Opposite the "Queen's Head," on the Chester-road, about a mile and a-half from Weedon, you descend at right angles with the main road. The descent is rapid; banks and tall trees fence it in on either side. Within a few hundred yards, you come to a cluster of fine lofty elms, and, turning short to the left, you ascend a gravelled path, which brings you to the churchyard. Crossing the churchyard diagonally towards the North-West corner, you see beneath you, on the right, the Vicarage, a tall mansion of the last century, and, East of it, a smaller, but still rather large, building, dating from about the beginning of the 17th century. It is long and low, with a deep porch in the centre of the same height as the building, and having rooms above it. Venerable evergreens tower up in the South-Western angle; climbing plants clothe and adorn its walls; and a spacious sweep of grassy lawn lies fair before it. It is now a farm-house, occupied by Mr. Thomas Russell, and looks as if it were well cared for, and not subjected to the fancies of innovation. The original door is still beneath the porch.

Leaving the churchyard by the corner gate already mentioned, you enter a path fenced in by tall hedges, and rapidly descending. It emerges, to your surprise, upon a gravelled space, where a skittle board let into the ground indicates the neighbourhood of an inn. Before you, a couple of willows stand upon the bank of a brook which runs rapidly past, and beneath a wooden foot bridge, rounding the corner eastward. Just to the right is the corner of a very rustic hostelrie, and at its right angle swings its sign—"The Swan."

Even if the month were not August, and the sunshine not hot upon your back, and your walk had not been a longish one, you might be tempted to enter so clean and so secluded a resting-place, but, combining all these arguments, the invitation is irresistible. There are rooms right and left: the "tap," we believe, is to the left. We turn to the right, and passing a little private parlour, enter an old-fashioned room, with seats all round, and a large, ample fire-place. A casemented window looks into a little garden that slopes upwards, and is all flowers and shrubs. The neatness and cleanliness of the place are an example for inn-parlours. In short, the interior of "The Swan" more than realises the promise of its exterior. If ever you relished a country crust of good bread and excellent cheese, you will relish it here, and Mr. Foster's home-brew'd does credit to the house. The Swan is just the inn for the bright summer time. The scent of flowers fills the air, and the brook babbles music as it flows. One thinks how balmy there the night air must be, and how the little rill, as it tumbles over the miniature dam, must realise Coleridge's verse—

"A noise like to a hidden brook
In the leafy month of June,
That to the sleeping woods all night
Singeth a quiet tune."

The waking up next morning, in such a spot, must be delicious. But as we do not propose to take a bed at the Swan (if beds are to be had there), and we have finished our glass, we bid our host "Good day," and, crossing the little bridge, turn into the village. Nothing can be more rural, not even the approaches to it. The brook runs quite through it eastward, occupying the entire roadway, and rippling over a bed of pure gravel. The southern bank is all hedge and trees, and wild flowers and aquatic plants; the northern is the foot-path, or main street, and lying partly under the wall of the vicarage garden. It is a pleasant saunter truly. The stream, very shallow as it is, shows the small milky stones which waken it into song, and make it catch the sparkling sunshine. The water-wagtails glance about—

"Sipping 'twixt their jerking dance,"

and a couple of ducks, white as the driven snow, seem to felicitate themselves as "monarchs of all they survey." The cottages look clean, and healthy, and cheerful, old, thatched, picturesque, and whitewashed.

Morton said the inhabitants of Dodford were long-lived, "generally living to 70 or 80." We do not know what later statistics say to this; but we do not see any reason to contradict it. Dodford lies in a valley sheltered from extremes of cold, and a running water is supposed to be healthy, reversing the conditions and effects of a stagnant stream, and maintaining a free circulation of air. The testimony of the inhabitants is in this direction; people live to a good old age hereabouts they say, and the Anno Domini seems the chief ailment; you don't hear of ague, nor rheumatism.

What is the etymology of Dodford? In Doomsday-book it is called Dodeford; "so named, as I take it," says Fuller, "from a Ford over the Avon (Nen), and Dods, water-weeds, commonly called by children cat tails, growing hereabouts." Baker has no hesitation in rejecting this explanation as puerile, but he confesses that it would be no easy task to substitute one more rational. Mr. Pretty (Wetton's Guide Book) suggests Dob, the Gaelic for stream, and Ford, a shallow place in a river. The ford is obvious enough, and "Dob" is singularly applicable to the place, the ford for some distance following the stream instead of crossing it at right angles. The "Stream-ford" is indisputably there. There is, of course, the difficulty of the difference in the final letters of Dob and Dod; but in former times letters did duty for each other in a very friendly and free-and-easy sort of way. It must be admitted that there is great ingenuity and probability in Mr. Pretty's suggestion, and that he has accomplished the task which Baker thought so difficult, of substituting a more rational etymology than Fuller's. At the

same time rational etymologies are not always to be looked for—
—rational that is in the sense of obvious appropriateness. Trivial circumstances, no doubt, gave names to places in old as well as in modern times. If "Dods" be the ante-Norman name of an aquatic weed common along the course of the brook in question, we see no inherent improbability in the ford acquiring a name from it. In our own day very odd and very puerile circumstances govern the naming of places. The *Builder* recently noticed the following names in the neighbourhood of Camberwell and Dulwich—Red-post-hill, Half Moon-lane, Dogkennel-lane, Goose-green, and Cut-throat-lane; at Wadsworth there are Matrimony-place, Lavender-sweep, and Pig-hill-path. In this town we have a Quart-pot-lane and a Narrow-toe-lane; and Cut-throat-lanes abound in all parts, rather, it would seem, from the convenience which they apparently offer for that process than from any actual throat-cuttings in them. Fuller's etymology of Dodford is not really more puerile than any of these, though we do not know upon what authority he gives "Dods" as the name of an aquatic plant there. Miss Baker's Glossary does not help us. "Dod," she says, means a bog or quagmire, but this would hardly apply to the character of Dodford, which is certainly not boggy, nor from the gravelly nature of the soil should we suppose it likely ever to have been.

Dodford church is as much a surprise as the village. Its exterior presents no feature to command special attention; as usual it has a variety of styles, the north aisle, which is Early English, being the oldest. Entering, however, by the north door you find yourself in the midst of ancient tombs of great interest. In the north chapel is the recumbent effigy of Sir William Keynes, who died in 1344, cross legged, and in complete armour. He wears a hauberk of ringed mail, and with one hand he grasps his scabbard, into which the other has just returned his sword. This noble monument is of Purbeck marble, and in fine preservation, the hardness of the material having withstood the wear and tear of upwards of five centuries, though from the lowness of the table the liabilities of the figure to injury during that long period must have been great and many. Farther eastward, on a high altar tomb of alabaster, lies the effigy of Sir John Cressy, who died in 1444. He is in complete armour, excepting that his helmet lies beneath his head; his hair is cut short equally all round. On the ledge of the altar is the inscription:—Hic jacet Johannes Cressy, miles d'nus isti ville quondam capitani de Lycieux, Orbef et Pontiesque in Normandia ac consiliarii d'ni regis in Francia—qui obiit apud Tove in Loreina iijo dei Marcii anno d'ni MCCCCLIIII. cuj' ani'e p'picietur deus. Amen. In the north wall is a sepulchral decorated arch, with deep mouldings, ornamented with the four-leaved flower characteristic of the period. Beneath lies a wooden effigy of a female. "Her head," to quote the accurate description of Baker, "rests on two cushions—the under one square, the upper lozenge-shaped. She has on a veil straight over her forehead and pendant to her shoulders, uniting near the temples to a wimple, which covers the lower part of her chin and the whole of her neck. Her vest hollowed out at the side, and partially disclosing her kirtle and band conforms to her shape down to the waist, and from thence descends in formal perpendicular folds to her feet, which press on a mutilated animal." Both the arms of this interesting figure are gone, and of the features only the mouth remains. Closely adjoining this tomb is another, on which is also a recumbent figure of a female, in stone. The costume," says Baker, "bears a general resemblance to its companion, but the veil is confined round the head with a fillet; there is no wimple, and the hair flows in ringlets to the top of the vest, which is so low as to leave the neck wholly exposed. Her head reposes on cushions sustained by two angels, and at her feet is a mutilated animal. The front of the tomb is divided by piers into five compartments, in which are alternately placed a knight holding a sword and a female veiled." Baker thinks these effigies represent the grand-daughter Wentiliana of the Sir William Keynes, of whose tomb mention has just been made. Both these ladies, however, died within a year of each other. Wentiliana in

1375, and Elizabeth in 1376, and there are some marked differences in the costumes, which would seem to indicate a wider interval. The wimple or gorget of the wooden figure belongs rather to the reign of Edward I. or II., and the dress generally of the stone effigy is that of the time of Edward III., though it is of course quite possible that the garment may have extended until the later time. The reign of Edward III. was remarkable for the variety of its costume, and Elizabeth, who was 50 when she died, may have adhered to the fashion of her younger days after it had been abandoned by her younger contemporaries. We cannot endorse the criticism of the historian in reference to the execution of these monuments. The wooden figure he describes as "rude," and the stone effigy as "no less rudely executed than the preceding." The former is, in our opinion, a skilful and graceful carving; the latter is of inferior workmanship, the arms being disproportionately small—a not uncommon error in the sculpture of the time. But it can scarcely be said to be "rudely" executed. Since Baker's time a curious wall painting has been discovered in the wall space beneath the canopy. It represents two angels supporting a dead body, from which rises a small figure representative of the soul of the deceased, with the hands in the attitude of prayer, and the head looking upwards towards an outstretched hand descending from the heavens. A shield is on either side, one charged with a cross, the other with two bars, apparently gules. The arms of Keynes were, vaire Argent and Azure, two bars gules; of Sir Philip de Aylesbury, temp: Edward 3; Azure, a cross argent. Margaret, daughter of Robert de Keynes, of Milton Keynes, married in 1330, 4th Edward 3, this Sir Philip de Aylesbury, and died in 1349. Is there not some evidence here that the wooden effigy may have been intended for this Margaret.

Above this sepulchral arch is a monumental tablet to the memory of John Wyrley, who was Sheriff of Northamptonshire, and died in 1655. It contrasts, not favourably, with the earlier memorials by which it is neighboured. Those prostrate warriors, "in the habit as they lived;" those stately ladies, with hands clasped in prayer; those pious supplications for God's mercy, awaken feelings more in harmony with the sacred edifice than the nude female caryatides, with one hand carrying three shields like a bucket of water, and the other applied to the eyes like a blubbering child. As mere works of art the later monument has the advantage. The figures are skilfully sculptured, but their unreal classicality ("too much in the style of Rubens") has little of the religious sentiment about it.

The churchyard contains nothing remarkable in the way of monumental records, if we except a series of tomb-stones connected with the family of the Hewitts, going back for a century and a quarter. They have all been recently restored with care and judgment.

The Manor of Dodford became connected with some eminent names in the 17th century. In 1677, Jane, daughter of Wm. Colley, Esq., of Glaiston, Rutland, a lord of the manor of Dodford, married Caius Gabriel Cibber, the sculptor of the celebrated figures of Raving and Melancholy Madness at Bedlam, and became the mother of Colley Cibber, the poet laureate to George II., and author of "The Careless Husband;" she was thus the grandmother of Theophilus Cibber, the actor, whose second wife was sister of Dr. Arne, the composer of "Artaxerxes," "Rule Britannia," the pretty music in "Love in a Village," the graceful setting of Ariel's lovely song—"Where the bee sucks," and a host of other compositions, which constitute in themselves an English school of music.

At the entrance to the village, or a little below the five elms by which you turn up to the church, on a bank, is a cluster of very old thatched cottages. In one of these is an oaken cupboard, with the door pierced with apertures of the Perpendicular period. It "goes with the house," and both are probably between three and four hundred years old. The parish clerk lives in the cottage, and his predecessors in the office may have lived there time immemorial.

Lines for the Fly-leaf of a Diary.

(Written about the year 1842).

RECORDED here keep all the days
On which or friendship, love, or joy,
Shall cast the glory of its rays,
Leaving no shadow of annoy:

Make every page a fountain, bright
With happy thoughts, where memory
May come in summer's sunset light,
And drink refreshed, and blessing thee.

But if sad hours *should* come—(Alas
Dark storms will cloud the sunniest sky)—
Leave the blank white untouched, and pass
With hurried hand the spectre by.

Grief with its own stern hand will score
Its own stern record on the heart
With truth minute,—oh far before
Thine accurate pencil's happiest art.

No cause have thou to intermit
One day throughout the year's long rank,
Be every page of thine o'er-writ,
As mine will surely all be blank.

About John Clare.

HELPSTON lies between six and seven miles N.N.W. of Peterborough, on the Syston and Peterborough branch of the Midland Railway, the station being about half a mile from the town. A not unpicturesque country lies about it, though its beauty is somewhat of the Dutch character, far-stretching distances, level meadows, intersected with gray willows and sedgy dikes, frequent spires, substantial water mills, and farm houses of white stone, and cottages of white stone also. Southward, a belt of wood with a gentle rise beyond, redeems it from absolute flatness. Entering the town by the road from the east you come to a cross, standing in the midst of four ways. On a base of four steps stands an octangular structure panelled, with angular heads crocketted and with finials, and crocketted pinnacles between each angle. The cornice is battlemented. From the centre rises a tall thin octangular spire. Before you and to the left stretches the town, consisting of wide streets or roadways, with irregular buildings on either side, interspersed with gardens now lovely with profuse blooms of laburnam and lilac. To the right is the Church, on a rising ground, commanding from the churchyard, a general view from the town. The Church, dedicated to St. Botolph, is a singular structure of all styles of architecture. It has a tower, nave, north and south aisles, and a large chancel. The lower stage of the tower is Norman ; the upper corners having been canted off, the next stage is octagonal, with Decorated windows, from which rises a stunted sexagonal spire with blind dormer-like windows of the Perpendicular period. Excepting the south porch, which is

Decorated, there is no feature of interest in the rest of the exterior. The interior is better than the outside. The tower arch is carried on Norman semi-pillars, three on each side. The nave is separated from the aisles by Early English arches, three on each side; the chancel arch is of the same period. The chancel, which is large, has some very interesting features. On the north are three sedilia, and on the south are three others and a piscina with double water drain and credence shelf. These sedilia are Early English, and very elegant; trefoil headed arches beautifully moulded are supported on clustered pillars, disengaged. On the altar steps are curious fragments of designs in tesseræ ot vari-coloured stone. There are long stone seats in the chancel, with elbows grotesquely carved. The chancel is ceiled so as to cut off the head of the east window. In the north aisle is a slab bearing an inscription which even in Bridges' day was so dilapidated that only the Christian name and two letters of the surname were traceable. It is given thus:—ICI: GIST: ROGER: DE: HE . . . . DE: KY: ALME: DEU . . . E: KY: PUR: SA: ALME: PRIERA . . JOURS: DE: PARDON: AVERA. It seems not unlikely that the missing portions may be thus filled in:—Ici gist Roger de Hecham de ky alme Deu eit pitié. Ky pur sa alme priera quarante jours de pardon avera—"Here lies Roger de Hecham, on whose soul may God have mercy. Whoever shall pray for his soul shall have forty days of indulgence." Roger de Hecham, or Higham, was patron of the living in 1296. In the middle of the 18th century there was a maker of monuments at Peterborough, named John Loveing, who seems to have done a tolerable stroke of business at Helpston. The tomb-stone sculpture of that day was none of the choicest either in design or execution, but we do not remember to have seen anything so ludicrously bad as the art of John Loveing. Some specimens in this chancel make one open one's eyes with astonishment. His cherubim look as if he had got his grandfather to sit as a model. Here you see the old man with the expression of the mouth of one who seems amused at the absurdity of his occupation, while the adjoining countenance marks the weariness and disgust of the sitter. The stone, which is adorned with the two heads just described, bears the following inscription:

"Here lies Interr'd the Body of Henery Watkin. Obijt September 18 Anno Domini, 1733, Ætatis Suæ 63.

Afore Desease his skin Orespread
which pierst unto his heart
and now he lies amongst ye dead
but free from pain and smart.
John Loveing, Peterboro' fecit."

One cannot help suspecting from the quatrain that John united in his own person the vocations of physician and poet, as well as that of tomb-stone cutter. His mantle seems to have fallen on his descendants, for there is in the same chancel some golden-haired cherubs bearing the same family likeness and the same marked genius for the bad and the ludicrous.

In the churchyard is a stone to the memory of Clare's mother, with this inscription—

"Sacred to the memory of Ann, wife of Parker Clare, died Dec. 18, 1835, in the 78th year of her age.

From off my bed of pain and grief
The Lord hath set me free,
And crown'd me with a heavenly wreath;
A happy change for me."

So recently as 1824 an epitaph was admitted into the churchyard with such literature upon it as below:

"Upon the Road I met cold Death,
Which soon reliev'd me of my breath,
It was a sudden death you no (sic)
For God had set my time to go.
Weep not, dear friends, it is in vain,
Your loss is my eternal gain."

The first two lines were evidently suggested to the poet by a highway robbery. "Cold Death" is the highwayman, who in ordinary newspaper phraseology "relieved him" of his property.

Clare's sonnet, "Helpstone Churchyard" may be fitly introduced here:—

"What makes me love thee now, thou dreary scene,
  And see in each swell'd heap a peaceful bed?
I well remember that the time has been
  To walk a churchyard when I used to dread;
And shudder'd, as I read upon the stone
  Of well-known friends and next-door neighbours gone.
But then I knew no cloudy cares of life,
  Where ne'er a sunbeam comes to light me through;
A stranger then to this world's storm and strife,
  Where ne'er a charm is met to lull my sorrow;
I then was blest and had not eyes to see
  Life's future change, and Fate's severe to-morrow;
When all those ills and pains should compass me,
  With no hope left but what I meet in thee."

The cottage in which John Clare was born is in the main street running south. The views of it which illustrate his poems are not very accurate. They represent it as standing alone, when it is in fact and evidently always has been a cluster of two if not of three tenements. There are three occupations now. It is on the west side of the street, and is thatched. In the illustration to the second volume of "The Village Minstrel" (1821), an open stream runs before the door, which is crossed by a plank. Modern sanitary regulations have done away with this if it ever existed, and was not a fancy of the artist. Neither this etching, nor the wood-cut to the "Rural Muse" (1835) gives the bow window, which may have indicated the principal room, or perhaps a small shop. Helpstone is probably a good deal changed from what it was in Clare's early day; new and rather imposing houses have been built, the Green is destroyed at the Southern extremity of the village, where also there was a pond, into which it is possible the stream which the artist in the view alluded to has represented as running before Clare's Cottage, may have drained. Clare, whose local attachments were intense, bewails in indignant verse the demolition of the Green:

"Ye injur'd fields, ye once were gay,
When Nature's hand displayed
Long waving rows of willows grey
And clumps of hawthorn shade;
But now, alas! your hawthorn bowers
All desolate we see,
The spoiler's axe their shade devours,
And cuts down every tree.
Not trees alone have owned their force,
Whole woods beneath them bow'd;
They turn'd the winding rivulet's course,
And all thy pastures plough'd."
* * * *

The first poem in his first volume is in the same strain:—

"Hail, scenes obscure! so near and dear to me—
The church, the brook, the cottage, and the tree:
Dear native spot! while length of time endears;
The sweet retreat of twenty lingering years.
* * * * *
These joys, all known in happier infancy,
And all I ever knew, were spent in thee;
And who but loves to view where these were past?
And who that views but loves them to the last?
Feels his heart warm to view his native place?
A fondness still these past delights to trace?
The vanish'd green to mourn, the spot to see
Where flourish'd many a brook and many a tree?
Where once the brook—for now the brook is gone—
O'er pebbles dimpling sweet, went whimpering on;
Oft on whose oaken plank I've wondering stood
(That led a pathway o'er its gentle flood)
To see the beetles their wild mazes run
With jetty jackets glittering in the sun:
So apt and ready at their reels they seem
So true the dance is figured in the stream."

Helpstone was unknown to fame before Clare sang it, as "Sweet Auburn" was before Goldsmith charmed the three kingdoms with the beauties of that "loveliest village of the plain" —

> "Caret quia vate sacro."

or as Clare in the vernacular gives it :—

> "Hail, humble Helpstone! where thy vallies spread
> And thy mean village lifts its lowly head ;
> Unknown to grandeur and unknown to fame ;
> No minstrel boasting to advance thy name ;
> Unlettered spot! unheard in poet's song ;
> Where bustling labour drives the hours along ;
> Where dawning genius never met the day ;
> Where useless ignorance slumbers life away."—

Not a flattering exordium : but the rest is all eulogy of the natural beauties of the place, and denunciation of its spoilers. Clare's remains are fitly buried in conformity with his expressed wishes, all leading to his native "Home of Homes." Connecting with his melancholy later history the following early lines, there is something very touching in their affectionate and vain aspiration :—

> "Thou dear beloved spot! may it be thine
> To add a comfort to my life's decline,
> When this vain world and I have nearly done,
> And Time's drain'd glass has little left to run ;
> When all the hopes that charm'd me once are o'er,
> To warm my soul in extacy no more,
> By disappointments prov'd a foolish cheat,
> Each ending bitter and beginning sweet ;
> When weary age the grave a rescue seeks,
> And prints its image on my wrinkled cheeks,—
> Those charms of youth that I again may see,
> May it be mine to meet my end in thee ;
> And as reward for all my troubles past,
> Find one hope true—to die at home at last.

Clare's removal to Northborough, well intended as it was, was not fortunate in its results. Although but three miles distant from Helpstone, he bewails the change as if he had been exiled to the Antipodes. Almost the last poem in his last volume is a lament "On leaving the cottage of his Birth." The verses record no "idly feigned poetic pains"; they are evidently the effusion of a heartfelt sadness. We must quote some passages :—

"I've left my own old Home of Homes,
Green fields and every pleasant place:
The summer like a stranger comes,
I pause—and hardly know her face.

* * *

I miss the heath, its yellow furze,
Mole-hills and rabbit-tracks, that lead
Through besom-ling and teasel burrs
That spread a wilderness indeed.

The woodland oaks, and all below
That their white powder'd branches shield,
The mossy paths—the very crow
Croaks music in my native field.

I sit me in my corner chair,
That seems to feel itself alone;
I hear fond music—here and there
From hawthorn-hedge and orchard come.

I hear—but all is strange and new;
I sat on my old bench last June,
The sailing puddock's shrill 'pee-lew,'
O'er Royce wood seemed a sweeter tune.

I walk adown the narrow close,
The nightingale is singing now;
But like to me she seems at loss
For Royce wood and its shielding bough.

I lean upon the window sill,
The trees and summer happy seem.
Green, sunny green they shine—but still
My heart goes far away to dream

Of happiness—and thoughts arise
  With home-bred pictures many a one—
Green lanes that shut out burning skies,
  And old crook'd stiles to rest upon.

* * *

I dwell on trifles like a child—
  I feel as ill becomes a man.
And yet my thoughts like weedlings wild
  Grow up and blossom where they can."—

Is there not in these last lines something like a forecast of the calamity that was so soon to manifest itself? Home sickness surely never more nearly became monomania.

Helpstone derives its name from Helpo, a stipendiary knight, of whom we know nothing more. Future time will know it better in its intimate connection with the poetry of poor John Clare.

From Helpstone, where Clare was born, to Northborough, where he last resided in a home of his own, the distance is but three miles. A pleasant three miles; along a road level and far-stretching, with the tall slender spire of Glinton in the distance; through the pretty village of Etton; and along "the bank," one of those works peculiar to the country, constructed for the purpose of directing and governing the flood waters. Before we speak of Northborough let us say a word or two of these objects of interest by the way.

Etton is one of those nestling villages which, with no pretence to scenery, properly so called, suggest to us that

—" if there's peace to be had in this world
A heart that is humble might hope for it here."

The church is not large, but has features of much interest. An Early English or late Norman tower carries a broach spire. Round the tower runs a curious corbel table with a great diversity of corbels; heads, Fleur de Lis, the dog tooth, and oddest of all, on the south side, a figure lying lengthwise, extremely rude in form but apparently intended for a Crusader wearing the flat-topped cylindrical helmet. A nave, with large quatrefoil windows in the clerestory north and south aisles, and a large chancel. Aisles and chancel are lighted by two-light lancets under one hood moulding with a trefoil in the head. There is an Early English priests' door in the chancel, and one of the low side windows with a fleur de lis finial to the hood moulding, and corbels. The east window has five lancet lights under a pointed hood moulding with delicate shafts on either side. In the north aisle is a good door way, now blocked up. The church-yard might make one "half in love with easeful death:" it has none of the repulsive fulness of populous burial grounds, and the tall healthy grass covers with its graceful clothing the mounds beneath which "the forefathers of the hamlet sleep." But its main charm is a beautiful avenue of limes on the north side, about whose sweet scented blossoms the bees make a perpetual hymning. East of the church is a Tudor farm-house, looking, like all its class, very comfortable and picturesque, with its pointed gables and deep stone porch. A stone stile in the church-yard wall directly opposite, allows of a pathway across the church-yard to its western entrance. This stile is formed of a tombstone apparently of the seventeenth century, from which the inscription is not wholly effaced. The coping of the church-yard wall is in part formed of fragments of stone coffins, of which, according to Bridges, many were dug up in that and neigbouring parishes, and commonly used as copings.

From Etton to Northborough there is a course of roadway, straight and level as a bowling green, but it is a pleasanter as well as a nearer route for pedestrians to go along "the bank" already mentioned. This is a characteristic of the country, and tells of a neighbourhood of meres and washes. It is a very long mound of earth, with a deep ditch of clear running water on one, mantled over with all kinds of water-plants, and on the other a border of willows; the slopes are covered with tall "bents," which indeed cover the whole embankment, except where, from its connecting two roads, it is commonly used as a footpath. There is something striking in these long lines of willow, bank, and ditch stretching their far perspective till they converge into a point. A painter would find studies for "bits" without end—grey willow, tawny water, and luxuriant growths of all weeds that become gigantic in abundant moisture. The Yellowhammer and Waterwagtail glance about like specks of sunshine and silver-light.

The road curves as you enter Northborough, and you are startled with coming upon an imposing edifice on your right, now occupied as a barn and other farm buildings. There is a noble gate-house, with an outer gateway of very large span, and within two smaller ones, one for carriages and the other for pedestrians. Originally there must have been three massive gates to be opened before an entrance could be obtained into the court-yard. The house is a fine old structure of various dates. In the passage entrance are three doorways, the central one more imposing than the rest, having heads of the Decorated period, with hood mouldings, crocketted and with finials. The windows had at one time been apparently of the same style, but they were altered many times. The last alteration was probably made in Charles the First's or the Cromwellian period, when the piercings of the flowing tracery of the heads were filled in, and the windows converted into tall upright parallelograms, divided into four compartments by a mullion and transom. This Manor House, very interesting architecturally, is not less so historically, for here lived the Claypoles, one of whom married Betty, the youngest daughter of Oliver Cromwell. Here, too, the Protector's widow found a retreat after the Restoration, and here she died. In the parish register is the following entry:

"Eliz., the relict of Oliver Cromwelle, sometime Pro. of England, was buried November the 19th, 1665."

Northborough Church is a singular structure. It is of no great size; but has a nave, north and south aisles, south porch, chancel, and a chapel at the eastern end of the south aisle, with a low tower, embattled, and finished with a stunted pyramidal spire at the east and west corners. The nave and aisles are terminated at the west end with a wall diminishing as it rises by stages, and ending in a double bell-cot containing two bells. The blankness of the wall is relieved by buttresses, and there is a west window to each aisle, but not to the nave. In the porch is a stoup for holy water. Against the wall of the south aisle is a recess, canopied by two pointed arches with deep mouldings, and directly opposite, in the wall of the north aisle, is another, under two trefoil heads with a quatrefoil in the intersection. The Claypole aisle or chapel is a large addition to a small church. It has two low arched recesses in the south wall, and a piscina in the south-east corner. Against the east wall are two elaborate perpendicular canopies, with brackets beneath, upon which, in all probability, statues once stood. An altar tomb against the east wall, at the northern end, with an arch over, supported by columns, bears on an escutcheon a chevron between three roundles, with the inscription—

ALL . GOOD . BLESSIN
GS . VNTO . MAN
COMETH . FROM . THE .

On one of the columns are the initials IA/CL and on the other 15/94.
In the south-west corner of the chapel is a doorway, which opens upon stone stairs ascending and descending: the latter leading to a sort of crypt or bone-house, with grated openings; the former to one of the turrets and the roof. A door midway opens upon the sill of the large window in the chapel, which has a corresponding wooden door in the opposite jamb. This latter opens only into a recess. What the purpose of these doors could be we do not know.

Bridges states that the entries in the register from 1613 to 1646 are torn out, and the following memorandum inserted in it:—

"The reason of this defect in the register was because Mr. John Cleypole, a factious gentleman, then living in the parish of Northborough, caused the register to be taken away from mee, John Stoughton, then rector; for which I was, by the ecclesiastical court then holden at St. Martin's, adjudged for satisfaction the summe of two pounds ten shillings.

"The money was paid at the charge of the parish by Robert Cooke, then churchwarden.

"Sic testator,

"JOHANNES STOUGHTON,

"Rect. ibm."

John Stoughton was inducted rector November, 1659, and held the living till March, 1695, when he died. The manor of Northborough became the property of the Claypoles by purchase in 1599, and John Claypole, who married one of the daughters of the Protector, would seem to be the "factious gentleman" spoken of by the rector in this curious memorandum. What his object could be in mutilating the record, Mr. Stoughton does not tell us; nor is it easy to understand what title the rector had to receive satisfaction at the cost of the parish for an injury done to the parish property. Four of Clare's children are buried in the churchyard.

Northborough is a large village—not in the sense of its number of houses or its population—but of the space of ground which it covers. The houses are mostly cottages, half hidden in orchards and luxuriant gardens, having a prodigality of ground. There is not an eminence loftier than a mole-hill throughout, yet the spacious roads and the wealth of trees and flowers make it a very picturesque and happy-looking locality. Clare's cottage stands in the midst of ample grounds. You enter from the road by a gate, and proceeding up a roadway, find the cottage with its front turned from the road, southward. The cottage was built for Clare by the kindness of the Earl Fitzwilliam, and it was at Clare's express desire that it has a southern aspect. Altogether it answers the ideal which the Poet sketched in the verses we quoted above. It is a real cottage—not the "cottage of gentility" which Coleridge satirized—but very comfortable, and homely, and rural. The roof is thatched, the windows are casemented, roses climb the wall, and there is a seat outside. In the pleasant and spacious garden are two yews trimmed into millstone-like circles and cones after the fashion of our forefathers. Poor Clare himself taught his sons how to shape these trees, giving his instructions in the topiary art as he sat on the garden seat. With these exceptions the garden is thoroughly a cottage garden, luxuriant, and free, and compound—flower, orchard, and vegetable intermingling in friendly and informal sociality. Within are snug and comfortable rooms, with cupboards for the books, all you might suppose that a mind like Clare's, unambitious of elbowing rank and fashion, and finding his enjoyment in the recesses of poetic feeling, and association with the woods, and fields, and flowers, would revel in. About the walls hang pictures connected in one way or another with the Poet; a beautiful portrait in water colours, from which the print prefixed to the Village Minstrel was engraved; an Indian ink drawing, from which was engraved the frontispiece to the "Shepherd's Calendar;" a clever Indian ink drawing of Helpstone Church, by Mr. Simpson, an artist of Stamford, and a friend of Clare's; prints of the Earl Spencer, the grandfather of the present Earl, and of other patrons. Yet, as we have said, to this pleasant place poor Clare never took kindly. In no respect can his Helpstone home compare with this of Northborough, excepting that the latter was wanting in early associations, and this want with Clare seems to have been fatal. The malady, however, which clouded so large a portion of his life manifested itself before he went to Northborough. It is a great question whether it was not connected with his organization, growing with his growth, and strengthening with his strength. He may be cited as a remarkable instance in support of Dryden's famous couplet:

> "Great wits are sure to madness near allied,
> And thin partitions do their bounds divide."

At Helpstone he used to bury himself in the woods throughout the day; and it was the hope of diverting his increasing moodiness that suggested his removal to Northborough, where it was thought the occupation of a little land would afford him a healthy excitement. When the time came, however, that he was to leave Helpstone, he showed the strongest reluctance to quit his "home of homes;" such a reluctance, that at one time Mrs. Clare thought she would be compelled to resign the Northborough cottage, and return to Helpstone. He was brought over at length by the kind compulsion of a friend. Yet at this time his poetical powers may be said to have culminated. His best verses were written at this period—those most remarkable for refinement of thought, truth of colouring, and closeness of expression. Among his books carefully kept by his widow are several presentation copies—one (Doddridge's Family Expositor) from Mr. Taylor, Clare's first publisher and kind friend always; another from Lord Radstock, with this entry:—"The gift of Admiral Lord Radstock to his dear and excellent freind, John Clare, Aug. 1, 1822;" a copy of the first edition of Keat's Endymion has written in it "John Clare, Helpstone, 1821."

The story of John Clare's life may be briefly told. He was born at Helpstone, in this county, on the 13th of July, 1793, and was the only son of Parker and Ann Clare, of that place. His father was a farmer's labourer. A poetical imagination manifested itself in John Clare at a very early age, from hearing his father read to him a poem which he used to say he thought was one of Pomfret's, though in after life he could not connect any poem of that author with the faint impression of it which he retained. He paid for his own schooling, by extra work as a ploughboy and thresher. His schoolmaster was a Mr. Seaton, of Glinton, an adjoining parish, who seems to have been very kind and liberal to him, giving him occasional rewards. One of his earliest favourites was "Robinson Crusoe." When he was thirteen years of age a boy showed him Thomson's "Seasons," which so excited his feeling for poetry, that he could not rest till he had accumulated a shilling with which to purchase a copy for himself. On a fine spring morning he set out for Stamford to buy the coveted treasure, and arrived there before any of the shops were open. His first poem is said to have been composed on his walk home through Burghley Park. His early education did not extend to writing or arithmetic, for both of which he was indebted to an Excise officer—Mr. John Turnill—then at Helpstone. In 1817 he was employed at Bridge Casterton, in Rutlandshire, at nine shillings a week, and here he fell in love with Martha Turner, the daughter of a cottage farmer, who afterwards became his wife. Love seems to have stimulated him to the endeavour to turn his poetical faculty to pecuniary account, and he contrived to get three hundred copies of a prospectus printed, which obtained him but *seven* subscribers. Indirectly, however, it led to the accomplishment of his object. He had appended to it a specimen sonnet, and a copy having accidentally fallen into the hands of Mr. Edward Drury, a bookseller at Stamford, through his intervention the MS. of the proposed volume was put into the hands of Messrs. Taylor and Hessey, who liberally gave Clare £20 for it, and published it in 1820. These early poems are remarkable, considering the circumstances under which they were written, for their powers of description, for their enjoyment of Nature, for their refinement of expression, and for their maturity of rhythm and general accuracy of rhyme. There is in them little evidence of imitation, though one can scarcely doubt that the writer of "Helpstone" had read "The Deserted Village." The hunting song, "To-day the Fox must Die," is obviously an echo of the fine old song, once so popular, beginning, "Bright Chanticleer proclaims the Morn," with its refrain, "To-day a Stag must Die." "Crazy Nell," too, reminds us of Southey's celebrated "Mary the Maid of the Inn." The volume was favourably reviewed in the Quarterly Review; and in the London Magazine by Mr. Gilchrist, of Stamford; and in 1821 two more volumes were published by Messrs. Taylor and Hessey, which shewed a considerable advance over the first. The form of the principal poem, "The Village Minstrel," seems to have been suggested by Beattie's "Minstrel," but there is no absolute imitation. Many of the miscellaneous poems in these two volumes are very beautiful. We may point especially to the verses after reading "Proposals for Building a Cottage":

Beside a runnel build my shed
  With stubbles cover'd o'er;
Let broad oaks o'er its chimney spread,
  And grass-plats grace the door.

The door may open with a string,
  So that it closes tight;
And locks would be a wanted thing
  To keep out thieves at night.

A little garden, not too fine,
  Inclose with painted pales;
And woodbines round the cot to twine,
  Pin to the wall with nails.

Let hazels grow, and spindling sedge
  Bent bowering overhead;
Dig old-man's-beard from woodland hedge,
  To twine a summer-shade.

Beside the threshold sods provide
  And build a summer seat;
Plant sweet-briar bushes by its side,
  And flowers that blossom sweet.

I love the sparrow's ways to watch
  Upon the cotter's sheds,
So here and there pull out the thatch,
  That they may hide their heads.

And as the sweeping swallows stop
  Their flights along the green,
Leave holes within the chimney-top
  To paste their nests between.

Stick shelves and cupboards round the hut
  In all the holes and nooks:
Nor in the corner fail to put
  A cupboard for the books.

Along the floor some sand I'll sift,
To make it fit to live in;
And then I'll thank ye for the gift,
As something worth the giving.

These pleasant verses in a striking manner mark the simple and thoroughly rural nature of the poet. For grandeur he not only did not care, but it was utterly distasteful to him. To wander about his native fields, and find in them the poems which made the happiness of his life, was all he desired. When he became for a time a wonder in the fashionable world he was bewildered, and when dinner was over he would rise, thrust his hands in his pockets, and saying, "Well, I'll goo"—"goo" accordingly. He never exulted at having "dinner'd wi' a lord," not from any disrespect towards lords, but because the humblest meal with the fields and birds about him, and the blue sky overhead, was to him far more congenial than all the splendours of artificial life. He had, indeed, no reason for not holding the aristocracy in grateful respect, for the noblemen connected with the county were very kind to him, and conferred upon him substantial benefits. The Marquis of Exeter, Earl Fitzwilliam, Earl Spencer, the Duke of Bedford, Prince Leopold, the Earl of Cardigan, the Duke of Northumberland, the Earl of Winchelsea, the Earl Brownlow, Lord John Russell, the Earl Rivers, the Earl Manvers, the Earl of Egremont, Lord Kenyon, Lord Northwich, and Lord Radstock were among a number of subscribers to a fund which ultimately produced for him an independent income of £40 a-year. At one time he engaged in farming, with ill success. He was, in truth, wholly unfitted for business which required competition with his fellow men. His mind was active enough, but not in the direction by which money is made.

In 1827 he published "The Shepherd's Calendar and other Poems," a still farther advance on his previous publications; and in 1835 a small volume entitled "The Rural Muse," the last and best of all. It is full of exquisite pictures of rural life and scenery, painted with a mature and masterly hand. "The Pettichap's Nest," is as lovely a little poem in its way as our language possesses:

WELL! in my many walks I've rarely found
A place less likely for a bird to form
Its nest—close by the rut-gulled waggon-road,
And on the almost bare foot-trodden ground,
With scarce a clump of grass to keep it warm!
Where not a thistle spreads its spears abroad,
Or prickly bush, to shield it from harm's way;
And yet so snugly made, that none may spy
It out, save peradventure. You and I
Had surely passed it in our walk to-day,
Had chance not led us by it!—Nay, e'en now,
Had not the old bird heard us trampling bye,
And fluttered out, we had not seen it lie,
Brown as the road-way side. Small bits of hay
Plucked from the old propt haystack's pleachy brow,
And withered leaves, make up its outward wall,
Which from the gnarl'd oak-dotterel yearly fall,
And in the old hedge-bottom rot away.
Built like an oven, through a little hole,
Scarcely admitting e'en two fingers in,
Hard to discern, the birds snug entrance win.
'Tis lined with feathers warm as silken stole,
Softer than seats of down for painless ease,
And full of eggs scarce bigger even than peas!
Here's one most delicate, with spots as small
As dust, and of a faint and pinky red.
—Well! let them be, and Safety guard them well;
For Fear's rude paths around are thickly spread,
And they are left to many dangerous ways.
A green grasshopper's jump might break the shells,
Yet lowing oxen pass them morn and night,
And restless sheep around them hourly stray;
And no grass springs but hungry horses bite,
That trample past them twenty times a day.
Yet, like a miracle, in Safety's lap
They still abide unhurt, and out of sight.
—Stop! here's the bird—that woodman at the gap

Frightened him from the hedge :—'tis olive-green.
Well! I declare it is the Pettichap!
Not bigger than the wren, and seldom seen.
I've often fonnd her nest in chance's way,
When I in pathless woods did idly roam;
But never did I dream until to-day
A spot like this would be her chosen home.

Equally beautiful is "The Nightingale's Nest," in which the fruitless search for the warbling bird is charmingly described :

——"I watched in vain.
The timid bird had left the hazel bush
And at a distance hid to sing again;
Lost in a wilderness of listening leaves."

The nest is found at length :—

"These harebells all
Seem bowing with the beautiful in song;
And gaping cuckoo-flower, with yellow leaves,
Seems blushing of the singing it has heard."
* * * * *

"Deep adown
The nest is made, a hermit's mossy cell,
Snug lie her curious eggs, in number five,
Of deaden'd green or rather olive brown;
And the old prickly thorn-bush guards them well.
So here we'll leave them, still unknown to wrong,
As the old woodland's legacy of song."

Not long after the publication of this charming little volume, to which Clare's fame as a poet may be safely entrusted, the hallucination commenced which gradually increased until the sad necessity came of subjecting to restraint a nature as little calculated to endure it as that of the bird whom he describes so appreciatingly. Poor Clare: In this very volume he says :—

"I love to walk the fields; they are to me
A legacy no evil can destroy."——

Little did he imagine how dire an evil was even then threatening him, destined ultimately to remove him from all that he loved so dearly, and to deprive him even of the legacy which he fancied indestructible.

Clare died on the 24th May, 1864, in the Northamptonshire Lunatic Asylum, of which he had been an inmate for many years; and was buried on the following Wednesday in the churchyard of his beloved Helpstone, thus realizing his early wish to rest in his "own old Home of Homes."

By the Canal.

BY the Canal I love to go,
Where the willows and sedges grow;
Where in the glassy stream the sky,
As in a mirror, seems to lie;
Storm or sunshine, or rainbow bright,
Amber evening or moonshine white,
Heaven above and Heaven below—
By the Canal I love to go,
By the Canal.

By the Canal, under the bridge,
Through the mountain's sever'd ridge,
Over the valley, gazing down
Into the hamlet, on to the town;
By where the wharf in the morning bright
Tinctures the stream with a blood-red light,
The red brick wharf which the waters lap
And delve into many a wounded gap
By the Canal.

By the Canal in the early morn,
When the young Spring sun leaps up new born,
And chases the ripples the crisp wind makes,
Till into a thousand lights it breaks,
And a merry dance of nymphs it seems
To him who closeth his morning dreams
By the Canal.

By the Canal in the Summer's ray,
When the sun is high on the traveller's way;
Pleasant to leave the dusty road
And loosen the knapsack's heating load,
And under the willows woo the air
That cooled by the waters wanders there
By the Canal.

By the Canal in the Autumn light,
While the clouds with sunset hues are bright
Amber and red, and green and gold,
And thousand tints, unmatch'd, untold;
And all in glory see them lie
Repeated, as in another sky,
In the Canal.

By the Canal, when the day is done,
And the worn steed's weary rest is won,
And the boat is moored to the water's edge,
Under the leaves, among the sedge,
And all is quiet and all is dark
Save one red gleam in the long low bark
On the Canal.

Holdenby.

"Whanné that Aprill with his showers sote
The drought that March had piercèd to the root,
And bathèd every veyne in swich liquor
Of which virtue engendred is the flower;
When Zephirus eke with his sweetè breath
Enspirud hath in every holt and heath,
The tender croppès and the youngè sun
Hath in the Ram his halfe course i-ronne,
And smalè foulès maken melody
That slepen all the night with open eye,
So pricketh them Nature in their coràges,
Then longen folk to go on pilgrimages."

SO sang Geoffrey Chaucer five hundred years ago; and so sings the heart of man to this day. Let us resume our rambles round about.

Holdenby is always associated with the memory of Charles I.; but its interest begins much earlier than the stirring days of that ill-starred monarch. In Domesday Book it is called Aldenesbi, which Baker supposes to mean the "bye," or home of the Saxon possessor. A family, taking its surname from the place, was located here at least as early as the beginning of the 13th century, and continued in the direct male line till the 16th century, when, through the marriage with the sister of a Holdenby, the estates passed to a branch of the Hattons, an ancient Cheshire family. At Holdenby, in 1548, was born the celebrated Sir Christopher Hatton—

> "Whose bushy beard and shoe-strings green,
> Whose high-crown'd hat and satin doublet
> Moved the stout heart of England's Queen
> Though Pope and Spaniard could not trouble it."

He was a student of the Inner Temple, when at a masked ball his handsome person, graceful dancing, and prepossessing manners won the heart of Queen Elizabeth, and he was introduced into the Royal household. He continued to advance in favour till in 1587 he was made Lord Chancellor, to the great heart-burning of the legal functionaries over whose heads he was promoted to this high office. How great the dissatisfaction was we may judge from the fact that the sergeants at first refused to plead before him. He had reached his exalted station at a leap, without any of the probation which is conceived, with good reason, to be needful for it. "He rather," says Fuller, "took a *bait* than made a *meal* at the inns of court whilst he studied the laws therein." "But his parts," says the same quaint writer, "were far above his learning, which mutually so assisted each other that no manifest want did appear." He seems to have had a passion for building. It was he who built Holdenby House, of which we have still a stately ruin, and Kirby, also a ruin. As he blossomed by the sunshine of royal favour, so he perished by its withdrawal. The Queen ("who seldom gave boons, and never forgave due debts") demanded of him the immediate payment of an old debt, and the vexation which it occasioned brought on a fever. Elizabeth relented when informed of his danger, and carried, as some said, cordial broths to him with her own hands, but without effect. "Thus," adds Fuller, "no pulleys can draw up a heart once cast down, though a Queen herself should set her hand thereto." Sir Christopher died in 1591, and was buried in St. Paul's. His estates were bequeathed to his nephew, Sir William Newport, with remainder to his godson and heir male, Sir Christopher Hatton. In 1608 this Sir Christopher conveyed, upon certain conditions, the greater mansion-house and manor to James I. for life, remainder to Charles Duke of York, his second son, in tail male, with remainder to his Majesty's heirs and successors. The nomination of the Duke of York was ominous. In 1625, by the death of his father, he became King of England, and Holdenby was destined to be his prison. In the struggle between him and his Parliament, Holdenby was seized, with the rest of the royal demesnes, and, after the decisive battle of Naseby, Charles having surrendered to the Scotch army at Newark-on-Trent, was removed thither. James Harrington, the author of Oceana, was one of the Parliamentary Commissioners employed on this occasion. The captive King was treated with liberality. His household included, besides the usual staff attached to the kitchen and out-houses, yeomen ushers, yeomen of the guard, yeomen hangers, pages of the presence, cup bearer, carver, sewer and esquire of the body, physician, apothecary, and chirurgeon. An estimate of the expense for twenty days, commencing 13th February and ending 4th March inclusive, was submitted to Parliament as follows :—

	£
His Majesty's diet of xxviii dishes, at £xxx per diem	700
The King's voydy	32
The Lords' diet of xx days	510
For the clerke of the green cloth, kitchen and spicery, a mess of vii dishes	40
Dyetts for the household and chamber officers, and the guard	412
Board-wages for common household servants, pot-scowrers, and turn-broachers	36
Badges of Court and riding wages	140
For linnen for His Majesty's table, the Lords, and other diets	273
For wheat, wood, and Cole	240
For all sorts of spicery store, wax lights, torches, and tallow lights	160
For pewter, brasse, and other necessaries incident to all offices, and for carriages	447
	£2990

The Communion plate, formerly set on the altar in the King's Chapel, at Whitehall, consisting of "one gilt shyppe, two gilt vases, two gilt euyres, a square bason and fountain, and a silver rod," were melted down to make plate for His Majesty's use at Holdenby. The first monthly remittance was made in accordance with the above estimate: but the expenses were afterwards cut down to one-third, viz., £50 a day. Charles's favourite amusement was bowling: it was the fashionable amusement of the day, and the Green being out of order at Holdenby, he used to ride over sometimes to Althorp and sometimes to Boughton. It was on one of these occasions that a Major Bosville, disguised as a countryman, awaited the King on Brampton Bridge, with a fishing rod in his hand, as if he had been angling, and endeavoured to convey to him letters from the Queen and Prince Charles. About a month afterwards another similar attempt was made to convey secret information to the King by Mary Cave, the daughter of Mr. William Cave, of Stanford. Of both these circumstances Major Whyte Melville has availed himself in his brilliant romance of Holmby House, but with the license of the novelist. Bosville was captured, and orders were given by the House of Commons to send for him from Northampton by the Sergeant-at-Arms, but how he was disposed of does not appear. Mistress Cave, in order to attain her object, says Baker, "engaged a female friend, who resided in the neighbourhood of Holdenby, to visit the landlady of Captain Abbot, one of the King's Guards, and through the landlady's influence to persuade the Captain to procure her the honour of kissing the King's hand: which having accomplished she apprised Mrs. Cave of her success, and contracted with her landlady to receive her as a visitor, and endeavour through the Captain to obtain for her also the honour of an introduction to His Majesty, by which means she hoped to put the letter into his hands. Mrs. Cave came, and the Captain had good naturedly, but unsuspiciously, acceded to the request; when the landlady imparted the plot to her husband, who, though a royalist and favourable to the design, dared not run the risk of detection, and divulged the secret to the Captain. On the appointed day (11th May) the Captain, who had apprised the Commissioners of the circumstance, accompanied Mrs. Cave, who had no suspicion of having been betrayed, to Holdenby; and on her arrival she was carried into a room, but, notwithstanding the most diligent search, nothing was found upon her. The letter was accidentally discovered a few days after behind the hangings of the room, where it seems she contrived to slip it whilst she stood with her back to the hangings conversing with the ladies who searched her."

On the 3rd of June the King was forcibly taken out of the hands of the Commissioners, at Holdenby, by Cornet Joyce, under circumstances which form not the least interesting chapter in the story of his unhappy life. We must sketch it briefly. On the 2nd of June a party of 700 horse arrived at Kingsthorpe, and at night they rendezvoused at Harlestone Heath. Soon after midnight they advanced into the park and surrounded the house. At break of day on the 3rd of June the horses were drawn up in front of the great gates at the back yard. The Commissioners had troops of their own stationed there, but they fraternized with the new comers. Joyce stated that their object was to bring the Governor, Colonel Graves, to trial before a Council of War for having scandalized the army. Graves was already aware of the hostile feeling against him, and had taken flight. Joyce, on learning this, concluded that he had gone for succours, and at ten at night demanded an audience of the King. He found the King in bed, and apologized for having disturbed him; to which the King replied, "No matter, if you mean me no hurt." He then announced his intention of removing the King from Holdenby. Next morning by six o'clock the troops were drawn up in the first court before the house. The King, addressing them from the top of the steps, said that Cornet Joyce having proposed to convey him to the army, he was come to give his answer in the presence of them all; he protested that he came to Holdenby not by constraint (though not so willingly as he might have done) for the purpose of communicating with the Parliament; and that having sent several messages to them, he considered himself in some degree bound to wait here for answers; yet if satisfactory reasons could be given he would go with them, even though opposed by the Commissioners. Joyce replied that their only motive for securing His Majesty's person was to prevent the kingdom being involved in another war; a plot contrived by some members of both Houses of Parliament having existed for the last four years to overthrow the laws of the kingdom, and convey His Majesty to a new army to be raised for that purpose. The King denied all knowledge or belief of any such design or intended army; and turning to the Cornet, who stood at the foot of the stairs in front of the troops, desired to know his authority for securing his person. "The soldiery of the army," said Joyce. The King replied that he knew no lawful authority in England but his own, and next under him the Parliament; but asked whether he had any verbal or written authority from General Fairfax? "He is only a member of the army," rejoined the Cornet. "Then deal ingenuously with me," returned the King, "and tell me what commission you have." "Here is my commission," Joyce answered. "Where?" enquired the King. "Behind me," retorted Joyce, pointing to the soldiers. The King, smiling, observed it was a fair, well-written commission, legible without spelling. Joyce had, in his interview with the King, the preceding night, promised that he should be treated with honour and respect, and not be forced in anything contrary to his conscience, and on the King repeating these stipulations, they were carried by general acclamation. And so King Charles departed from Holdenby. The vicissitudes of the monarch's life have furnished many a subject for the canvas; yet we are not aware that this most picturesque and striking incident has ever been treated by any artist. An early June morning, a troop of sturdy horsemen, with helm and cuirass and buff jerkin, and furniture of war, with fair fields and distant woods for a background; a quaint Elizabethan doorway, with steps, on the uppermost of which stands the stately figure that Vandyck loved to paint—the monarch with the sallow, melancholy, yet handsome visage ; and the resolute Cornet Joyce at the foot pointing to "his commission:"—here, surely, are materials for as fine a picture as ever was painted by Maclise or Millais.

What Holdenby House was in its magnificence we learn from Norden. He describes it as "a very beautiful building erected with such uniformity and so answerably contrived as for the quantity and quality is not to be match'd in this land. In the hall there are raised three peramides very high standing instead of a shryne, the midst whereof ascendeth unto the roofe of the hall, the other two equal with the syde walls of same hall, and on them are depainted the arms of all the gentlemen of the same shire, and of all the noblemen of this land. The situation of the same house is very pleasantlie contrived, mounting on an hill environed with most ample and large fields and goodly pastures, manie young groves newlie planted, both pleasant and profitable; fish ponds well replenished, a park adjoining of fallow deer, with a large warren of coneys not far from the house, lying between East Haddon and Long Bugbye. About the house are greate store of hares, and above the rest is especially to be noted with what industry and toil of man the garden hath been raised, levelled, and formed out of a most craggy and unprofitable ground, now framed a most pleasant, sweete, and princely place, with divers walks, manie ascendings and descendings, replenished also with manie delightful trees of fruite, artificially-composed arbors, and a distilling house on the west end of the same garden, over which is a pond of water brought by conduite pipes out of the field adjoyning on the west, a quarter of a mile from the same house. To conclude, the state of the same house is such and so beautiful that it may well delight a prince." Baker adds the following details:—"From a careful inspection of the remains, aided by the personal and traditionary information of an old inhabitant whose father and grandfather resided on the spot, I have been enabled satisfactorily to retrieve the original outline of this interesting mansion. The principal front faced the east, and the two archways now standing were the lateral entrances to the principal court. The foundations of the central entrance my informant remembers being dug up close to the wall which bounds the adjoining field; the postern gate at the north end of this wall communicated with the stables and coach-houses which ranged eastward, nearly on the site of the cottages on the south side the green; eastward of these was a large gateway, removed within these few years [this was written circa 1822]; beyond which were the malt-house, and probably the dairy and other buildings, the remnants of which are converted into a farm house: the whole of the premises stretching considerably above a furlong in length." Buck's View (1729) gives one of the pyramids spoken of by Norden, and other ruins, south-east of the present remains, which have long since disappeared.

In May, 1650, the trustees for the sale of Crown Lands sold the mansion and estates to Adam Baynes, of Knowsthorpe, Esq., a captain in the Parliamentary army, and M.P. for Leeds in the only Parliament in which it was ever represented prior to the Reform Act of 1832. The sum given for the whole was £22,299 6s. 10d.: the materials of the mansion were valued at £6,000 over and above the expense of taking them down: the park contained 500 acres, and was stocked with upwards of 200 deer of different kinds, worth £200; and eleven cows and calves of wild cattle worth £42. Baynes demolished the building, and with part of the materials three houses were erected in Northampton—one in the Drapery, one in St. Giles's-street, and one in Gold-street. They were all standing within living memory, but that in Gold-street (now in the occupation of Mr. Muscott) is the only one remaining. The house in St. Giles's-street stood on the site of the houses now occupied by Miss Markham and Mr. Terry, jun., and was always known as "Little Holmby." At the Restoration the alienated Crown Lands were resumed, and Holdenby was given by Charles

II. to his brother James Duke of York, afterwards James II., who sold it to Lewis Duras, created Baron Duras of Holdenby. He died in 1709, and Holdenby was purchased of his representatives by the Great Duke of Marlborough, whose descendants sold it in 1802 to Henry Welbore Agar Ellis, second Viscount Clifden. In the Clifden family it still remains.

"If," says Fuller, "Florence be said to be a city so fine that it ought not to be shown but on holidays, Holdenby was a house which should not have been shown but on Christmas Day. But, alas! Holdenby-house is taken away, being the emblem of human happiness, both in the beauty and the brittleness, short flourishing, and soon fading thereof. Thus one demolishing hammer can undo more in a day than ten edifying axes can advance in a month."

Evelyn, writing from "my Lord Sunderland's seat, at Althorpe" (1675) says—"The park full of fowl, especially herns, and from it a prospect of Holdenby House, which being demolished in the late civil wars, shows like a Roman ruin, shaded by the trees about it, a stately, solemn, and pleasing view." Since then, as we have seen, the ruin has lost very much of its magnificence, though the two lateral gateways bearing the Hatton arms, and the noble chimneys, still give a character to the view from Althorp. Baker describes the portion of the House not demolished, "as only a portion of the attached offices;" reserved by Adam Baynes "probably for his own habitation." But, traditionally the large stately upper room of the eastern half of the building is known as King Charles's bedroom. Considering the history of the House the distinction between the windows of the eastern and western portions is curious. The western windows retain the stone mullions of the Hatton period; the eastern are of the time of the Charleses.

What Holdenby House was in its grandeur we can but faintly guess at; but its splendid site is still a magnificent reality. Major Whyte Melville breaks into a prose poem in describing it. "The slope of the ground," he says, "which declines from it on all sides, offers a succession of the richest and most pastoral views which this rich and pastoral country can afford. Like the rolling prairie of the Far West, valley after valley of sunny meadows, dotted with oak and elm and other noble trees, undulates in ceaseless variety far as the eye can reach; but unlike the boundless prairie, deep, dark copses, and thick luxuriant hedgerows, bright and fragrant with wild flowers, and astir with the glad song of birds, diversify the foreground and blend the distance into a mass of woodland beauty that gladdens alike the eye of the artist and the stolid gaze of the clown. In June it is a dream of fairyland to wander along that crested eminence and turn from the ruins of those tall old gateways cutting their segments of blue out of the deep summer sky, or from the flickering masses of still tender leaves upon the lofty oaks yellowing in the floods of golden light that stream through the network of their tangled branches, every tree to the up-gazing eye a study of forest scenery in itself, and so to glance earthward at the fair expanse of homely beauty stretching away from one's very feet. Down in the nearest valley, massed like a solid square of Titan warriors and scattered like advanced champions from the gigantic array profusely up the opposite slope, the large old oaks of Althorpe quiver in the summer haze, backed by the thickly wooded hills that melt in softened outlines into the southern sky. The fresh light green of the distant larches blooming on far Harlestone Heath, is relieved by the dark belt of firs that draws a thick black line against the horizon. A light cloud of smoke floats above the spot where lies fair Northampton town, but the intervening trees and hedgerows are so clothed in foliage that scarce a building can be discerned, though the tall sharp spire of Kingsthorpe pierces upwards into the sky. To the west a confusion of wooded knolls and distant copses are bathed in the vapoury haze of a declining sun, and you rest your dazzled eyes swimming with so much beauty, and stoop to gather the wild flower at your feet. Ah, 'tis a pleasant season, that same merry month of June! Then in December—who doth not know and appreciate the merits of December at such a spot as Holdenby? Of all climates upon earth it is well known that none can produce the equal of a soft mild English winter's day, and such a day at Holdenby is worth living for through the gales of blustering October and the fogs of sad November with its depressing atmosphere and continuous drizzle. Ay, these are rare pastures to breathe a goodly steed, and there are fences too hereabouts that will prove his courage and your own. But enough of this. Is not Northamptonshire the very homestead of horse and hound, and Pytchley but a synonym of Paradise for all who delight herein?"

The terrace walks from which the eye takes in all this beauty are still traceable. What a brilliant scene they must have presented when they were thronged by the ladies and gallants of Elizabeth's time, all gorgeous in silks and satins, velvets and laces! The natural slope of the ground was artificially increased; far beneath are the fish ponds, and you look down upon the Church tower.

The Church is a small structure of various dates, the earliest portion being of the fourteenth century. It consists of an embattled tower, a nave, north and south aisles, and a chancel. The latter has been recently restored in the Early English style, and is large and lofty—loftier than the body of the structure. At the entrance is a ponderous oak screen, elaborately carved, which was set up by the Rev. Daniel Amiand, rector from 1690-1 to 1730. It is a good specimen of the Renaissance style of the day, and has no feature in harmony with the rest of the building. Among its adornments are two figures in Roman costume, each with a hand resting upon a shield. A large square pew is probably of Sir Christopher Hatton's time. The font is octagonal, with a projecting kneeling stone, and is covered with shields blazoned, which were restored in 1860, by the son of the late rector, Mr. Hartshorne, as we learn from the following inscription on one of them:—"Albertus Hartshorne, hunc fontem repinxit 1860." In the chancel are eight stalls with misereres. The under brackets have been mostly mutilated, but one retains the grotesque bust of a man wearing a hood or cap with two asses' ears. He is clothed in a doublet with hanging sleeves, and plays on a small drum. On his left shoulder sits a cat; a pair of wings form the ends of the bracket. The carving is very spirited. Neither Bridges nor Baker makes any allusion to it, though the latter speaks of the stalls and the turn-up seats, of which in his day there appear to have been five on each side. The oldest monumental record now in the church is a white alabaster slab in the south aisle, on which are out-lined two figures—male and female, with the hands in the attitude of prayer. The man is in plate armour, with fan elbow and knee pieces: his head is uncovered, his hair, long and lank, falls straight in a line over his forehead: the woman is plainly dressed with a bodice fitting close down to the hips, and a skirt falling in straight folds; she wears a cap with lappets. The slab is partially covered with a pew, and the inscription which borders it is in part hidden and altogether much worn. Bridges gives it as follows :—

"Hic jacet Willi'us Holdynby et Margareta uxor ejus, que quidem Margareta obiit . . . die mensis . . . Anno Domini MCCCCLXXI. Et Willi'us obiit . . . die . . . mensis MCCCCLXXXX quorum a'i'abus propitietur Deus. Amen."

Bridges states that the engraving of the figures is in brass, which is an error, and Baker is also mistaken in describing them of the size of life. They have, Bridges tells us, a boy and girl at their feet: this is the portion now covered with the pew. On a brass in a slab at the east end of the nave next the chancel is the following quaint inscription :—

Tu quis es? Hattonus: que te pronomine dicis?
Franciscum: genitor cui Gulielmus erat.
Viventi que cura? mori meditabar, avebas
Deserere hanc vitam? non: sed adire deum.

This Francis Hatton was an elder brother of the great Sir Christopher Hatton, and died, aged 14, in 1547. On a brass tablet on a slab in the south aisle is the following inscription :—

Hic Holdenbei castissima nominis heres
Hattoni Conjux Elizabetha jacet.
Legerat hæc talem non inconsulta maritum
Ut foret huic generis majore origo sui.

Another slab records the death of the grandson of this Elizabeth as follows :—

"Heare lyeth William Hatton, sonne of John Hatton, sonne of Elizabeth Hatton, daughter and heire of William Holdenbie, on whose soule Jesus have marcie."

He died in 1546. On another slab is the following verse :—

Corpus eras pulchrum, sed non sine pectore corpus
Sic tibi re Thoma, laus ab utraque fuit,
Te juvenem terris raptum Deus intulit astris
Et sacra Civem fecit in arce suum.

There is an arch in the wall of the south aisle which probably once canopied the founder's tomb. Bridges states that it contained a wooden statue of a man in a buttoned gown, with an iron sword and head-piece laid by him, but without any inscription. At a small distance, he adds, upon a raised pavement, is a black marble, on which was the effigies of a man in brass, with a coat of arms on each side of his head and a brass tablet at his feet; but the whole he says, is now gone.

There is assuredly no finer site for a mansion in the whole county of Northampton than Holdenby, and something like the revival of its Elizabethan glories was, we believe, at one time contemplated by the late Viscount Clifden. He built a family vault there, and transferred to it the remains of his grandfather, who purchased the property, father and sister, and buried there his mother, the late Baroness Dover. There, too, his own remains, and the remains of one of his twin children, are deposited. In the churchyard is a slab to the memory of Florence, daughter of the eminent antiquary, the Rev. C. H. Hartshorne, some time rector.

Holdenby village consists of a few cottages, skirting a spacious green—healthy-looking and pleasant.

In the house are two interesting relics found at different periods in the immediate neighbourhood. One is apparently a kind of *couteau de chasse*. The handle of horn, with silver rivets, is about eleven inches long, and is grooved for a clasp blade, of which traces remain. At the other end is an axe curved at the blade like a cheese-cutter, and on the top a pole-axe. It was probably used in stag-hunting. The other is a sword of, we believe, peculiar construction. The blade is waved, and is 22 inches long; the guard is a sort of gauntlet of iron, with a cross bar of the same metal within, at right angles with the blade, for the grasp. The blade springs from the upper part of the gauntlet, and a flap of iron in front is closed from within by putting a finger through a ring in the centre. There are guards on the gauntlet in the centre, and a steel point on either side, within which are curved cutting blades on joints, apparently devised to cut the knuckles of an antagonist grasping the weapon at close quarters. This elaborate weapon is calculated less for cutting than for thrusting.

Songs by the Way-side.

SONGS of love I used to sing thee
In those early days;
Votive flowers I used to bring thee,
Songs of love I used to sing thee.
Winter's grasp hath left no flowers,
Care's hath left no lays,
Like the songs and like the bowers
Of those early days.
Yet beneath this death-like seeming,
Warmth and life remain;
Flowers will burst at summer's beaming,
And the heart, with love still teeming,
Wake to song again.

Worn and weak with travel
Through the live-long day,
Thinking with a sad heart
Of the onward way,
Sudden from a lattice
Looked an angel face,
Such as in his happiest hour
Guido loved to trace.
Fount of inspiration!
From thy radiant source
Heart and mind and weary limbs
Drew unwonted force.
Thankless they who tell us
Beauty's gifts are vain;
Making bliss itself more blissful,
Giving bliss to pain.

Gayton.

TURN to the right on leaving Blisworth Station; take the descending road between Blisworth Gardens and the Towcester railway embankment, and a walk of a mile will bring you to pleasant Gayton. A mile, it is called, though most pedestrians, we believe, think it a long one—a mile and a bittock, as the Scotch say—about half a mile further. There is music in Blisworth Gardens always, the freshest and truest and purest being that from the orchestra in the boughs up above, when beautiful with the bright bursting of the Spring leaves. Cross the first roadway at right angles, descend the path by the new railway bridge, and follow it over undulating fields till you reach the next road, running east and west. Your way lies westward; turn to the left, and you will soon see direct before you the tower of Gayton church, the outline of its fine old Manor House, and a picturesque boundary of trees.

A few paces, and a glorious scene opens upon you. The road crosses fields now under the plough, affording a rich brown foreground, alive with the busy crow. To the right is a magnificent panorama, sweeping a vast extent of country to the north and north-west. We are upon high ground here: here, if anywhere, a breeze may always be found; in winter, one that for keenness might vie with the cutlery of Sheffield itself. In the early Spring, with a strong east wind blowing, the air is chill, but the fair beauty of the prospect, and the rural sights and sounds all round us, make up a happy and thoroughly enjoyable whole.

Gayton is a goodly village, with comfortable cottages within it, though some of them elbow their neighbours rather too closely. Here and there you find an old substantial house with good gables and mullioned windows. But its glory, in this respect, is the fine old Manor House at its eastern extremity, the way by which we entered. It stands north of the church, and is an imposing feature of the landscape. Originally it was a cruciform building with four gables, faced by a narrower gabled projection from roof to basement, affording a bay window to every room. The windows have stone mullions and a label above; they are of three lights—five in the bay. Lofty and imposing, with that air of comfort and domesticity which characterises the Elizabethan structures, one can imagine no more desirable residence, certainly none finer in respect of situation. There are large cheerful windows all the house over, though half of them are blocked up. In early times, when every man's hand was against his fellow, people were compelled, for the sake of security, to be content with dwellings dimly lighted by narrow loopholes in massive walls. With the dominion of law came the recognition of the blessedness of ample light, and our ancestors of the Elizabethan era revelled in the gladness of spacious windows. Half the picturesque beauty of these old mansions is due to this cheerful characteristic. But a time came when, although the brute force of war was not known in this country, the cost of it was, and people were compelled to take refuge in darkness against the tax-gatherer, as they had done formerly against the man-at-arms. Pitt's window-tax did irreparable mischief to our dwellings, old and new. It set builders to devise how light might be most generally dispensed with, and it blocked up the windows of our old mansions, shutting out the wholesome light and air, and consigning long passages and cosy nooks and corners to dinginess and damp. How it is that the cause being removed, the effect is not removed also—why these bricked-up windows are not re-opened, and air and light and health again admitted into them—is not difficult to understand. The restoration would cost much money; the casements are gone, and in some cases the mullions; the rooms to which they belong have been devoted to uses, perhaps, for which light is not absolutely necessary; or they have been wholly deserted and abandoned, and are mouldering to decay; and lastly, long habit and the unacquaintance with a brighter condition of things have blunted the sense of inconveniences and evils which must have been sorely felt by those upon whom the dismal duty first fell of blocking out the cheerful day. All good is not of necessity immediately recognised. The trail of evil remains long after the evil itself has passed away. Our domestic architecture has not even yet returned to the knowledge of the value of abundant windows.

This Gayton mansion was probably built by the Francis Tanfield whose monument is conspicuous in the church. The Tanfields were possessed of the manor from about 1452 to 1607, when a Sir Francis Tanfield sold it to Sir William Samwell. When the occupation of its early owners filled it with life, and the brawls and revels of the time brightened every window with light, the house must have shone like a beacon of brightness and joy to the far-surrounding country.

Exteriorly the Church is of small promise to the archæologist. It has been much restored at various periods, and the traces of the original structure are not many. The western door in the tower has a triangular head, but on the top two stones are engraven the words, "1725, William Ball, churchwarden," implying that a restoration was made at that time. It is probable, however, that Mr. Ball may have followed the form of an original Anglo-Saxon door. The tower was restored, apparently, about the same time to a large extent; nearly all its windows have evidence of eighteenth century work about them. In the main the Church is Decorated, but in the north wall there are traces of a circular-headed door, long since walled up, which may have belonged to the original building. It is divided by a Decorated buttress partly built, apparently, of some of the stones of the arch. In the same buttress, also, may be traced the dedication-stone, marked with five crosses.

The interior, however, has many features of interest, although that, too, has in its day suffered by restoration. The nave, for example, is ceiled and coloured in a fashion more suitable to a drawing-room than a Gothic Church. The font is late Norman, and is rimmed with the cable moulding; the sides have an arcade of intersecting arches, the head of each having a curve at the termination not unlike the incipient idea of a cusp, forming a somewhat rude trefoil head. The chancel arch is lofty and spacious, and on the south side, immediately within the arch, is a long narrow confessional window, divided by a transom. The chancel is full of interesting work. A reredos of rich dark oak, elaborately carved, extends along the entire width. It is divided into panels with arches and a kind of drapery pattern, and a centre separated by two buttresses, pinnacled and crocketted. Under a canopy in each of these buttresses, and standing on a slender column as a pedestal, is a figure about six inches high, also carved in oak. One is habited in a tunic reaching to the knees, a mantle over the shoulders, and a cap with a long end, as if to draw down over the face like the cap of a chimney-sweep. The legs are cased in tight hose, and the shoes are high-lows without lacing. The other figure is clothed in a vest, closed in front, and having large hanging sleeves; a tunic falling in large, straight, regular folds to the knees, tight hose, and shoes like the other. His head is covered with a huge mass of clustering hair, crowned with a kind of trencher cap. On each side of the chancel are three stalls, with carved elbows and misereres, in excellent preservation. These misereres have all curiously grotesque carvings. Beginning at the east end on the south side, the subject appears to be the entry into Jerusalem. At a window above is apparently a priest with clasped hands. No. 2 represents a sitting figure with uplifted hands, and on either side a cluster of praying figures as if in panniers. No. 3: three figures seated under a canopy; above, the fragment of a curled head, similar to the one on the reredos. On the north side, beginning at the west end, is a stern-looking draped figure, with both arms extended, spreading an ample mantle, beneath which on either side cower naked and terrified figures; the central miserere affords a grotesque group—an animal, which may be meant for a dog or possibly a bear, has been seized by a lion, which in its turn is seized by a winged dragon. The ends of the carving, which in the instances already mentioned are flowers, and oak-leaves, and acorns, are here formed of nondescript animals—one of them a dragon, biting his own tail; the other, a winged creature, with a hood or cap on its head. The last of the series is a figure in scale armour, a personification, probably, of the Evil one, with bird-like claws instead of hands and feet, and carrying a kind of heraldic shield, with traces on it of a bend and bordure. He sits astride prostrate figures, wearing caps and tunics, and one holding a coil of beads. One of the ends is formed of an animal something like a bear; the other, of a figure with folded arms, having a scroll in his lap, from behind which projects an axe. His legs are demoniacal claws. We have already said that these curious sculptures are in excellent preservation; they seem, indeed, to have been the objects of a more intelligent care than such relics ordinarily meet with; but we may call the attention of the authorities to the fact that one of the feet of the figure on the south side of the reredos is broken off, and a remarkably well-carved mask from one of the elbows of the stalls is lying on the credence shelf of the piscina in the south wall. Five minutes and the glue-pot will save them from the peril to which their present unsecured state subjects them.

Separating the chancel from the north chapel is an altar tomb under an open trefoil-headed ogee arch, upon which lies the wooden effigy of a cross-legged knight, with his feet on a dog, and his hands pressed together, in devotion. He wears a round filletted helmet and camail; a tunic girt round the middle by a belt, and a sword, broken, suspended by a baldrick. Baker supposes it to represent the last of the Gaytons, Sir John de Meaux, of Gayton and of Bewyk in Holderness, Yorkshire, who died in 1379, leaving no children. Opposite this tomb, in the south wall, is an altar tomb of Purbeck marble, under a depressed Tudor arch embattled, and bearing four blank escutcheons. It has no inscription, and apparently has been blank always. Against the north wall of the north chapel is an altar tomb of alabaster, on the face of which are incised the effigies of Francis Tanfield and Bridget, his wife, with their eighteen children. Eight of them, having died in infancy, are represented in swaddling clothes, bound with cross straps, like the wrappings of a mummy. The initials of the Christian name of each child is engraved beneath :—C. F. A. F. B. A. L. I. T. Y. A. M. E. M. I. B. S. I. The knight is in plate armour, with chain mail tassettes, and slashed sollerettes, with the frightful broad toes characteristic of the time of Henry VIII. His feet rest on a greyhound, and those of his lady on her lap-dog. The figures are very interesting as illustrative of the costume of the period. Round the ledge of the tomb is the inscription :—"Hic jacent Franciscus Tanfield, Armiger, et Brigetta, ux' ejus, qui quidem Franciscus obiit diem Ao dni 1558 Novebris 21 die quorum vita Christus est, Brigetta v'o obiit ao dni 1583 Junii 20 die. Requiescant in pace." The arms of Tanfield and Cave appear on lozenges within square panels at each end of the tomb, the lady having been a daughter of Richard Cave, of Stanford, Esq., and sister of Sir Ambrose Cave. Eastward of this interesting monument, beneath an arch in the wall, is the recumbent figure of a female, her head supported on a square cushion, and her feet resting on a lion. She wears, says Baker, "a long Paris hood or veil, falling gracefully on her shoulders, and confined round the head by a studded fillet, from which a smaller fillet rises over the forehead, disclosing her parted hair in front. Her robe is loose, with tight sleeves from the elbows, and close buttoned at the wrist. Her mantle is fastened across the breast by a cordon, which she holds in her left hand: her right reposes by her side, and the folds of her drapery are gathered under each arm." The historian is of opinion that this figure must have been imitated from, if not the actual production of, the sculptor of the Royal females on the Queen's Cross, and has little hesitation in assigning it to Scolastica de Meaux. If by this Scolastica is meant the wife of Godfrey de Meaux, and mother of Sir John de Meaux, the last of the Gaytons, whose monument we have already described, and who died in 1354, the inexorable logic of figures makes it impossible that the work should be that of the sculptor of the Eleanor Cross figures. All the Eleanor Crosses were built between 1291 and 1294; and the intrinsic evidence also is against the supposition. The sculpture on the tomb is artistically inferior to that of the Crosses. Of course the argument is not equally good as against the question of imitation. But the fashion of the day will, we think, sufficiently account for any resemblance without assuming direct copy. A terrible tragedy is connected with this Scholastica. Her sister Juliana married Thomas Murdak, of Edgcote, and in the 26th year of her age was burnt for the murder of her husband. On a bracket over this figure is a remarkable little effigy of a young female not two feet long. It had been built into the exterior east wall of the north chapel, and was discovered by Dr. Butler, the incumbent, during some reparations in 1830. Like the figure just described, she wears a veil confined across the forehead by a studded fillet. One of two shields discloses her connection with the Gaytons. On the ledge may be traced in Lombardic characters—" H— jacet in tumba Mabila filia Thomæ "—

The section of the Northampton and Banbury Railway from Blisworth to Towcester skirts the southern boundary of Gayton. Owing, however, to the line being in a cutting at this point, and the swelling of the intermediate fields, little of the village is visible from it besides the summit of the church tower.

Simon, the Piping Crow.

(An Inscription for a case containing a Piping Crow that used to whistle "The Girl I left behind me.")

THIS is Simon, the Piping Crow:
These are his feathers, this is his toe,
This is his beak so sharp and strong;
But where, alas! ah, where is his song?
A strange, mysterious bird was he,—
The song he sang in his native tree
He never sang in slavery,
But he solaced himself with a captive strain,
"The sweeter for a taste of pain."
It told of a girl he left behind,
Rocked by the rude Australian wind;
He learnt it of a bold Jack Tar,
Who had also left his girl afar,—
A man in his way a bit of a trim-beau,
Who used to stand with his arms a-kimbo,
And looking up at the young May moon,
Whistle his love in that plaintive tune.
And Simon caught, not merely the lay,
But Jack's identical, nautical way,
And kimboed his wings and lifted his beak,
As if he were shouting his strange *musique*
To a messmate, mast-headed above,
Purely for liking and for love.

This is Simon, the Piping Crow:
He died—as possibly you know,
Or he wouldn't be sitting mumchance so.
He died—yet we didn't "lay him low,"

As the common phrases of epitaphs go,
But had him stuffed with wool and tow,
And made him a kind of a sort of a show,
To make you cry "I never!"—"Oh!"
Why he died we never could tell!
He never complained of feeling unwell.
One doleful day we took to his house
A dish he was partial to—a mouse;
And at it he went with his mighty beak,
And then we heard a terrible shriek,
Such as we never heard before,
And it thrilled our hearts to the very core;
And before we could speak he was on the floor,
And we plainly saw that all was o'er.
Never did Simon whistle more.

Down he fell, to the mind recalling
At Pompey's foot proud Cæsar falling;
For dying he held his lordly will,
And mantled his wings about his bill;*
In death Australian Simon still.

And since Australian Simon died,
A bold Jack Tar I never have spied,
With arms a-kimbo and legs astride,
And his head upraised and a little aside,
And never I hear the warlike fife
Pipe farewell to maid or wife,
But my heart will with the music go,
In memory of "Simon, the Piping Crow."

---

* . . . . Then burst his mighty heart,
And in his mantle muffling up his face,
Even at the base of Pompey's statue,
Which all the while ran blood, great Cæsar fell.

JULIUS CÆSAR.

Abington.

NOT so many years ago, a walk to Abington was a perfect country walk. Abington-street, cheerful in itself (its eastern half at all events) with an occasional scrap of garden, Mr. Markham's somewhat quaint house, with its evergreens and creepers, and garden wall, peaked-roof summer-house, and trees overhanging the footway, and, at the extremity, on one side Dr. Kerr's garden, terminating in the Dutch-fashioned *lusthuis*, of the kind which still border the canals of Holland, and which came in with William the III., and on the other the late Mr. Percival's house, with its ample garden also next the street—Abington-street, pleasant and country-like, had, so to speak, one foot in the fields. The "Bantam Cock" was a way-side inn, with fields and gardens all about it. Church-lane, as the turning down to St. Giles's Church was called, was overhung with a noble row of elms in Mr. Percival's garden, all the way down to the Churchyard, on the site now magniloquently called St. Giles's-terrace, on the *lucus a non lucendo* principle, because it is not terraced, just as Albion-crescent is called a crescent because it is not crescented. Keeping under Mr. Percival's wall, at the north boundary of St. Giles's Churchyard, there were continuous paths through market gardens and fields nearly all the way to Abington. The paths remain, but changed from what they were. For hedge-rows we have houses, and brick walls, and cinder paths. A whole suburb has sprung up in our track, and we cross at right angles street after street, having the advantage, however, let it be noted, of a sight of trees and allotment grounds at either extremity, north and south. Many, too, of these small suburban houses have neatly-kept gardens in front, and look very clean and cheerful, and well-to-do. Some of them still look over orchards and market gardens, and must have delightful up-stairs rooms, though they will hardly retain the advantage many years. Of the streets crossing our path north and south, the last ought to be the pleasantest, being built at present on one side only, and having the privilege of looking over gardens, and onwards to distant fields. Somehow, the inhabitants seem to have a custom of breaking their windows and mending them with brown paper and dirty rags, which is certainly not ornamental, nor, we should think, much more useful. Crossing a stile, old memories revive; we get at length into the old garden grounds, odorous of the bean-flower and that *essence de mille fleurs*, which no chemist can elaborate like the great chemist Nature. Then comes a good liberal hedge-row, interspersed with elms, and fields with nibbling sheep. Another stile, and we are in sight of Abington Park. And now we are fairly in the country, and in a very beautiful nook of it too. The trees are magnificent in their abundance, their size, and their luxuriance. Broad-leaved chestnuts make a shade, resting in which we can survey in the early summer the glory of the white cones of flowers scattering delicate showers of white beauty on the vivid grass. Huge elms, making an avenue from the Rectory to the Abbey, fling their giant arms across the road. "A circular array" of pines,—

> "— so fixed,
> Not by the sport of Nature but of man,"

gives special character to the scene. Down the slope to the left is a farm-house, looking like snugness itself; but conspicuous over all are the abbey (upon what authority it is called an abbey we do not know) and the church tower. It is a picturesque group. The grounds of the abbey are on a sort of terrace, and in the wall which embanks it is an arch, covering a long stone trough, fed by a spring, to which the cattle resort. The church, standing in the grounds of the abbey, and very near it, is clustered about with tall trees, and we see the tower only, partly clothed in ivy. It is embattled and has decorated windows and gurgoyles, and is the best part of the structure, the rest having in the main been re-built in comparatively modern times, and with but scant architectural knowledge. It was blown down when under repair in 1821. Baker thus describes it previous to this calamity:—"The church, dedicated to St. Peter and St. Paul, is situated in a small church-yard, planted on the north and west to screen it from the mansion. It consists of a tower, nave, side aisles and chancel leaded, and a plain south porch tiled. The south front is mantled with ivy; the tower and east ends of the nave, chancel, and north aisle are embattled. Most of the windows are long and square-headed, divided by a single mullion; the eastern chancel window is of three lights, with plain arched heads; one of the windows in the north aisle is of a much earlier date than any other part of the building, being a double lancet with a drip-stone following the course of both arches." When the church was re-built it seems to have been shortened at the east end. It is difficult otherwise to account for the position of two altar monuments in the north chapel, which stand so nearly together as to preclude any passage between them, the east wall also being built close up to them. The inscriptions face the east, and are only legible by climbing on to the tombs themselves. There was, no doubt, access to them round the east end, unless we are to suppose that at the rebuilding of the church the top slabs were reversed. Bridges describes them as "at the south-*west* end of the north chapel." At present they occupy the whole depth of the chapel from east to west. They are to the memory of Dame Eleanor Hampden, mother of Sir John Bernard, who died in 1634, whose first husband was Baldwin Bernard, and her next Sir Edmund Hampden, of Great Hampden, Bucks, the uncle of the patriot; and to the same Sir Edmund Hampden who died in 1627. Neither Bridges nor Baker notices a carving on the stone panel of the west end of the lady's tomb, of a demi-knight in full armour on a wreath holding a tilting-spear, with the upper part broken. On the floor on a plain slab at the south-east end of the church is the following inscription beneath the Bernard arms now nearly defaced :—

M. S.
Hic Jacent Exuviæ Generosissmi
Viri Johannis Bernard, Militis
Patre, Avo, Abavo, Tritavo, aliis
Progenitorjb' per ducentos et
amplius annos huius oppidi de
Abingdon Dominis insignis. Qui
Fato cessit undeseptuagesimo
Aetatis suæ anno quinto nonas
Martii Annoque a partu B Virginis
MDCLXXIII.

Bridges mistakenly gives the date 1683. There is a peculiar interest in this inscription. Not that the father, grandfather, great-grandfather, great-great-grandfather, and other progenitors of the Sir John Bernard whom it records, for more than two hundred years were lords of Abington, nor that with him ended that distinction; but that he was the second husband of the last of the line of William Shakespeare. Shakespeare's favourite daugher, Susannah, who married Dr. Hall, had a daughter Elizabeth, who married in 1626 Thomas Nash, Esq., of Welcomb, in the county of Warwick. Mr. Nash died in 1647, and in 1649 his widow married this Sir John Bernard, whose first wife was also a daughter of a man of mark in his day, Sir Clement Edmonds, of Preston Deanery, the author of the Observations on Cæsar's Commentaries, and Remembrancer of the City of London in 1609. The second Lady Bernard died in 1669-70, and we find the record of her burial in the Parish Register as follows :—"Madam Elizabeth Bernard, wife of Sr. John Bernard, Kt., was buried 17th Feby., 1669." It is curious that the entry is somewhat cramped and crowded upon a record of the burial of one "Thomas Hoe, labourer:" it is the last in that year, and its appearance almost suggests that it was an interpolation between the entry of the burial of Thomas Hoe and the heading of the coming year "Anno Domini 1670;" as if the keeper of the Register had written the heading for that year, not expecting other burials. Of this last of the Shakespeares there is no other record. So far as we know, no stone ever marked the spot where she was buried. When the body of the church was blown down and the new building took place, we may take for granted that many inscriptions were destroyed; but that one to Lady Bernard was not among them we may accept as a certainty. Baker, who compiled his account of Abington before the destruction of the church, makes no mention of any inscription, as he undoubtedly would have done had any existed; and Bridges is equally silent. Sir John Bernard sold the Abington property in this same year of Lady Bernard's death. There may be nothing in the coincidence: there may have been a recording stone, which, in the hundred years and more between the burial and the compilation of Bridges' history, may have become accidentally destroyed. But it is difficult to repress the feeling that something of a domestic romance has been lost. The entry of the burial of Sir John Bernard is as follows:—

"Sr. John Bernard, Knight, my noble and ever honoured patron, was buried 5th March, 167¾."

It is written in a distinct and good hand, obviously by the rector, John Howes, who was inducted in 1652. There is an entry in the register, under the date of 1654, that "Robert Joyce, servant to John Bernard, Esq., aged about one hundred years, was buried 27th Nov., anno predicto."

Abington came by marriage through Elizabeth, only daughter and heiress of Sir Nicholas Lillyng, who was member for the county in 1381-2, into the family of the Bernards of Isleham, co. Cambridge, about the beginning of the 15th century, and continued in their possession till 1669, when Sir John Bernard sold the manor, lordship, and advowson of "Abbington alias

Abingdon," with the court-leet, court-baron, and fishery in the river of Nen from Northampton Meadow to Weston Meadow, to William Thursby, then of the Middle Temple, London, Esq., for £13,750. Mr. Thursby was a native of Holt, in Leicestershire, and was educated at Uppingham Grammar School; he was twice married, but had one child only, who died an infant. He was member for Northampton in 1698. His estates were devised to his nephews, William and Richard Thursby, successively, in tail male, with remainder to his niece Mary Harvey. The nephews died without children, and the settled estates devolved to John Harvey, Esq., the son of the niece Mary Harvey, who thereupon, in pursuance of an express proviso in the will of the devisor, assumed the name and arms of Thursby of Essex. Ralph Thoresby, the celebrated Leeds antiquary, was of the Thursby family.

Baker suggests, with much plausibility, that the south and east fronts of this fine old mansion were built by the first Mr. Thursby; and the late Mr. Pretty (a sufficient authority) thought it probable that they were designed by Francis Smith, an architect of Warwick, of whom a portrait is engraved by A. V. Haecken, in mezzotinto, and dedicated to Wm. Thursby, Esq., 1730. But much of the interior belongs to an earlier time. The hall, a lofty gothic room, has an open timbered roof, a recess and dais at one end, and mullioned windows. The staircase is of the Elizabethan period. But the glory of the place is a room at the south west corner, so elaborately and beautifully pannelled that nobody, through the centuries of its existence, has found heart to deface it. There are the three pikes naiant of the Lillyngs; the bear rampant of the Bernards, and a whole gallery of grotesque devices besides. Among them are a fool carrying a child in swaddling clothes, with women following; a fox in a pulpit; a dog with his head in a pot; groups representing the seasons and their occupations—ploughing, sowing, mowing, carrying grapes, beating the mast from the oak for the swine beneath; mummers and antics dancing and tumbling;

a dancing bear; boys blowing bubbles, &c. It is not easy to determine the date of this interesting room. The chimney front may be as late as James I., but it does not follow that the entire room is of that date. We should rather believe it to have been the work either of the John Bernard, who died in 1485, or of his son, also named John, who died in 1508. Our reason for fixing on these particular individuals, apart from the evidence of the workmanship itself, is that on one of the shields are the initials I. B., with, a little below, M., which may be interpreted John and Margaret Bernard. Both the Bernards in question married a Margaret, and no later Bernard had a wife whose name had the same initial. In this curious and beautiful room, however, precisely as we see it, by whomsoever panelled, it is certain that the last of the Shakespeares sat. The possibility indeed is that Shakespeare's own favourite daughter herself, Susannah Hall, may have looked upon its quaint carvings. Her daughter, the widow of Mr. Nash, married Mr. Bernard (he was not knighted till twelve years later) on the 5th of June, 1649, while her mother was still living. Mrs. Hall died in little more than a month afterwards (July 11) at Stratford-upon-Avon, in her 67th year. A journey from Stratford to Abington was not, in those days, to be performed with the ease and speed of our railway times; but whatever convenience the times afforded would have been at her service. Wedding tours had not yet become the fashion, and after her marriage Mrs. Bernard, with a goodly company of friends and relations, would proceed direct to her new home. It is not impossible that Mrs. Hall, should have been among the most honoured of the guests there.

Mr. Halliwell, we have heard, entertains an opinion that behind the wainscoting of this room may be found a solution of the question—What became of Shakespeare's MSS. and correspondence? Among the curiosities of literature there is nothing, perhaps, more curious than the total disappearance of every scrap of Shakespeare's writing, his autographs excepted attached to legal documents, and the one in his copy of Florio's

Montaïgne. A completer clearance could not have been made had his will contained a clause directing that all his papers should be burnt. Whatever his supposed indifference to the preservation of his writings, it is impossible that at his death there should not have been a vast accumulation of papers and correspondence. We agree with Mr. Knight in altogether disbelieving the assumption that after his retirement to Stratford, Shakespeare wholly ceased to write. The argument to the contrary is unanswerable—"Is it reasonable to believe that the mere habit of his life would not assert its ordinary control?" Assuming, which we have no right to assume, that Mrs. Shakespeare took no interest in her husband's miscellaneous papers, and set no value upon them, regarding them indeed rather as lumber to be got out of the way of good housewifery as speedily as possible, it is not probable that his daughter, Mrs. Hall, should not understand, and duly estimate them. She and her husband were Shakespeare's executors, and in that capacity had possession of the house in which the testator died, New Place, with all the goods not specially otherwise bequeathed, "and household stuff whatsoever." Susannah Hall was "witty above her sex;"—

Witty above her sex, but that's not all,
Wise to salvation was good Mistress Hall;
Something of Shakespeare was in that, but this
Wholly of Him with whom she's now in bliss—

says the epitaph on her tombstone. All her father's papers must have fallen into her hands, and she lived more than thirty years after his death. At Mrs. Hall's death they would go to her daughter, Mrs. Bernard. What did she do with them? Mr. Halliwell, we have understood, thinks it not improbable that she deposited them somewhere behind this antique wainscoting, and that they may be there still. The question arises—What was her motive for such a concealment? Was she a person of eccentric habits? Had she tastes not in common with her husband's? She was a woman of education, to judge by her bold, masculine autograph. Sir John had lived through the times of the

Commonwealth. Had he adopted the prejudice of that day against the drama? Did his lady put her grandfather's papers out of the sight of good Mr. Howes, the rector, who was "a moderate Presbyterian," and dedicated some sermons to his "ever honoured patron?" Are there behind that panelling other Hamlets; other Merry Wives of Windsor; Letters from Ben Johnson: from my fellows John Hemynge, Richard Burbage, and Henry Cundell?" A mere Midsummer dream perhaps, but to say the least, a dream strangely tantalizing. Whenever Mr. Halliwell brings out his magnificent projected work—"Illustrations of the Life of William Shakespere," we shall no doubt have these possibilities and probabilities discussed with all the fulness that zeal and knowledge and unsparing research can give them, and we may expect to see thorough pictorial justice done to this beautiful room.

This fine old mansion has for many years been occupied as a "Retreat"—a happy name for a place so peculiarly adapted to "minister to a mind diseased." The grounds about are very large and very diversified in their character; every turn affords a new and pleasant picture. The very kitchen gardens, surrounded with lofty walls, are yet so wide and so bounded with trees that they look thoroughly unconfined and inviting to a stroll in them. The many roofs of the mansion seen from them are pleasing in their combination with the church tower beyond. Among the old and ample outhouses is a Dovecot, with a good Tudor doorway to it. The present occupant, Dr. Prichard, has made vast improvements in the grounds of the most judicious kind.

On the lawn before the east front is a mulberry tree, which was planted in 1778 by David Garrick, and had suspended to it a copper plate with the following inscription:—

"This tree was planted by David Garrick, Esq., at the request of Ann Thursby, as a growing testimony of their friendship, 1778."

Eighty-eight years is not a great age for a mulberry tree. There are some three hundred years old still flourishing and bearing, and as long as it continues vigorous, the older the tree, we believe, the richer the fruit. But this tree which the great actor planted is, we are sorry to say, by no means in a thriving condition. Its leaves are small, and have a dwindled appearance; the foliage is scanty, and the fruit does not ripen kindly.

In the Dunciad is at once immortalized and libelled one Leonard Welsted, in these lines :—

> " Flow, Welsted, flow ; like thine inspirer, Beer,
> Tho' stale, not ripe ; tho' thin, yet never clear ;
> So sweetly mawkish, and so smoothly dull,
> Heady, not strong ; o'erflowing, tho' not full."

This is a parody on Denham's famous apostrophe to the Thames :—

> " O could I flow like thee, and make thy stream
> My great example as it is my theme :
> Tho' deep, yet clear ; tho' gentle, yet not dull ;
> Strong without rage ; without o'erflowing, full."

Leonard Welsted was the son of the Rev. Leonard Welsted, the incumbent of Abington, and was born there in 1689. He was educated at Westminster School, and very early in life obtained a place in the Ordnance Office. In 1724 he published a volume of poems entitled "Epistles, Odes, &c." One of his Odes was highly commended by Steele, and so generally admired as to be attributed to Addison. In Dr. King's Works is included a poem on "Applepie," which Chalmers claims for Welsted, who, it is said, wrote it while he was yet at Westminster School. Bell's "Edition of the Poets" (1781) retains "Applepie" among Dr. King's poems, with the following note :—"'This poem hath been claimed as Mr. Welsted's in 'The Weekly Oracle,' August 6th, 1735, with a remark that 'Dr. King, the Civilian, a gentleman of no mean reputation in the world of letters, let it pass some years without contradiction as his own.'" Whether Chalmers had other authority besides the "Weekly Oracle" for claiming it as Welsted's, we do not know. As Welsted published many poems in his life time, he had frequent opportunities of asserting his title to his poem, which, however, he does not appear to have done. He was twice married; first to a daughter of the eminent musician, Henry Purcell, who composed, among so much other delicious music, the lovely air to Dryden's words, "What shall I do to show how much I love her," and the music to "The Tempest;" and secondly to a sister of Bishop Walker, the defender of Londonderry. He died in 1747.

It was apparently a merry time when the nephew of the purchaser of Abington was in possession of the property. In one of the early volumes of the *Northampton Mercury* occurs the following advertisement:—

"On Tuesday in Whitsun-week, being the 26th of May, 1724, will be run for from the gate of William Thursby, Esq., leading into Wellingborough-road, down Abbington-street, to the Pump upon the Corn-market Hill, in Northampton, a plate of £5 value by any bull, cow, or bullock, of any age or size whatsoever, that never won the value of £5 in money or plate. Each rider to have boots and spurs, with a goad of the usual size. Every bull, &c., to pay one shilling entrance, which is to be given to the second best bull, &c.; the winning beast to be sold for £20 (if desired) by the subscribers. They are to start at the gate above-mentioned, at five o'clock in the afternoon. If any disputes arise, to be decided by the majority of the subscribers then present."

Those were the days of open fields, and the farmers along the line of the proposed route were naturally somewhat alarmed at what might happen to their crops if the bull were to bolt from the appointed course, and choose one for himself across country. They appear to have remonstrated, and the programme was accordingly modified. In a subsequent number of our paper there appeared a second advertisement, as follows:—

"Complaints having been made that great Damage will be to the Corn by the Bulls, &c., starting at the Gate of William Thursby, Esq., it is ordered by a great many of the Subscribers that upon Tuesday in Whitsun Week, being the 26th instant, at 4 in the afternoon, the Bulls, &c., are to start from the Bridge near Swallbrook Spring, run down Abbington Street into Northampton, and end at the Pump upon the Corn-Market-Hill. The winning Bull, Ox, or Cow to be rid by the rider from the said Pump, by the Hind Inn, and down the Drapery to the George Inn: where the Treasurer will be to deliver the Plate, Five Pounds in Money; and the Stakes to the second best Bull, &c. The Bulls, &c.,

to enter at Hill's Coffee House, in Northampton, at Nine in the Morning the Day of Running, and pay One Shilling entrance each Bull, &c., which goes to the second best Bull, &c., as aforesaid. No less than Four to start for the Plate."

If, as is certain enough, we are not a whit better than we should be, it is consolatory to know that in some respects, at least, we are a little better than our forefathers. We have abandoned bear-baiting, and bull-running, and bull-racing. Northampton in 1724 was a somewhat aristocratic town, and the route chosen for this extraordinary race was through its most aristocratic portion. It was a town of large inns mainly, and of the residence of the smaller gentry. The intercourse with London was not so easy as in later times, and Northampton was a kind of metropolis for its surrounding neighbourhood. Balls and assemblies were frequent, and they brought hither the surrounding aristocracy. Hill's Coffee House, wherever it stood, was no doubt the fashionable resort of the bloods of the day. In reference to these bull races, however, we must bear in mind that cattle in those days were commonly used for draught, at the plough, and in carts and waggons employed in agriculture. The racing bull, therefore, was to a certain extent a trained animal, and the race was not exactly the same thing that it would be with animals taken fresh from the pasture or the stall. Still no amount of education could make a seat on bull-back very secure or agreeable, and the fun must have mainly consisted in the frequent unshipping of the riders; perhaps in the animal making a sudden raid among the spectators, overturning some and scattering the rest in all directions, amidst shrieks and laughter. The triumphal ride from the Pump to the George was not the worst devised part of the programme. To make a bull, hot from a pell-mell chase, march with stately step and slow down a street, thronged with shouting and laughing people, argues a skill in "noble horsemanship" which might well "'witch the world."

Abington, and nearly all its pleasant domains, is now the property of Lord Overstone.

The Monks of Yore: a Ballad.

A Pleasant life it must have been,
The life of the monks of yore,
Or sauntering on the Abbey-green,
Or over the purple moor;
Or with a book beside the stream,
The trout-stream gushing clear;
Or in the morning's earliest beam,
With an eye on the plump red deer.
Oh, a merry life he must have led,
The monk of long ago;
If he didn't get nigh to the heaven o'erhead,
He made heaven of earth below.

They gifted his cell with broad, rich lands,
The richest in the shire;
And they came to his service with willingness,
To fashion his desire;
And he dream'd sweet dreams of a fane that seems
Wrought by a breath divine;
By the holy rood, the love was good
Whence sprang so fair a shrine.
Oh, an earnest life he must have led,
The monk of long ago;
If he didn't get nigh to the heaven o'erhead,
He made heaven on earth below.

Jolly at eve, at the ample board,
  In the high refectory;
When the party came, and the wine's red hoard,
  Who would not do as he?
He has echoed the anthem through the aisles,
  He has told his rosary;
And the pilgrim cheer'd with food and smiles,
  And a benedicite.
So a merry life he must have led,
  The monk of long ago;
If he didn't get nigh to the heaven o'erhead,
  He made heaven on earth below.

They tell that in the dead midnight,
  The hind that wends his way,
Sees many a strange, unholy sight,
  He dare not tell by day.
Strange deeds were done beneath the sun,
  As fearful legends tell;—
Aye, there was crime in the olden time,
  But in modern times as well.
So deem the best of the life he led,
  The monk of long ago;
And hope that he thought of the heaven o'erhead
  When he made a heaven below.

Rothersthorpe.

TRAVELLERS by rail between Blisworth and Northampton discern, lying northward, a church tower rising from a cluster of trees. It is especially remarkable in having a pack-saddle roof. Any rambler would be attracted by its picturesqueness. A rambler with an antiquarian bias would be sure to seek it out. From Blisworth there is a pleasant walk of a long-ish mile—pleasant whether you follow the road, or take the shorter cut over the fields. A cluster of poplars is a sufficient land-mark. Rothersthorpe is the most rural of villages—small, scattered, quiet, clean, intersected with fields and trees and gardens; with none of the unagreeable accompaniments of large towns. The farm-houses look prosperous and very pleasant, and happy. Some of them have stately gables, and windows with drip-stones and mullions of the Tudor period. As we pass an open homestead, we see its mistress, who has just entered, welcomed by a simultaneous winging downwards of pigeons, and rushing towards her of fowls, and frolicsome homage of dogs. We get glimpses, too, of orchards, white and pink with blossom, and lawns which they overshadow and keep green. Dwellers in towns contrast them, with a shrug of the shoulders, with their own poor endeavours at gardens in pots on the window sills, which, however, if they are wise, as well as observant men, they will cherish none the less, remembering the sage maxim—"Quand on n'a pas ce que l'on aime, il faut aimer ce que l'on a"—when we haven't got what we like, we must like what we have got.

Rothersthorpe, secluded and out of the world as it now is, must at some remote period have been a place of importance and turbulent assemblage. In Domesday Book it is called simply Torp, the Saxon name for a village, but at an earlier date than that famous record it had been the site of extensive earthworks. A camp, occupying about four acres in the centre of the village, and evidently dictating its form, had probably a connection with the camp on Hunsborough Hill, known as Dane's Camp. It is wedge-shaped, the highest part of the embankment being on the west and north-west. The late Mr. Pretty, F.S.A., who twenty years ago published in the *Archæological Journal* a very careful account of the village, accompanied by two admirable etchings of the church, points out that several of the earthworks in the vicinity are more or less of a similar shape—those at Burnt Walls, Alderton-Bury, Lactodorum, the station of Antoninus at Towcester; and Dane's Banks, towards Brickhill. The highest part of the embankment at Rothersthorpe is at the north-west corner. The feet of many generations must have traversed the footpaths intersecting the enclosure, and the cattle of centuries grazed upon its mounds, but it is still boldly defined, and manifests its once formidable character. It is known as the Burys, a modification of the word Burh, the Anglo-Saxon name for a fort or settlement.

The Church, which attracts the eye at a distance, by no means disappoints a closer inspection. Its aspect is singularly venerable. The peculiar gable of its pack-saddle roofed tower, its sancte bell cot, and its generally grey and weather-stained walls, impress one strongly with a sense of its antiquity. Its architecture is mainly of the Decorated period, with introductions, of course, of a later date; while its Norman font, and an Early English doorway within the porch, tell of an antecedent structure. It consists of nave, chancel, north and south aisles, with a chapel at the east end of each; a tower and a south porch. The three arches on either side, which separate the nave from the aisles, are carried by clustered pillars, the shafts of which are painted in a grey oil colour. Wonderful things are sometimes done under the delusion of improvement. In Towcester Church there are two early Norman pillars, with the shafts ornamented with the zigzag ornament, as in the tower arch of St. Peter's, Northampton. Somebody, no doubt, fancied he was putting things as they should be when he turned these unhappy pieces of work upside-down, and set them on their heads, as they are at this day. The chancel arch appears to have recently had some attention bestowed upon it, and presents the original stone. A squint or hagioscope, on the south side of the chancel, afforded a view of the ceremonial from the south chantry. In the chancel are two sedilia and a piscina; and on the north side is an aumbry, with its original oak door, and wrought-iron hinges of horse-shoe form, the ends being snake's heads. In the south chantry is another piscina, and a third in the south wall of the north chantry. Beneath an ogee arch, crocketted, and with Decorated mouldings, in the south wall, is the founder's tomb. As late as 1835 the par-close screens were in existence: they were of the late Decorated period. The tower arch is closed. In the belfry are four bells, with the following inscriptions:—"1 God Save our King 1638;" "2 Russel of Wotton made me;" "3 God Save our King 1630;" "4 Som Rosa polsata monde Maria vocata." The fourth bell of Pattishall Church, about four miles further on the Banbury Lane, bears the same legend. An Englefield once held both those manors, and Mr. Pretty conjectures, with great probability, that he was the donor of both bells. Prior to 1841, when the Church was new-paved, some of the figured tiles of the pavement remained. Two of them were of rather a bright-red earth, covered with a chocolate-coloured ground, impressed with a yellowish pattern of deer running and two cocks fighting. The Norman font is in good preservation. Its lower half is plain: the upper has an arcade of intersecting arches: the brim has the cable moulding. The Church is barren of monuments. One flat stone records the deaths of nine children of Daniel and Elizabeth Howes, five of them in one year,

1717. One of the Rothersthorpe incumbents, George Preston, was ejected by the Parliament Commissioners, and died in gaol at Northampton. The churchyard is considerably higher than the roadway, which surrounds three sides of it—by nearly a man's height. The accumulated dust of generation after generation has thus mounded it up. Like the Church, it does not seem to contain any remarkable records of illustrious dead; but it is a true village churchyard, in which one loves to linger. "Neighbourhood is at hand without noise; the fields stretch away into quiet remoteness; birds sing as cheerfully as in the homestead; and, in truth, the churchyard itself seems but another homestead, into which fathers and mothers and brotherhoods and children have gone to rest, just as they might do into another and most quiet room." Grass and flowering weeds clothe the graves with their luxuriant beauty, and some pious hand has planted one of them with shrubs and flowers —a graceful innovation.

"Shall I not take mine ease at mine inn?" After a long walk and an exploration of the place, which is the object of it, Falstaff's exclamation seems natural enough. Perhaps the merry countenance and sufficient proportions of mine host of the Chequers is suggestive of it. No true rambler is exacting in the matter of his inn accommodation. So that the interior is clean, and the hostess good-humoured, and the host wears a proper host's welcome in his visage, almost any modest refreshment will pass. One objects only to a room that is at once very new, very formal, very bare, and very pretentious, with nothing to support its pretence. Rusticity and antiquity, the older and the more rustic the better, are sure to content us. Give us a room so old that we can people it with guests of past generations, and link it with some point of historical interest, and we care not how humble its present estate may be. A more humble hostelrie than the Chequers you will not readily find, but it is a pleasant place to dream in and to bring before us the "forefathers of the hamlet" for generations gone by. Its exterior shows a rambling thatched cottage, which is approached through a sort of fore-court, partaking of the character of a straw yard. On the right is a cow-house; on the left some excellent pig-sties. A pebbled pathway leads to the inn door, which has a wicket before it, to protect it, we suppose, from possible invasions of the denizens of the straw-yard. Lift the latch of the door on the left within the wicket, and you will find yourself in a room decidedly of other days. It is not very large, and is diminished by a "settle," which gives an air of snugness to its huge fire-place. The chimney-piece is of black oak, and low enough to make you cautious how you lift your head when you pass under it. The "chimney-corner," of the cosy comforts of which we know rather in books than in reality, is here before us, though one is apt to think it might have been pleasanter when wood was burnt on the hearth than now that coal feeds the grate. The windows are deeply recessed in the thick walls, and the shutter loops up to the ceiling, the black oaken rafters of which are crossed with bars to hold in the bacon. Artists love such "interiors;" and think how the Dutch masters would have treated them, and how surely, if some of our living good men and true were to drop in here, they would turn the scene to account.

St. John's Hospital, Northampton, was possessed of property in Rothersthorpe as early as the time of Henry II., and we believe it holds some portion of it to this day.

Autumn in Kent.

A nest
Built in a Paradise; a home where love
In its first wedded happiness might come
And find all Nature like its own pure heart,
A sanctuary for sorrow, seeking rest
And quiet, and all balmy influences.
For me, too, wandering with no other aim
Than to enjoy, and jot my sketch-book full
Of notes of pleasant places: it has charms
To make me linger day by day, nor care
(Though the bright heath and the all-glorious ocean
Lie in the distance) to pursue my way—
So be it; all sufficient for the time
Be the time's happiness.

The sun is high,
And lovely is this lane, chequered with shade,
From the o'er-hanging hop, our English vine,
Than which no vine clusters more gracefully.
What a bright bower it is! The amber flowers
How well contrasted with the azure sky
Seen through the interstices! The distant pickers
Dot with a bright red cloak or apron blue,
The green monotony. The air is redolent
Of that fine aromatic bitterness,
Gratefullest in the draft at early noontide,
And grateful now to the scent; the wind, methinks,
Tastes of the wholesome herb.

My little room too,
Wherein the morning beams come sparklingly,
And sunset's calmer glories; whence I see
The dim grey grandeur of the ruined castle
And purple heaths of distant Tunbridge Wells.
Well could I rest me here content for ever,
So sunlights lingered here, too, all the year round;
But the fierce winter comes, to calm delights
Of inland landscape hostile. Where the sea
Flings stern defiance to the angry sky
My winter haunts and winter home must be.

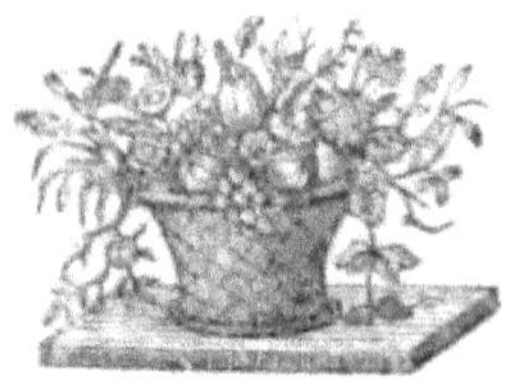

Cotterstock.

OUNDLE Station is nearly equidistant between the handsome town whose name it bears and the pretty and thoroughly Northamptonshire village of Cotterstock—if the latter is farther it has the advantage of having the most rural walk thither. A pedestrian has a choice of ways. He may follow a lane running parallel with the railway till it is intersected by the road, or he may go round by the road itself. Both are pleasant. The Warmington and Peterborough road is as level as a bowling-green; wide, skirted with greensward and bordered with trees. A picturesque turnpike (turnpikes may be picturesque if they have been built long enough for Nature to tint them) crosses the road. A little beyond, where you turn to the left, the road is more of a bye-way—narrower, more rugged, and with hedges and trees wandering more at their own sweet will. Crossing the railway we meet the lane already mentioned as the shorter cut, and, turning to the right, continue along a country road with gnarled trees in the hedge-rows, and pollard willows, such as the sketcher loves, and fresh meadows in the intervals. Another turn to the left, and before you is the mill, and on your right the stately church, with its noble chancel. You cross the river by a sufficient bridge, but the length of planking which precedes it tells what the frequent willows had told before, of its liability to floods, and how it was that the Poet Dryden thought the country thereabouts might be agueish. Two centuries ago, however, the Nene was less under control than it now is, the lands adjacent more frequently and continuously flooded. A mill is always a picturesque object, more or less; the very nature of its calling making it so:—

"The sleepy pool above the dam
The pool beneath it, never still,
The meal-sacks on the whiten'd floor,
The dark round of the dripping wheel,
The very air about the door
Made misty with the floating meal."

The hooded window for the hoisting apparatus; the tilted waggon, with its four horses; the white sacks; the millers themselves, help the picture, and Tennyson's admirable portrait inevitably comes to one's memory:—

"I see the wealthy miller yet,
His double chin, his portly size,
And who that knew him could forget
The busy wrinkles round his eyes?
The slow wise smile that round about
His dusty forehead drily curl'd
Seemed half-within and half-without,
And full of dealings with the world."

Quiet meadows, through which the river winds its slow and tortuous length, stretch right and left. The sites of mills are of remotest antiquity, though the mill itself may be modern. The present one is, we believe, comparatively so, not being over 60 years old. Its predecessor was destroyed by fire. Two mills, one of which no doubt stood here, are mentioned in the endowment of a chantry in the time of Edward III. (1337). Crossing the mill-stream, the road winds to the right, and then to the left, with somewhat of an ascent, and then Cotterstock village begins very prettily. A lane in an easterly direction, over-arched with ancestral elms, leads to the church, its highly picturesque tower terminating the vista. Busy rooks build in the lofty branches, and caw what seems an intelligible and emphatic language. Now it is like the soothing of a mother to her crying babes; now a remonstrance against some grievous wrong; now an admission of redress obtained, and a sense of satisfaction. The church, dedicated to St. Andrew, has some very interesting features. A Norman doorway in the tower speaks its early original: it has the chevron moulding well preserved. In the upper stage of the tower, which is flanked by two remarkably bold buttresses, is a late Norman window of two lights. The disproportionate size of the immense chancel, with its grand profusion of noble windows of the Decorated period, is very noticeable. The south porch, of the Perpendicular period, has a groined roof, with bosses, the central one being sculptured with a representation of the Trinity. The chancel has a piscina and three sedilia, under crocketted trefoil-headed canopies, on the south side. On the north is an aumbry, and a door which formerly led into the chantry or college founded by one John Giffard in 1339, the remains of which have been converted into cottages and farm buildings. Bridges says of it—"Contiguous to the east end of the church, with a door out of the chancel, is a house belong to Mr. Kirkham, supposed to stand upon the site of the chantry." A brass record near the altar points out the resting-place of a Provost of this chantry in 1420. The inscription runs thus:—"Hic. jacet. magister. Robertus. Wyntrynghm. nuper. canonicus. ecclie. cath. Lincoln. Prebendarius. de. Ledyngton. ac. Prepositus. prepositus. sive. Cantarie. de. Cothrestoke. qui. obiit quinto, die. Julii. Anno. Domini. Millimo. CCCCo.XXo cujus anime, ppicietur. deus. Amen." Leland mentions it and says—"One Nores clayming to be founder, even of late hath gotten away the landes that longged to it. So that now remaineth only the benefice to it." In the north east nook of the north aisle is a curious bracket, à propos to nothing so far as we can see, but which may have at some time carried a statue of a saint. It represents the head and to the middle of the body of a man in a tunic, with a belt round the waist, a cloak over his shoulders, a cap, and flowing hair. With his left hand he forces aside his mouth: with his right he plunges a dagger into his bosom. The action of the left hand is that of a person in sudden agony; the eyes are staring in accordance with such an emotion. At first sight the impression is very grotesque. The heft of the dagger is round, and it has the appearance of a huge bolus, to enable him to gulp which the holder is stretching his mouth with the left hand. A close investigation only reveals the blade of the dagger. To what story or fancy this grotesque sculpture refers—for grotesque it is, whether its meaning be grave or burlesque—it is impossible to say. The bolus fancy would not be an extravagant one, considering what extraordinary license was allowed to the carvers of all kinds of corbels and gargoyles in connexion with edifices the most sacred. Near the porch is the base of a churchyard cross, with the remains of an inscription, of which the following words alone are legible:—

Iohs leet et * ' *
* * uxor ejus hanc * *
fecerunt fieri

So much time has left us to this day, and the lapse of nearly a century does not appear to have diminished the inscription. Bridges gives no more words and does not give them accurately. He gives leef for leet—Leete being still a name in the neighbourhood—and for "fieri" he writes "Eclam"—(ecclesiam), as if John Leef and his wife made the church, instead of, as is clearly intended, John Leet and his wife caused the cross to be made which bears the inscription. Two monumental stones, one sculptured with a human figure, with the hands crossed on the bosom, and the other with a cross fleury, lie at the West end of the church, just outside the tower. The churchyard is neatly kept. It is considerably elevated above the surrounding meadows, and one corner is protected by a piece of wrought iron-work of excellent workmanship and taste. Cotterstock belfry rejoices in four bells, double the number of that of Tansor. The churches are within ear-shot of each other, and when they ring they are said to keep up the following colloquy. Cotterstock, conscious of its superiority, proudly and tauntingly asks with all its four bells:—"Who rings the best? who rings the best?" To which little Tansor answers, with a rapid and vehement defiance—"*We* do, *We* do, *We* do."

Returning from the church into the village we pass a pleasant house, with the date 1720 on its front. Adjoining it is a farm yard, very complete, compact, and under the hand of the master, and evidently under a master's hand.

> "A troop of pigeons, separate, three parts white,
> Round the glad homestead wheeling at their ease,"

add to the pleasantness of the scene. Beyond, the houses are sufficiently separate, though in a line, to have gardens and trees about them. A stranger would have some difficulty in finding the shops, though there are such places, and a public-house, distinguished by its sign, "The Gate," with the legend:—

> "This Gate hangs well, and hinders none;
> Refresh and pay, and travel on."

A sober injunction with which nobody but a very rigid teetotaller would quarrel. In the centre of the wide and very rural street yet still thoroughly in the country proper, we see on the right, on a rising ground, a stately and very attractive building, which has memories connected with it more stately and attractive even than itself. Cotterstock Hall has an Elizabethan character, though it may be of a somewhat later time. At all events its gables and projections are very picturesque in their forms and play of lights and shadows. It stands, as it were, in a park, which the high road intersects, cutting its way through an avenue of high trees, in fields sloping westward. From the house the road would probably be visible only as a path giving life, in its not over frequent passengers, to the landscape. In this mansion, according to Bridges, John Dryden wrote his Fables. Malone contradicts this statement in words, though scarcely in substance. "In the autumn of the year 1698," he says, "Dryden made an excursion from Titchmarsh to Cotterstock, and appears to have passed a few weeks there; and in 1699 he spent full six weeks at the same house. Perhaps in that time he wrote two or three hundred verses of the volume afterwards published with the title of FABLES, but that was the utmost; for he himself has told us that in his visits to the country his object was to unweary himself, not to drudge." Bridges is not fairly to be held to the letter of his statement. Two or three hundred verses is, after all, a fairish cantle, especially if they included (which, all the circumstances considered, is probable), the three famous opening lines of Cymon and Iphigenia, in which the poet speaks in his own proper person:—

> "Old as I am, for ladies' love unfit,
> The power of beauty I remember yet,
> Which once inflamed my soul, and still inspires my wit."

Cotterstock Hall was built by Norton, says Bridges, and Malone echoes him. But neither tells us who Norton was, and we have no clue to his identity. By whom, however, and when it was built, this, at least, we know, that in 1698 it was the residence of Elmes Steward, Esq., or Stewart, or Stuart, for Dryden, with the careless orthography of those days, spelt the name all ways. Mr. Steward married Elizabeth, eldest daughter of John Creed, Esq., of Oundle, secretary to Charles II., for the affairs of Tangier, by Elizabeth Pickering, his wife, only daughter of Sir Gilbert Pickering, Bart., Dryden's cousin german. Dryden, therefore, called Mrs. Steward cousin, or as he usually wrote it, after the French fashion, *cousine*. She appears to have been an accomplished lady: wrote poetry, and was an artist. Malone says, the Hall at Cotterstock was painted by her in fresco in a very masterly style, and she drew several portraits of her friends in Northamptonshire. When Malone wrote, towards the close of the last century, there was her own portrait, painted by herself in the possession of a lady named Ord, who lived in Queen Anne-street, and who was a kinswoman of hers. We have never had the fortune to get inside the house at Cotterstock, but we fear the frescoes have long since been obliterated. Towards the close of the seventeenth century, Dryden used to visit this cousin and her husband, and there are several letters of his to both still extant. The earliest is dated October 1st, 1698, at which time Mrs. Steward had been married and had lived at the Hall six years. Her distinguished cousin begins with the formal politeness of the time.

"Madam—You have done me the honour to invite so often that it would look like want of respect to refuse it any longer. How can you be so good to an old decreped man [Dryden was at this time in his 68th year] who can entertain you with no discourse which is worthy of your good sense, and who can only be a trouble to you in all the time he stays at Cotterstock. Yet I will obey your commands as far as possibly I can, and give you the inconvenience you are pleas'd to desire, at least for the few days which I can spare from other necessary business which requires me at Titchmarsh. Therefore, if you please to send your coach on Tuesday next, by eleven o'clock in the morning, I hope to wait on you before dinner. There is only one more trouble, which I am almost ashamed to name. I am oblig'd to visit my cousin Dryden, of Chesterton, some time next week, who is nine miles from hence and only five from you. If it be with your convenience to spare me your coach thether for a day, the rest of my time till Monday is at your service, and I am sorry for my own sake it cannot be any longer this year, because I have some visits after my return hether, which I cannot avoyd. But if it pleases God to give me life and health, I may give you occasion another time to repent of your kindness, by making you weary of my company. My sonn kisses your hand. Be pleas'd to give his humble service to my cousin Steward, and mine, who am, madam,

"Your most obedient, oblig'd servant,

"John Dryden.

"For my Honour'd Cousine, Mrs. Steward, att Cotterstock, These."

The next letter is dated November 20 in the same year (1698), and is addressed to Mr. Steward—"My honnour'd cousin," as it begins. Dryden appears to have spent the few days mentioned in the former letter with his Cotterstock friends, dispatched his business at Titchmarsh, returned to Cotterstock, and spent four or five weeks there. The present letter was apparently written after his return to Titchmarsh, and as he was about to set off for London. "And now," he says, "you are pleas'd to invite another trouble on your self which our bad company may possibly draw upon you next year if I have life and health to come into Northamptonshyre, and that you will please not to make such a stranger of me another time. I intend my wife [Lady Dryden was in London] shall tast the plover you did me the favor to send me. If either your lady or you shall at any time honour me with a letter, my house is in Gerard-street, the fifth door on the left hand comeing from Newport-street." And he concludes, "My sonn and I kiss my cousin Steward's hand, and give our service to your sister and pretty Miss Betty." "Pretty Miss Betty" was a little lady under six years old. Three days after, November 23, the Poet writes again to Mrs. Steward. Referring to his recent visit, he says, "If your house be often so molested, you will have reason to be weary of it before the ending of the year, and wish Cotterstock were planted in a desart an hundred miles off from any poet." He contrasts the happiness of her company with his solitary condition on his return to Titchmarsh. "I had no woman to visite but the parson's wife; and she who was intended by nature as a help meet for a deaf husband was somewhat of the loudest for my conversation; and for other things I will say no more than that she is just your contrary, and an epitome of her own country." His journey to London, he says, was yet more unpleasant than his abode at Titchmarsh, "for the coach was crowded up with an old woman fatter than any of my hostesses on the road. Her weight made the horses travel very heavily." He writes again on December 12th, acknowledging another present—"I," he says, "being eternally the receiver and you the giver. I wish it were in my power to turn the skale on the other hand, that I might see how you who have so excellent a wit, cou'd thank on your side. Not to name myself or my wife, my son Charles is the great commender of your last received present: who, being of late somewhat indisposed, used to send for some of the same sort, which we call heer marrow-puddings, for his suppers; but the tast of yours has so spoyl'd his markets here, that there is not the least comparison betwixt them. * * I am very glad to hear, my cousin your father, is comeing or come to toun: perhaps this ayr may be as beneficiall to him as it has been to me: but you tell me nothing of your own health, and I fear Cotterstock is too agueish for this season." On Candlemas Day, 1698-9, he writes again. Mrs. Steward was evidently a favourite, and the liking was reciprocated. She was a beauty as well as a wit, and was, says Malone, "esteemed one of the finest women that appeared at Queen Mary's Court." The opening sentence of this letter is evidently the germ of the triplet already quoted:—

"Old as I am, for ladies' love unfit," &c.

"Old men," he says, "are not so insensible of beauty as it may be you young ladies think. * * I would also flatter myself with the hopes of waiting on you at Cotterstock sometime next summer; but my want of health may perhaps hinder me. But if I am well enough to travell as farr northward as Northamptonshyre, you are sure of a guest who has been too well us'd not to trouble you again. * * I pass my time sometimes with Ovid and sometimes with our old English poet, Chaucer; translating such stories as best please my fancy; and intend besides them to add somewhat of my own; so that it is not impossible but ere the summer be pass'd I may come down to you with a volume in my hand like a dog out of the water with a duck in his mouth. As for the rarities you promise, if beggars might be choosers, a part of a chine of honest bacon would please my appetite more than all the marrow-puddings, for I like them better plain, having a very vulgar stomach."

In July of the following year (1699) he writes again. Amiable Mrs. Steward continued to make presents, proud, no doubt, of her distinguished kinsman, who would seem sometimes to have forgotten to acknowledge them. But how gracefully he atones for his short-comings:—

"Madam,—As I cannot accuse myself to have received any letters from you without answer, so, on the other side, I am obliged to believe it because you say it. 'Tis true I have had so many fitts of sickness, and so much other unpleasant business, that I may possibly have received those favours and deferred my acknowledgment till I forgot to thank you for them. However it be, I cannot but confess that never was unanswering man so civilly reproach'd by a fair lady. I presumed to send you word by your sisters of the trouble I intended you this summer, and added a petition that you would please to order some small beer to be brew'd for me without hops or with a very inconsiderable quantity, because I lost my health last year by drinking bitter beer at Titchmarsh. It may, perhaps, be sour, but I like it not the less, though it be small enough. What els I have to request is, onely the favour of your coach to meet me at Oundle, and to convey me to you, of which I shall not fail to give you timely notice. My humble service attends my Cousin Stewart and your relations at Oundle."

Dryden only shared a general prejudice against bitter beer, occasioned by the supposition that hops were a pernicious drug. The use of them in beer was forbidden by Henry VIII., but their value in the preservation of liquor was so great that the prohibition had small effect. A writer in 1649 says, although "hops were then grown to be a national commodity, it was not many years since the famous city of London petitioned the Parliament of England against two nuisances,—and these were Newcastle coals in regard to their stench, &c., and hops in regard they would spoyl the taste of drink and endanger the people." Prejudices die out very slowly, and half a century later we find Dryden imagining that the fragrant bitter was injurious to his health, though it scarcely appears that he thought it spoiled the taste of the drink. His fancy that sour beer was the wholesomer is curious. His injunction that it shall be "small enough" was wise in a time when people were proud of having ale of the strongest possible quality. On the 5th of August he writes again:—

"Sunday, Aug. 5, 1699.

"Madam,—This is only a word to threaten you with a troublesome guest next week: I have taken places for myself and my sonn, in the Oundle coach which sets out on Thursday next the tenth of this present August, and hope to wait on a fair lady at Cotterstock on Friday the eleventh. If you please to let your coach come to Oundle, I shall save my cousin Creed the trouble of hers.

All heer are your most humble Servants, and particularly an old cripple who calls himself your most obliged Kinsman and Admirer,

"JOHN DRYDEN.

"For Mrs. Stewart, Att Cotterstock near Oundle in Northamptonsh: These. To be left with the Postmaster of Oundle."

Travelling was a cumbersome process in those days. Dryden took his place in the Oundle stage five days before his proposed journey, and the coach was to be two days on the road. Dryden appears to have remained at Cotterstock over a month. His next letter affords some amusing incidents of travel in those days. On the 28th of September he writes:—

"Madam,—Your goodness to me will make you sollicitous of my welfare since I left Cotterstock. My journey has in general been as happy as it cou'd be without the satisfaction and honour of your company. 'Tis true the Master of the Stage-coach has not been over civill to me; for he turn'd us out of the road at the first step and made us go to Pilton: there we took in a fair young lady of eighteen and her brother a young gentleman; they are related to the Treshams, but not of that name; thence we drove to Higham, where we had an old serving-woman and a young fine mayd: we din'd at Bletso, and lay at Silso, six miles beyond Bedford. There we put out the old woman, and took in Councellour Jennings his daughter; her father going along in the Kittering coach or rideing by it with other company. We all din'd at Hatfield together, and came to toun safe at seaven in the evening. We had a young doctor who rode by our coach and seem'd to have a smickering to our young lady of Pilton and even rode before to get dinner in readiness. My sonn Charles knew him formerly a Jacobite and now going over to Antigoo with Colonel Codrington having been formerly in the West Indies. Which of our two young ladies was the handsomer I know not. My sonn liked the Councellour's daughter best: I thought they were both equall. But not going to Titchmarsh Grove and afterwards to Catworth I missed my two couple of rabbets which my cousin your father had given me to carry with me, and cou'd not see my sister by the way: I was likewise disappointed of Mr. Coles's Ribadavia wine, but I am almost resolv'd to sue the Stage-coach for putting me six or seven miles out of the way, which he cannot justify. Be pleas'd to accept my acknowledgment of all your favours and my Cousin Stuart's; and by employing my sonn and me in anything you desire to have done, give us occasion to take our revenge on our kind relations both at Oundle and Cotterstock. Be pleas'd, your father, your mother, your two fair sisters and your brother, may find my sonn's service and mine made acceptable to them by your delivery; and believe me to be with all manner of gratitude, give me leave to add, all manner of adoration, Madam your most oblig'd obedient servant John Dryden."

In October he writes again, beginning in the same gallant strain:—

"I have been," he says, "so sensible of the loss of your charming conversation ever since my departure that I assure you in all my travells I never left any place with more reluctance than Cotterstock and never found any satisfaction equall to what I enjoy'd there. * * Dr. Radclyff calls Northamptonshire a shineing country, I doubt not but he means for hospitality: and yet he has never been at Cotterstock. The two young gentlemen who sayd they were almost starv'd with you had better fortune than I found, who can complain of nothing but too much of a variety of daintyes. But you it seems were sparing to them of your company which had certainly been thrown away upon them; that I confess I had, and of that only I can never surfeit."

In November, 1699, Mrs. Steward's husband was appointed sheriff of the county of Northampton, and on the 14th of December Dryden writes:—

"I am heartily sorry that a chargeable office has fallen on my Cousin Stuart. But my Cousin Driden comforts me that it must have come one time or other, like the small pox and better have it young than old. I hope it will leave no great marks behind it and that your fortune will no more feel it than your beauty by the addition of a year's wearing. My cousine, your mother, was heer yesterday to see my wife, though I had not the happiness to be at home."

The poet's last letter to his cousin was written on the 11th of April, 1700. On the 1st of the following May he died.

Nobody who can spare an hour or so between the trains should fail to pay a visit to Cotterstock: for its own sake as a characteristic Northamptonshire village with characteristic Northamptonshire surroundings; for the sake, too, of the great Northamptonshire writer who was so welcome there, and who loved it and his fair kinswoman, the life and charm of its picturesque hall. It is seldom that the lapse of well-nigh two hundred years changes so little the haunts of our great men. Some inclosures possibly, better farming, an additional house here and there, or a substitute for the older one; the mill larger probably, the river less wide-spread and sedgy,—these, we may believe, make up the sum and substance of the difference between Cotterstock as it is and Cotterstock as it was in Dryden's day. The hall, the avenue, the far-stretching meadows, and all the varied charms of country life, are in the main as when he pondered there his noble verses. We can without difficulty figure to ourselves the whole little drama—the arrival of Cousin Steward's coach, probably with four stately horses, for coaches in those days were heavy and solid in their build and their weight, and and the rough roads which they had to travel required more horse-flesh than our modern light-springed vehicles; and a costly equipage was part of the necessary state of a squire of rank enough to be high-sheriff of the county. There are outriders too, and when the coach draws up before the hall, liveried servants are at the porch to receive the visitor, and, better than all, the smiling beauty of Queen Mary's court, in all the glory of stomacher and looped gown and flounces and falbalas and lofty laced cap in tiers, comes forward with cordial hand and bright intelligent eye. The squire is following the chase, of which he is very fond, and of which there are ample tokens in the hall, crowning the frescoes of his lady. Dryden's fine countenance is set off by an ample wig, the curls of which flow over his shoulders. He lifts gallantly his hat, cocked all round and trimmed with feathers, as he alights. His coat and waistcoat reach to the knees, and the long stockings over-lap his nether garments. He wears high-heeled shoes, with a tongue coming over the instep, and fastened with a rosette. Dogs of many kinds, among which the diminutive King Charles's breeed is conspicuous, yelp a choral welcome to the hospitable mansion.

Such, at least, is the fancy that besets us passing the hall, and we take off our hats reverentially, alike to the poet and the beauty, though the place knows them no more.

All this part of our country was evidently long in the hands of the Romans; traces of these masters of the world crop up everywhere. At Cotterstock, about the beginning of July, 1736, a very fine pavement was discovered, of which a very particular account was given in the *Northampton Mercury* of March 28, 1737. The site was at the edge of the lordship, adjoining to Glapthorn field, on a headland commonly called The Guild Acre. "The verge or margin of the work was seven feet wide on each side, and consisted of red, light blue, and grey stones, all of them about an inch and a quarter square. The work within the margin was ten feet square exactly, and consisted of lesser stones and bricks, each about the bigness of dice, or six-tenths of an inch square, of three different colours, viz., white, red, and blue, and set in various and most beautiful figures, as chain work, maze work, &c., in the midst whereof were placed in a circular order the figures of four hearts, beautifully wrought, and pointing with their vertices towards the centre." So much for our description contemporary with the discovery. The Society of Antiquaries published an engraving of it, by Virtue, after drawings by George Lynn, of Southwick, and Wm. Bogdan, Esq., by which we find that the "chain work" was what is known as the guilloche border, and the "maze work" an interlaced Greek fret. Animal bones, ashes, pieces of urns, three or four oyster shells, and as many large nails were found among the rubbish. The pavement was soon destroyed by the ignorant curiostity of a multitude of visitors. "Some ingenious workmen," however, as the narrative continues, "were employ'd by a certain person of great distinction (with the leave of the owner) to take up about a yard square of this admirable work, that a specimen of it might be preserv'd. The owner was a Mr. Campion, who is described as "a gentleman farmer," and who may be the "John Campion, gent," who lies buried in the south-east aisle of the church, and who died in 1766, and was recorded as "An honest man, who bore a painful decline." Some brass coins of Valentinian, with different reverses, were also in the "find" and "a very large freestone," which Mr. Campion converted into a watering trough for cattle, and several stones like foundation stones, from which the writer of the account inferred "that the particular edifice which the pavement did formerly adorn was most probably an Ædes Sacra."

Turning to "Gibson and Gough's Castor," we find the inscription on the base of the cross at the church porch quoted from Bridges, with the addition of "et Jacklen," as the missing name of the wife and "fieri," which does not appear in Bridges. These words are said to have been supplied "from another copy" (what copy is not stated), and the writer adds, "but this inscription is not now to be distinguished." Nor are the two antique stones, on one of which is cut a rude figure of a man with his hands on his bosom, and on the other a cross to be seen in the yard near the west end of the church, unless the latter be the cross at the end of the stone bench. Between Bridges' time and the publication of Gough's book, the inscription on the cross and the figure of the man had got buried in the increasing earth. We believe their recovery is due to a former churchwarden, Mr. Everest.

Bath. Evening from Cleveland Bridge.

THE purple mists of evening on thy walls;
The parting sunbeam on the Abbey-towers,
And touching with brief gold these Avon bowers;
The poplar shade that in the river falls
With deepest darkness; distant childhood's calls;
The bather's splash among the water-flowers;
The chimes that sweetly knell the dying hours;
Weave a strange spell that all the heart enthrals.

'Tis like the lotus-land of poesy!
Fair city! when the time that thou art not
Poetic land? morning's first brilliancy
Lifts us to heaven upon thy hills; and what
A crown of radiance shines at night on thee,
Cresting thy circling hills with starry glee.

Towcester.

TOWCESTER lies upon the "right noble street," as Drayton calls the Watling-street, and like most towns situated on a great thoroughfare, which retains its character of an ancient way, is a pleasant place. Towns which have a manufacture grow about equally on all sides; space is an object; house crowds upon house; gardens are few and far between, and are shut in by tall walls; fortunate if they are not neighboured by a tall chimney to fill the roses with "blacks," and disfigure the young mistress who goes out in the morning—

> To gather flowers partie white and red,
> To make a sotel garland for her head—

with soot and sneezes. When the chief business of the inhabitants is dependent on the through traffic, the houses keep chiefly in a line, and do not extend laterally. So in the rear are large inn yards and pleasant gardens, with the country stretching far away behind them, and the breath of Heaven smelling "wooingly." This form of town has grown of course, out of the old modes of travelling—by pack-horse, waggon, stage-coach, mail. The railway revolution will necessarily change it in process of time. When it is no longer to people's interest to have their houses lying specially along the main road, streets will spring up at right angles and wrong angles of all kinds, as in manufacturing towns. But that time is not yet with Towcester. Let us sketch it, not as it may be, but as it is.

The approaches to Towcester are pleasant on all sides, with the exception of that suburb which is like a long, lean arm stretching out towards London, and even that is not without interest to the saunterer. "Jubilee-row," to be sure, is not attractive in any sense, but there are plenty of olden houses, which have their history as it were written on the face of them, and there is picturesqueness in the irregularity and utter jumble of buildings of all dates, and sizes, and qualities; somewhat stately well-to-do houses elbowed by thatched cottages, and shops whose windows exhibit a few oranges, dingy bottles of lollipops, and biscuits, not of yesterday's baking. How thoroughly the town was once a town of inns may be sufficiently seen in this suburb. Those lofty gateways which now lead to tumble-down workshops, or to small tenements for the poorer classes, led, in the old time, to spacious yards for the reception of various merchandize, and were surrounded with stabling, and warehouses, and dormitories. The picturesque and comfortable-looking "Sun Inn" may be taken as the type of many others, which have ceased to exist, in its general aspect towards the street. We dare say, too, its landlord, may be taken as the type of many a genial host, who, during the two centuries that have elapsed since it was built (it bears the date 1650 on its front), has cheered the weary traveller with that welcome which, according to Shenstone, is found warmest at an inn.* "The Talbot" and the "Pomfret Arms" appear to be of later date, but they stand upon the sites of older inns, and retain the spacious yards and ample entrances so indispensable to the hostelries of old times. The Talbot indeed is really much older than its exterior would lead us to suppose. It was probably an inn in the time of Chaucer, for in 1440 it was sold to Archdeacon Sponne,

*Since this Ramble was written the "Sun" has also ceased to exist as an inn.

the good rector of Towcester, who in 1450-1 gave the house to the town, and in the deed it is described as the "Tabard," which was also the name of the poet's famous inn in the borough of Southwark. The latter changed its name in 1676. Through the courtesy of the feoffees of Sponne's Charity, we have obtained a sight of the very interesting series of documents connected with that trust. They are excellently kept in a box in the Church, and include a long series of deeds, with the seals, beginning with the early part of the fourteenth century; and the accounts of the receipts and disbursements of the feoffees from a very early date. From the latter we ascertain the exact time when the change was made of the name of the Tabbard for the Talbot. In 1642 it is entered on the accounts as the Tabbard; the next year, 1643, it is called the Talbot. All entries, previous to that date, call it the Tabbard; all subsequent the Talbot. With the reason for the change we are still unacquainted. It was made a considerable time previous to the date of the change of the Southwark Tabard, which did not take place before 1667. In that year occurred the great fire of Southwark, by which the inn was partially destroyed, and Aubrey, writing about it some years after, says:—"The ignorant landlord or tenant, instead of the ancient sign of the Tabard, put up the Talbot, a dog." The Talbot, a white hound, was the cognizance of the ancient house of Shrewsbury, which may have had something to do with the change of name. Nearly five-and-twenty years before the landlord or tenant of the Southwark Tabard manifested his ignorance, as Aubrey calls it, we find the feoffees of Sponne's Charity re-christening their inn in the same way. The two different names occur in adjoining pages of the same book, within a dozen entries of each other; and, as we have said, the Talbot continues to be the Talbot ever after, with the variations of spelling characteristic of the time, as "Talbut" and "Talbott." It never relapses into "Tabbard," as it might be expected to do if the change had been made, not of set purpose, but by ignorance. In 1642 John Talbot, the second Earl of Shrewsbury, fell in a fight before Northampton between the forces of the Parliament, who held the garrison under Lord Brooke, and the Cavaliers. A few months after the fire in Southwark, an event occurred which again made the name of Talbot familiar to the public ear. On the 16th of January, 1668, a duel was fought in a close near Barne Elms, between Francis Talbot, eleventh Earl of Shrewsbury, Sir John Talbot, and Bernard Howard, a son of the Earl of Arundel, on one side; and the Duke of Buckingham, Sir Robert Holmes, and Captain William Jenkins on the other. The Earl of Shrewsbury had challenged the Duke of Buckingham, who had supplanted him in the affections of his wife, the daughter of the second Earl of Cardigan. She is said to have held the Duke's horse, in the habit of a page, while he was fighting with her husband. "My Lord Shrewsbury," says Pepys, "is run through the body from the right breast through the shoulder; and Sir John Talbot all along up one of his armes, and Jenkins killed upon the place, and the rest all in a little measure wounded." The Earl died of his wounds on the 16th of March succeeding the duels. The Countess of Shrewsbury found a second husband, notwithstanding the infamous notoriety of her conduct towards the first, and died in 1702. A portrait of her by Lely, as Minerva, was bought by the late Sir Robert Peel, at the Stowe sale, for £68 5s. It does not follow that in either case the events led to the substitution of the name of Talbot for the original Tabard, but the double coincidence of the change of name with events connected with the Talbots is at least curious. Talbot may have been a mere corruption of Tabbard after the latter name had become obsolete with the disuse of the tabard itself. The tabard was a sleeveless coat, open on both sides, with a square collar, and winged at the shoulders; "a stately garment of olde time," says Stowe, "commonly worne of noblemen and others, both at home and abroade in the warres, but then (to witte in the warres) theyre arms embrodered, or otherwise depicte upon them, that every man by his coate of armes might be knowne from others; but nowe these

Tabardes are only worne by the Heraults, and bee called their coats of armes in service." We find by these interesting and valuable feoffee accounts, that in the 35th year of the reign of Henry the 8th (1544), the Tabard was in the occupation of one John Kyslingbury, at a yearly rent of £6 13s. 4d. In 1687 the rent had increased to £35, but it may have had land with it, which would account for the increased value. "The Tabard" was, no doubt, an ordinary sign formerly for an inn, and so was "The Bell." Chaucer speaks of—

—— "This gentil ostelrie
That highte the Tabbard faste by the Bell."

And there was a "Bell"" also in Towcester, as well as a "Tabbard." It is mentioned in an enfeoffment as "le Bell" in 1473. An inn called the "Old Bell," probably the descendant of "le Bell," stood, within these three years, at the corner of the Brackley road, at the north-west end of the town. In one of the upper windows at the Talbot are the arms of Archdeacon Sponne, with his name beneath, "William Sponn." In a tap-room, lying backwards in the yard, is a huge chimney beam, formerly belonging to the kitchen, upon which is carved the figure of a dog (the Talbot), and the initials on either side T. O. and G. S., with the date, 1707. One of the heir-looms of the house is an oak chair, with the back ornamentally carved, and the initials B., and underneath W. A., 1627. It is known as Dean Swift's chair, the tradition being that the Dean of St. Patrick's used to occupy it when he put up at the Talbot in his journeys to and from Ireland and London. Under the management of Mr. Tunnard the Talbot achieved a reputation of being one of those inns in which the traveller exclaims with Falstaffe — "Shall I not take mine ease at mine inn?" and to its host might be fairly applied the eulogy which Chaucer bestowed on his host of the Southwark Talbot—

"A fairer burgess was there none in Chepe"—

that is, there was not a more honest and upright tradesman in the market place. Mr. Tunnard left the Talbot for the Pomfret Arms, which had long been in sore need of a good landlord.

The Pomfret Arms is apparently not two centuries old, and was once the Saracen's Head. It stands advantageously to welcome comers from all the four points of the compass at the southern corner of the Brackley road, and Mr. Tunnard has added to its convenience by opening a new entrance towards the Brackley road. The figures of Apollo and Venus, in the niches on either side the gateway from the street, probably came from Easton Neston. They have the appearance of having, at some period, adorned a stately garden, and may have been removed when the Italian garden at the south front of the mansion was done away with. Bridges, referring to Morton's account of the ***Marmora Arundeliana***, which in part ornamented the gardens, says the statues were not all antique, for upon the pedestals of three were the inscription ***Egidius Morettus, Romanus faciebat***, whose "fine Roman hand," it is not unlikely, may be traceable in these figures. One of them, indeed, is what may be called an edition, with additions, of the Venus de Medici.

There was an "Aungell" Inn in Towcester in 1448. It adjoined the Talbot on the south, on the site of the premises belonging to Mr. J. M. Cooke, the solicitor. In the feoffee accounts occurs an item, in the reign of Henry VII., a payment to one Edward Dene, "for cleansyng of the guttyr betwyx the Tabard and the Aungell, 1d." Up to a comparatively recent period it was a waggon yard; greatly used before the opening of the Grand Junction Canal. Towcester must, at one time, have been almost entirely a street of inns. On the north of the Talbot stood the Swan; there was a "Bell," besides the "Old Bell" already mentioned; and a second "White Horse," on the site of the present residence of Mr. R. W. Watkin, the surgeon, directly facing the Pomfret Arms.

But the chief coaching and posting inn of Towcester, in the

palmy days of coaching, was the ***White Horse***, which was put, to use a pun of the period, ***hors de combat*** by the railway. The premises are now occupied as Wine Vaults by Mr. Vernon.

Bickerstaffe's Alms Houses have nothing in the way of antiquity (they were rebuilt in 1815) or architecture to recommend them, but they look comfortable. The tablet which the founder set up is still there, and is worth noting. It bears the following inscription:—

> **"He that earneth**
> **Wages by labour**
> **and care, by the**
> **blessing of God may have**
> **something to spare. T. B., 1689."**

Charitable Mr. Bickerstaffe, of course, meant only to explain how it came about that he was able to do this good work; but his doggrel verse will bear the additional meaning of a gentle reproof to the inmates that they too might have had something to spare if they had taken care.

It is in contemplation, we believe, to rebuild the Grammar School House. The house itself, much modified, is the original Chantry House founded by Archdeacon Sponne. Externally, it appears to be nothing more than an ordinary house of a couple of hundred years old, but one of the rooms retains very much of its Tudor character; the fire-place, ceiling, and doors are very interesting. The wall which encloses the house from the street is of the same period, and the entrance is under a very perfect Tudor arch. If the school-house should be rebuilt, it is to be hoped that this arch will be preserved.

Not the least interesting house in Towcester, however, is one on the west side of the Market-place, south of the Talbot, in the occupation of Mr. Joseph Key, and used as a butcher's shop. It is a good specimen of the ordinary houses in towns and villages in the days of Henry VIII. and Queen Elizabeth. The upper part has been modernized, and the timbering plastered over; but all beneath the pent-house remains as when it was originally built at least three hundred years ago.

This interesting relic of old time belongs, we believe, to Lord Pomfret, in whose custody, we hope, it is secure from destruction.

Towcester is mentioned in the curious journal of Drunken Barnaby, which was written in the early part of the seventeenth century, as "Tosseter where he sate up all night":—

"Veni Tosseter die Martis,
Ubi baccalaureum artis
Bacchanalia celebrantem
Ut inveni tam constantem
Feci me consortem festi
Tota nocte perhonesti."

"Thence to Tosseter, on a Tuesday,
Where an artful bachelor choos'd I
To consort with : we ne'er budged,
But to Bacchus revels trudged :
All the night long sate we at it,
Till we both grew heavy-pated."

"Towcester," says De Foe, "is a pretty town of Roman antiquity ; through which, in a straight line, runs the Watling-street. The inhabitants, of all ages, are here employed in a silken manufacture and lace-making." The silk manufacture has long since died out. Of the Roman antiquity of Towcester there can be no doubt. Its very form indicates its origin. The market place at once suggests the site of the forum; where the Church now stands, stood, in all probability, the basilica of our Roman conquerors; Berry Mount, Bury Hill, the Hill Garden, as it is variously called, being the site of the pretorium. One need not enter here into a question which may be considered as satisfactorily settled, whether Towcester is the Lactodorum of the Itinerary of Antoninus. All the evidence points to that conclusion; coins innumerable, fragments of pottery, and Samian-ware have been dug up from time to time; and discoveries of the same kind are continually being made. In the autumn of 1859, when the old Bell was pulled down, a beautiful little Roman lamp in terra cotta was found in excavating the foundations. It is as perfect and as fresh in appearance as when it came from the hands of the maker. From the handle to the extremity of the burner the length is about three and a-half inches. The potter's name—FORTIS—in very distinct characters, crosses the circle at the bottom. Mr. Roach Smith, in his Collectanea, gives the name as occurring on earthen lamps found in London. There was also found an article in iron, the use of which is somewhat doubtful, though it is now generally supposed to be a shoe for cattle. In Mr. Roach Smith's "Illustrations of Roman London," we find figured a similar article found in London, and in the "Collectanea Antiqua" is the figure of another in the Evreux Museum. Mr. Roach Smith states that they have been found at Stony Stratford, at Springhead, near Gravesend, at other places in this country, at Autun, Dijon, and other localities in France. He suggests that they were used only for temporary purposes, where the feet of the animal were diseased, or the ways were particularly bad. At the present day, in Holland, it is usual to bind, with a thong of leather, long flat iron shoes to the horse's feet. Catullus speaks of a mule leaving its iron shoe in the mud—

"In gravi derelinquere cœno
Ferream ut soleam tenaci in voragine mula,"

and he is of opinion that it is of this kind of shoe the poet speaks. It has been doubted whether the Greeks and Romans nailed on their horse-shoes, but horse shoes with holes for the nails have been found in the very places where these temporary shoes (supposing them to be so) have been met with. If they are shoes at all, we must infer that some of the roads at least were mere quagmires, so that it was necessary to have a kind of snow-shoe to prevent the animal from fairly sinking into the mud. Its length is six inches. The ears, which form a marked characteristic, would appear to be for the purpose of attaching the shoe by means of leather ligaments to the leg of the animal. A knife, probably of the time of Henry VII., and nine inches in length, has recently been found in an old drain. All these articles, and a beautiful coin of Vespasian, also found in Towcester, are in the possession of Mr. S. C. Tite.

People may be very familiar with Towcester without knowing anything of the Berry Mount, and know of its existence without being aware that it possesses any special interest. Yet it is, undoubtedly, connected with important events in the history of the little town. It lies out of the track of ordinary life. The visitor who would search it out must turn down the Church Lane, and take the turn to the left, instead of going down to the Mill. A little way down on the right, beyond the houses, is a garden, within which rises a mount of considerable height, with a circular top—

> —" Crowned with a peculiar diadem
> Of trees, in circular array, so fix'd
> Not by the sport of nature, but of man "—

a hollow has been scooped out of its southern side, and a cottage built in the gap. The mount is between twenty and thirty feet high, and its diameter about twenty-four feet. The summit commands a view of Lord Pomfret's park and the river Tove, a branch of which runs immediately beneath. It is easy to see that the hill has been moated all round.

The Church, dedicated to St. Laurence, like most of our churches, is of various styles; there are traces of all, from Norman downwards to Perpendicular. There is a noble tower and west door. The chancel arch springs from two corbels, representing figures of jesters in grotesque attitudes. Some fragments of painted glass in a window in the south aisle are the remains of a window which was destroyed by the puritanical zeal of one Robert Stichbery. Baker quotes a pamphlet published in 1642, which states that two days after his wife was seized with a sudden torment in her limbs, which, ultimately, " brought her to her last." Stichbery himself died howling mad. His sister, who had a Common Prayer bound up with her Bible, tore it out, upon which her hands, says the pamphlet, "began presently, in a most strange manner, to rot, the flesh flying from the bones: and so continueth up to this present, rotting in a most fearful and loathsome manner. And in regard great store of people come to see her, and being so extreme loathsome, that by the neighbours she is removed a mile out of the town, where she remains, lamenting much that she hath done so wretched and wicked a deed." The monument to Archdeacon Sponne, who was rector in the reign of Henry VI., represents that worthy ecclesiastic under two aspects—in his habit as he lived, on the upper part of the table, and as a skeleton, or nearly so, on the underpart. He has this inscription at his feet on a board against the wall :—

"In memory of Mr. William Sponne, archdeacon of Northfolk and rector of Towcester, who in the 29th year of King Henry the VI., gave the Talbot Inn, in Towcester, with the lands belonging to it, for the payment of the fifteens for the parish of Towcester, if any such tax be given by Parliament; if no such be given, then to pave and repair the pavements in the streets of Towcester, and the pavements being made good, the remainder to be given to the poor at the discretion of the feoffees appointed to manage the same."

Excellent archdeacon! Happy Towcester! Happy Northampton if a few of his worthy stock had belonged to it, and exempted it also from its "Improvement Rate!" In the chancel is a small mural monument, having the effigies of a man and a woman praying at a table. The inscription informs us that it is—

"The memorial of Hierom Farmore, Esq., and Jane, his wife. They lived together in wedlock forty-two years, and he attained to the honour of a great grand uncle, and after 74 years left this life for a better, September the 7th, 1602."

Then follow these two punning verses :—

"Terra subest pars parta mei, pars indita supra,
Terrea pars moritur, cœlica pars superest,
Sed periit pars parva mei, pars maxima vivit,
Vilior ista jacet, sanctior illa viget.

"Hierom thy joys all shine on high,
Thy faith and truth did shine before;
Jane lived thine and will so dye,
All praise thy life, thy life FARMORE."

The Latin verse may be Englished thus; the alliterative whim being impossible to render :—

Earth-sprung, a part of me in earth here lies
Part heavenward flies;
The earthly part is dead, the heavenly stays:
The smaller part decays,
The greater lives; the viler part lies here,
The holier blossoms in another sphere.

Pope Boniface was possessed of this benefice at the time of his promotion to the pontificate in 1294. He is said to have obtained the papal chair by a profane artifice. His predecessor, Pope Celestine V., had held his sacred office but five months and seven days. Boniface, according to the story, procured somebody to address the Pope through a concealed speaking trumpet thus—"Cœlestine, Cœlestine, dimitte papatum, si vis salvs fieri; negotium supra vires est." "Cœlestine, Cœlestine; lay aside the popedom if thou wishest to be saved; the duties are beyond thy strength." Cœlestine took the voice to be from Heaven, and resigned accordingly, and Boniface was installed in his place.

Towcester is peculiarly fortunate in its exemptions from local burthens. Not only has it no paving rates to pay, but Providence and charitable Mr. Bickerstaffe, who built the Alms Houses already mentioned, have saved it also from a water rate. Two excellent springs at the northern and southern extremities of the town keep up a constant supply of good water, and, by the will of Mr. Bickerstaffe, one of them is walled in, and an iron dish supplied for poor wayfaring people to drink out of.

Towcester, one of the most peaceable and social of towns, has seen its troubles. It was probably a strong place during the Roman dominion, and suffered the fate which befel the other places along the line of Roman occupation at the hands of the destroying Dane. About 917 King Edward, the son of Alfred the Great, rebuilt it. It gallantly withstood an assault by the Danes from Northampton and Leicester for a whole day, and succour arriving, the enemy were compelled to retire. Edward afterwards fortified it, and encompassed it with a wall of stone. It was probably of these remains that Leland was told as "certen ruines or diches of a castelle at Towcester." Baker thinks it probable that Edward's fortification followed the Roman line of circumvallation. Camden says that with all his seeking he could find no token of any such wall. In the civil war of the 17th century Towcester was the principal garrison of the royalists, under Prince Rupert, to keep in check the Parliamentarians, who were in considerable force at Northampton and Newport Pagnell, in the autumn of 1643. The prince made the town very strong, and brought the water round it. He must have been an unwelcome guest, for he levied contributions from the inhabitants, of man's meat and horse meat, and labour of all sorts, on pain of "the total plundering and burning of your houses, with what other mischiefs the licensed and hungry soldiers can inflict upon you." The Commissary General lay at Ambrose Burton's house, "over against the Talbot." We learn, also, from this warrant, that among the inns were the signs of "The Petty Bridges" and "The Running Mare." On the 12th of June, two days before the memorable battle of Naseby, Towcester was the head quarters of General Fairfax, and in January, 1646, of Colonel Whalley.

In Mr. Elliot's interesting Paper on "Parish Registers," the stationariness of the population of Northampton and the adjoining parts of the county is inferred from the existence in the town of very many surnames derived from neighbouring places in the county; and from names which, appearing in the town registers during the 16th and early part of the 17th centuries, are still familiar to the ear in Northampton. Of course Mr. Elliot refers to the peculiar stationariness of the population in question as compared with the populations of other places; he would hardly build a "pet theory" with reference to Northamptonshire upon facts common to all or nearly all other places. Is Northamptonshire, then, peculiarly stationary in its population? We suspect not. Our own observation, on the contrary, tends to the opposite conclusion. We should have said that Northamptonshire people were a very migratory race. We have met with them or heard of them pretty well all the world over. Great names of emigrants rise in the memory without an effort:—Washington, Franklin, Sir Paul Pinder, Sir William Laxton, Carey, Ryland—the latest representative of that honoured name, though resident till his death in Northampton, was born at Bristol, whither his father emigrated—

Clarke (the father of Cowden Clarke), a Northamptonshire man, emigrated to Enfield, where his eminent son, we believe, was born. We should not, indeed, be surprised to find some Northamptonshire Mrs. Hopkins

> "taking tea
> And toast upon the wall of China."

Mr. Elliot, by-the-bye, seems to have overlooked the probability that, where the names of persons are obviously taken from the names of places, the inference is, not that the population was stationary, but rather on the contrary, that it was migratory. John would hardly be called "of Lowick" or "Lowick," by way of distinguishing him from other Johns equally existent in Lowick. He would be called "John of Lowick" after he had migrated to Northampton or London, to distinguish him from the Johns of Northampton, or the Johns of Hockley-in-the-Hole. Names taken from callings may imply stationariness; names derived from places almost necessarily imply migration.

A village churchyard we have generally found to be the best guide to the nomenclature of the neighbourhood, and we suspect that what Mr. Elliot has discovered in respect of Northamptonshire would be discoverable also everywhere else. This is rather a long preface to a small but interesting circumstance which Mr. Elliot may claim in support of his theory. One of the feoffees of the Sponne charity, to whom we were indebted for the inspection of the documents connected with it, is Mr. Webb, who lives in the same house and carries on the same business of an ironmonger which his ancestors have owned for four generations. Occupations of the same farm often continue from generation to generation. The pleasant old song does not exaggerate a common fact—

> "And the farm I now hold on your Honour's estate
> Is the same which my grandfather till'd."

But such descents are not common in trade. Trade is more liable to vicissitudes and changes than agriculture; and the son of the prosperous tradesman is much more often disposed to abandon the father's calling than the son of the farmer. The property itself, also, is much more liable to the influences of change.

The stone staircases which led to the rood loft, still exist in Towcester Church. In the accounts to which we have alluded there are payments on the 10th of April, 1562—"Payd Robert Russel for taking down rode-loft, 7s. 8d." "Payd for car of the tymber of rode loft to Heath, 12d."

We close our gossip with an anecdote concerning the figures of Venus and Apollo in the niches over the gateway of the Pomfret Arms, of which we have already spoken, and which, by the bye, are cast in lead, accounting fully for the bend of the figure of Venus. When Mr. Tunnard's predecessor entered upon the house the statues naturally enough attracted the notice of the landlady, Mrs. Popple. She accordingly addressed herself to the hereditary post-boy for information respecting them. "I can't tell you anything about 'em, ma'am," was the reply; "but they calls 'm Junus and Venus." "And who was Junus and Venus?" was Mrs. Popple's further question. "I don't know who they was, mum," said the post-boy, "*but you can read all about 'em in the Bible!*"

The post-boy must have been a descendant of him who wrote the description of the "Groves of Blarney"—

> "There's statutes gracing this noble place in
> All heathen goddesses so fair—
> Bold Neptune, Plutarch, and Nicodemus
> All standing naked in the open air."

There are excellent accounts by Mr. Pretty, F.S.A., formerly of Northampton, of Roman remains discovered at Whittlebury, if testimony were wanting, to the fact that Towcester was once a Roman station, in the 6th and 7th volumes of the Journal of the British Archæological Association.

Not least among the advantages of Towcester is the vicinity of Lord Pomfret's beautiful park, with its noble trees and interesting mansion.

The Old Man and the Conqueror.

(From Béranger.)

CONQUEROR:

FOLLOWING the chase too eagerly, this wood
Has 'wildered me—Good Father, point its outlet.

OLD MAN:

You must dismount. The paths are narrow here
And dangerous. Assist my feeble steps.

CONQUEROR:

Am I unknown to you?

OLD MAN:

I never saw you.

CONQUEROR:

My features may be strange. My history
You surely know.

OLD MAN:

It is a quiet spot, Sir,
Where my hut stands.

CONQUEROR:

For more than twenty years
My glory has been bruited through the world;
Mine was the prowess bowed so many kingdoms;
Mine was the name which hath in war and peace
Shaken the universe.

OLD MAN:

I do not know you.
And yet mine arms are wearied with the toil
Of delving Mother Earth.

CONQUEROR:

You know me not!
Why more than twelve proud months have passed away
Since, conquering the land that gave you birth,
I changed the course of your long kingly line
And overthrew the throne—

OLD MAN:

Pray pardon me.
I did not know that I had changed my master.

CONQUEROR:

Why, how now leveller! What is your lot, then?

OLD MAN:

Born in this wood, I never left its shade;
In peace year after year hath been heaped on me;
My partner and two sons cheer my life's close;
Our wealth—six goats, and arms disposed for toil.
It has sufficed us ever, God be blessed,
And will. But here's the road, Sir. Fare you well.
Pardon an old man's ignorance.

CONQUEROR:

Farewell!
Happy old man!

Green's Norton.

THE tall spire of Green's Norton Church is a pretty object from Towcester, and Towcester reciprocates the pleasure, the square tower of its church being visible from Green's Norton. From Towcester to Green's Norton there is a pleasant walk of less than two miles, across flush meadows at this Spring season "painted with delight" by "daisies pied" and the golden gorgeousness of buttercups; by the side of a brook chattering over pebbles; by the low embankment of an embryo railway, under tall hedges white with May-blossom and skirting fields vividly green with the young wheat; and so out at length into the roadway opposite the bowery residence of the late Mr. John Elliott. A short walk along the road and we come into Green's Norton,—a long, straggling, wide, irregular village, with a brook crossing it, and roads branching out right and left. The church-spire rises above it, backed by a belt of trees in picturesque relief. From the Blakesley road, at the end opposite to that by which we entered, there is a considerable ascent, from which almost a bird's-eye view of the village is obtained. You turn eastward out of the High Street, if we may call it so, to reach the church, which is on an elevated table-land.

We live in an age of church-restoration. Will future times anathematize our restorers as we anathematize the restorers of half-a-century ago? What a grievous spectacle does Green's Norton

Church present without and within. At the time of our last visit the church was being not "restored," but cleaned and repaired. It is the best thing that can now be done. There is no restoration possible of what was murdered in the great churchwarden "beautifying" of the edifice in 1826. Before that time, indeed, somewhere in an earlier Georgian period, something a great deal rather—had been done to the tower, and possibly to other parts of the building also. We cannot altogether apportion the mischief of the two eras.

The church belongs originally to the Early English period, though there is the striking evidence, in instances of long and short work at the two western angles of the nave, of an Anglo-Saxon structure. We look in vain, however, for other traces of the same period, and marvel that these should still remain. In the south wall of the chancel, which is spacious, are two good Early English windows, with double lancets, a deep splay and a most graceful slender shaft dividing them. There were corresponding windows in the north wall, but they have been long since blocked up. The present east window is wholly devoid of architectural character. It is simply a large cluster of leaded square panes. The aisles are lighted by good windows of the Decorated period, the heads filled with flowing tracery. In the interior the devastation of the periods of which we have spoken is painfully manifest. The nave is divided from each aisle by two lofty pointed arches, borne by octangular pillars; eastward other arches formerly led into chapels. Both nave and chancel are ceiled. We were told by the workmen that the timbers of the original open roof are perfectly sound—so hard, said one, that you cannot drive a nail into them. At the west end is an Early English doorway, with very deep and picturesque mouldings. The font is of about the same date, and curiously ornamented with lozenge compartments enclosing a flower, the bands forming the divisions being studded with beads. It is figured in Simpson's fonts. At the west end of the north aisle is an enormous chest, iron-clasped and iron-bound, with excessive security. Along this end of the church runs a gallery of oak, the front ornamented with those arcades which are common on chest fronts of the time of James I.

Once the glory of the place was its noble array of monuments to the Greenes, who were lords of the manor from 1354 to 1512, and from whom its distinctive name was derived. Several at least of these interesting records existed so lately as Bridges' time. At what precise period they were destroyed is not known, but something of the kind was done so late as the year 1826, when the church was re-pewed and otherwise "beautified." All that now remains is the following:—In the wall of the north aisle is a depressed arch, with a shield in each spandril. In the recess beneath lies a recumbent alabaster figure of a female habited in a vest, which fits closely at the bodice and flows in straight folds down to her feet; over this is a mantle open in front, fastened across the breast with a cordon and clasps. Round her neck is a collar of SS. On her head she wears the mitred head-dress resembling a starched kerchief, folded so as to present a broad band over the forehead, a high peaked fold towards the crown of the head, and loose folds falling on to the neck behind. The hair is gathered into a kind of ornamental net work, which has been gilt. The head is supported by angels amply draperied. Beneath the same arch is a fragment of a recumbent male figure, broken at the waist, and propped up ludicrously on the broken trunk at the head of the female. He is in plate armour, with a mail gorget and collar of SS, pouldrons with the edges curiously turned up, and coudieres. His hair is short, and combed straight down all round; the head rests on his helmet and crest, a buck's head. A glance is sufficient to tell that the arch has no connexion with either of these effigies. In point of fact, the latter were removed hither in 1826. Originally the arch covered the tomb of Sir Thomas Greene, who died in 1457, and Philippa Ferrars his wife. The effigies are those of his ancestor, Sir Thomas Greene, who died in 1391, and his wife Mablethorp. At the back and one end of the arch are slabs of alabaster sculptured with long narrow trefoil-headed compartments, alternately charged with shields, from which the blazonry has been wholly obliterated. Baker gives these tombs before their demolition, copied from Halstead's Genealogies. We have no means of referring to that rare work, and cannot therefore pronounce upon the skill with which the copying has been done, but if Halstead's work is not a great deal more artistic than the etching of Baker, it gives but a very imperfect idea of the grace and beauty—we may even say of the form and detail—of the original effigies. Some day Mr. Albert Hartshorne will probably give us a more accurate representation of what yet remains of them. Mutilated as they are, they are alone worth a visit to Green's Norton.

In September, 1826, the late Mr. Gilbert Flesher, of Towcester, drew attention, in the *Gentleman's Magazine*, to the destruction of the monuments. In the October number of the same magazine the then curate of Green's Norton, the Rev. R. B. Exton, vindicated what had been done:—

"The appropriation," he says, "of a large portion of the sacred edifice to free seats for the poor, rendered it necessary to occupy some part of what was before vacant space. In the transept stood an ancient tomb of the Greenes who gave their name to the place. This was a massive slab, resting on four walls of sand-stone, once curiously carved and painted, but defaced anterior to the memory of any person in existence, and now (lately) in a state of insecure dilapidation. The slab was removed with all possible care, laid in the floor immediately over the vault of the persons it commemorates (its inlaid brass effigies and legend being in perfect preservation), and now forming a very handsome finish to the spacious centre aisle, and quite secure by its locality from the wear of footsteps. . . Now for the 'monumental effigies.' There were formerly two recumbent figures of soft white marble or alabaster lying by the side of the aforesaid tomb upon walls in a most dangerous state of decay, insomuch that the churchwardens long since thought it their duty to remove them. These figures afterwards lay in an obscure corner of the church, from which, probably, they would have had no resurrection, but for the proper spirit actuating the persons now in office, and under whose superintending authority a fine country church has been beautified, and made perfect for its sacred uses. The effigies, then, have not been replaced, it is true, on their original site, but removed to a very short distance, under a vacant arch in the north wall; and an inscription has been actually prepared to explain the occasion of their removal, to include a copy of the long-lost inscription, which Bridges, in his History of Northamptonshire, has alone preserved, as once attached to some part of this monument. I annex a copy, which will show how ancient a memorial this is; and I am happy to add that the researches of a friend have been rewarded by the discovery of the dates of these person's deaths, who were the grandfather and grandmother of the Sir Thomas Greene who lay under the adjoining tomb. He died Dec. 14, 1417, she April 13, 1433 :—

"Hic jacet Thomas Greene, Miles, filius et haeres Thomæ Greene, Militis, filii et haeredis Henrici Greene, Militis (quondam unius Justiciarorum D'ni Regis Edwardi Tertii), et Maria uxor ejus, filia D'ni Talbot, quorum animabus propitietur Deus, Amen."

From which we gather that the devastation began at an earlier period than 1826. Yet in the text to Simpson's Font, which was published in 1825, the effigies are alluded to as if then in situ. De mortuis nil nisi bonum. We dare say the churchwardens acted according to their lights in removing the "dangerous walls" and figures into obscure corners instead of putting them in repair at a cost probably not exceeding that of a year's sparrows' heads. And equally, no doubt, the churchwardens of 1826 were actuated by "a proper spirit," when they made the odd jumble of different relics now existing under the north wall. All we can do is to lament that the lights of those days were not a little brighter. We need not chuckle overmuch. With the best possible intentions we do much in our own time in the way of restoration which will make posterity stand aghast.

Against the north wall of the chancel is another interesting monument of a later date. Beneath a canopy, the curtains of which are withdrawn by two angels, is a double desk, at which a man in armour is kneeling on one side, and, on the other, two female figures, one behind the other. The inscription is as follows :—

"Heere lyes the bodyes of William Hicklinge, Esq., and Frances his onely wife (daughter of John Goodwin, of Winchinton, in ye county of Buckingham, Esq.), sonne and heyre of Jhon Hicklinge, of Green's Norton, in ye county of

Northampton, Esq., wch William departed this life August the 5th, 16.. Frances dyed August ye 25, 1603, leavinge issue behind them one onely daughter and heyre Christian, married to Thomas Elmes, son of Edmund Elmes, of Lileford, in ye county of Northampt., Esq,, by whome she had issue seaven sonnes and five daughters."

In the state in which we found the church, in the process of cleaning, we were not able to search for the brasses.

The churchyard is belted round by noble limes. The manor house of the Greenes stood near it, but no vestige remains. Nothing in the village calls for remark, except "The Butchers' Arms," which faces you as you descend the hill from the church. A pleasanter rural inn one would not desire; with a bow window commanding the street up and down, and one of those capacious old-fashioned fire-places which have seats in them, and give one the intensest idea of snugness and shelter and cosy warmth, and all that weary pedestrianism can desire in chilly weather. Grave is the mistake of landlords who, with a view to a little more room, or for the sake of being more spruce and modern, abolish these ample shelterings of our ancestors, which are none the less comfortable because the substitution of the coal fire in the grate for the wood on the hearth leaves more space for the sitters in the corners. Then, too, "The Butcher's Arms" is as spotlessly clean as a Dutch hotel, and, as the saying is, you might eat off the slabs of its flooring. A glass of excellent ale and perfect courteousness and attention are the climax to the other merits of this agreeable halting-place. We mentioned on our way hither the house of the late Mr. John Elliot. One cannot pass it without remembering the love of art which he possessed, and his natural gift for the practice of it. Many of our readers will remember the specimens of his remarkable ability in this direction—his close observance of nature and his skill in re-producing what he observed on canvas—exhibited in the Northampton Museum.

Egdon Hall.*

"*Era il detto luogo sopra una piccola montagnetta, da ogni parte lontano alquanto alle nostre strade, di varj albuscelli e piante tutte di verde fronde ripieno, piacevoli a riguardare: in sul colmo della quale era un palagio . . . . con pratelli dattorno, e con giardini maravigliosi.*"—Boccaccio.

VERT alleys with trim trees arching o'erhead,
And ending in a vista of blue hills,
Statue, or vase, or nook where grottoed rills,
Trickling from stone to stone, clear coolness shed;
Elsewhere a pleasaunce, with quaint patterns spread
Of rarest flowers; an orangery that fills
The air with that sweet odour which distils
From Lisbon or the Azores, seaward led.
There needs but laughter from the shrubberies coming,
Ladies, and rustling silks, a gorgeous show,
And mantled cavaliers chitarras strumming
Or whispering love in willing ears;—and lo!
A picture by Lancret or by Watteau,
Or tale recorded by Boccaccio.

---

* The seat of the Rev. C. F. Annesley when this Sonnet was written; now occupied by Colonel Henry Cartwright.

Wellingborough.

THE walk from the Wellingborough station—the old station that is—on the Northampton and Peterborough line—is pleasant enough fully to compensate for its distance. As a rule, country roads manifest small respect for the pedestrian; but here there is capital walking all the way from the Bridge foot to Swan's Pool. On the Bridge, it is true, you may get crushed by an omnibus or a waggon, if you don't look out, there being no footway, and the road being far from too wide. Once over the Bridge, however, and you are as safe as you can desire. A tall hedge protects you on one side from the dust and dangers of the road, and on the other you look over green Northamptonshire meadows. At the Dog and Duck you emerge into the road again, but for a few yards only, and then you enter a noble walk, straight as an arrow, bordered on either side with limes, and terminating in a vista of trees and the lofty spire of Wellingborough Church. Wellingborough has good reason to be proud of this beautiful entrance to the town.

Approaching the descent of the hill by the pretty Cemetery, the aspect of the town is novel and picturesque. Tall chimneys are not usually agreeable adjuncts to a landscape, but the tall chimney and the adjoining tower-like building at Mr. Dulley's Brewery, are really ornamental, and show how the most utilitarian and unpromising structures may be wrought into elegance and picturesqueness by a cultivated and artistic taste. Rising upwards from the dip along which the Swan's Pool stream meanders, the houses rising one above another, intermingled with trees, give an agreeable character to the scene.

Crossing the Bridge beneath which the rivulet runs, the eye is caught by a building on the right hand, which has historical, as well as picturesque, interest. It is an unostentatious structure, of one story only, with a gable projecting forwards about the centre towards the street. A sign attached to this gable tells us that it is the Inn of "The Golden Lion." There is quite enough of promise in the aspect of the exterior to make us desire to get a sight of the interior. Turning to the right on entering the passage, we find ourselves in a low room with a ceiling of black oak, and ponderous beams with elaborate mouldings. Across the fire-place is an immense piece of oak timber, which is said some years ago to have been raised considerably from its original situation. Cole's "History of Wellingborough" speaks of "a carved wood chimney-piece of curious workmanship," and it is possible that the carved work may have been removed to admit of the raising of the beam. There is no carving now, nor, so far as we know, any tradition of it. An old man of 80, who remembered the raising of the beam, did not remember any carving; but your "oldest inhabitant" is not always the best authority in such cases. It is possible for the eye to rest upon objects every day through many years without any impression being made upon the memory, unless the attention is specially awakened to them. In a room upstairs is a Tudor fire-place with an ornament in the spandrils. The quantity of timber in the house is enormous. At a short distance in the rear are the stables and granaries of the same date, and equally ponderous with timber, the gables being finished with finials. Cole states that the house was the residence of Thomas Roane, who died in 1676. The house, however, is at least a century earlier. Thomas Roane may have been the owner, but he could not have been the original builder; possibly an ancestor may. It is very interesting, as showing the modest residence of a country gentleman of the 17th century. Roane was a man of substance; he married a daughter of Wm. Law, Esq., of Glendon, and his daughter, who died in 1717, left £100 to the Girls' Charity School.

[Thomas Roane's House; now the Golden Lion.]

Nearly opposite the Golden Lion is another house, noteworthy, not for its antiquity, but as a successful adaptation of the Norman style to modern domestic architecture. It was built, we believe, originally for a factory, and afterwards converted into a dwelling house by the architect, Mr. Edwin Sharman. We trace the same tasteful hand in several of the new buildings in various parts of the town.

Higher up on the same side of the street is another eminently picturesque old house, respecting which we are sorry to say we are in the position of Canning's knife-grinder, having no story to tell. We believe it is "in Chancery," and, if so, we have a tolerable certainty that it will not be disturbed in a hurry. It is now occupied as a broker's.

[Old House in Sheep Street.]

The Hind Hotel, the next object of interest, stands well facing the Market Place, to which it is a decided ornament. It is stated to have been building when the Parliamentarians marched through Wellingborough, previous to the battle of Naseby, which would make the date of its erection about 1645. Its design is ascribed to Wm. Battey, a local architect, parish clerk and registrar, about the middle of the seventeenth century, and shows him to have been a man of considerable ability and taste in his profession. There was an older inn than this in the Market Place, existing within the last five-and-thirty years—the White Swan. It stood on the south side of the Market Place. When Charles the First and his Queen came to Wellingborough for the benefit of the Red Well waters, which were then in repute, they were lodged at the White Swan. It was the White Swan too, in all probability, that drew forth the bitter criticism of Horace Walpole, who was at Wellingborough for a night in 1763. "We lay," he says, "at Wellingborough—pray never lie there—the beastliest inn upon earth is there! We were carried into a vast bed-chamber, which I suppose is the club-room, for it stunk of tobacco like a justice of the peace! I desired some boiling water for tea; they brought me a sugar-dish of hot water in a pewter plate." We must not always, perhaps, take Horace Walpole's words literally, else we must infer that tea was not in general use in Wellingborough a century ago. But the inference is not a very improbable one; a century ago Wellingborough was at least two or three days' journey from the Metropolis. The only public conveyance was the stage waggon, of the pace of which some idea may be formed from the fact that the first coach which commenced running in 1776 was on the road from five in the morning to eight in the evening. In those days of comparatively infrequent intercourse with London, it would take a long time for a custom to send its roots so far. At the houses of the nobility and gentry we may well believe that tea was an accustomed luxury; but it is not unlikely that it may not have been ordinarily called for at inns, and that the mode of making it may have been but imperfectly known to the servants. It is rather in favour of this supposition, that Horace Walpole asks not for tea as a guest at an inn would now, but for "some boiling water for tea," as if he carried his own tea with him, and only required the means of making it.

Burystead Place, just beyond the Hind, is a suggestive name, and the antiquary would look about it for matters of interest. A stone in the Church records that "George Hodges de Burysteed, hic jacet. Sepultus 14 Feb. Ano Dni 1623." The site of Burysteed is indicated by some large sixteenth century outbuildings: when the house was demolished does not seem to be known. Near the same spot stood a Grange belonging to the Abbots of Croyland. A fine old building of the sixteenth century stands on the site. It has an oaken staircase in excellent preservation, and some good old panelling in the handsome and spacious hall. Its front faces the south, and its pleasant gardens are bounded by a moat supplied with clear water. Beneath (for it stands on the brow of a hill) slope picturesque grounds down to the Swan's Pool stream, and beyond are trees and pleasant country. All about it speaks of antiquity and country life as if it were far remote from towns, while in point of fact a stone might be thrown from it into the main streets of Wellingborough. Two doors from the corner of Burystead Place in Silver Street is another good old house with the gable towards the street: a house of a couple of centuries old at least, the inhabitants of which must have seen the great fire of 1738 raging around it. Following up the street, northward, to High Street and Broad Green, there is a picturesque jumble of houses of all kinds and degrees, with a spacious roadway between, that gives them a healthy and agreeable character. Broad Green, with the trees of Hatton House, and its own ample spaciousness, is a very pleasant place. St. John Street is said by Cole to have had an old house in it, on the front of which was a representation of the Crucifixion carved in stone, which was traditionally called St. John, from having, he thinks, been affixed to a wall in an edifice dedicated to St. John. House and carving are now gone, and the street has nothing in it requiring special notice. Gold Street running eastward, at quite the northern extremity of the town, is nevertheless an ancient way, and shows that Wellingborough three or four hundred years ago was at least co-extensive with its present boundaries. There is a house of some pretensions, with respect of length of frontage, in it, with excellent Tudor doorways at each extremity, the original oak door in one instance remaining almost perfect.

About this neighbourhood are what are called "Long Lanes"—a curious characteristic of Wellingborough. Large tracts of garden ground are intersected by tolerably broad lanes, fenced in with lofty old stone walls, covering an intermediate space between Gold Street on the north-east and Skitterdine on the south-west. Gold Street is evidently so ancient a way, that, considering also the situation of the Church, one would be led to suppose that at an early period—say the fifteenth century, this site was part of the town, and covered with houses. The lanes may indicate old streets. It is not easy to account for them upon any other hypothesis. Mere suburban gardens would have been fenced in with hedges; there are, however, very substantial old stone walls, for the most part well built.

Skitterdine! What an odd name for a street is Skitterdine! What does it mean? Has anybody anything to say about it? It is a place of some antiquity; that is, there are old buildings in it, though of no particular mark, but the way and the name are clearly older than any buildings in it. In the absence of all information, we beg to offer the following guess. Is it derivable from Sceat, Anglo Saxon for a corner or portion, and Dincg, new broken land; a sort of equivalent to our Northampton "Newland?" Wellingborough, it must be remembered, is a Saxon name originally. In Domesday Book it was called Wedlingeberil, and at other different times Wendlesberie, Wendyngburgh, Wendleberie. It is supposed to have become modified when the Red Well became famous, and people were perhaps anxious to make the name of the town itself declaratory of its waters. It does not seem to have been fixed in 1610, for Norden writes of "Wellingborrow, called of some Wedlingborow, of others Wenlingborowe," and says, "It may bc thought that the name of that should be Wellingborowe, so given in regard of the springs that rise in many places in and neare the town." If the change was made with such an object as that mentioned above, and was not a mere corruption of the original name (which, perhaps, is, after all, the most probable) it must have taken place at an early date, for Norden was evidently not aware of it. Drayton whose Polyolbion, was written about the beginning of the 17th century, calls it "Wellingborough, so called for its many wells or fountains," and makes no allusion to the earlier name.

Skitterdine debouches into Gloucester Place, one of those open spaces which contribute so largely to the health of towns. Gloucester Place obtained its aristocratic appellation in the following way. Formerly it was called Hog Hill, the Hog Market being held there; a public-house close by, called the Sow and Pigs, still attests the character of the neighbourhood. Between forty and fifty years ago the Duke of Gloucester was going to Cambridge on some public occasion; and the landlord of the Hind put his best horses to the carriage, which was honoured by the august person of His Royal Highness. The post-boy was duly apprised of the importance of his task, and directed to drive as it became a Duke to be driven. "Thou bearest Cæsar and his fortunes," was repeated by the worthy host, mutatis mutandis, and off the vehicle dashed with its noble freight, to the admiration and pride of the by-standers. Up the ascent of the Market Place, along Silver Street, the postillions' whips crashing, the four horses heels making a tattoo, as if

> "Played with iron sticks,
> On a kettle-drum of granite."

Hog Hill is reached, and now for the postillions' triumph, to sweep grandly round into East end, at showing-off-corner.

"— It's awful work!
It's faster than Turpin's ride to York
On Bess that notable clipper."

Round they go, never pulling a rein, and over goes the carriage with a sparkle and crash, depositing the Duke at the foot of the pump in the middle of the hill. How from all the fair dames who thronged the windows round the Hog Hill, there proceeded one simultaneous shriek of horror; and how all the loyalty rushed headlong on to the hill to assist the downfallen royalty, used to be graphically told by Mrs. Wells, the landlady of the Globe Inn, in 1862, who herself remembered the event, and whose father was one of the first and foremost to render help. Fortunately, though the chaise was smashed, the Duke was not, and in reply to the enquiry of the worthy citizen and cooper aforesaid, whether His Royal Highness was hurt, he very courteously thanked the enquirer, and assured him he was not. Another chaise was soon procured, and the Duke proceeded on his route. But Dukes don't get upset every day, and, to commemorate the event and the place, it was unanimously resolved for these reasons, and because Hog Hill was a name clearly unfitted to be handed down in connexion with the spilling of a Duke, that henceforward Hog Hill should be called by the style and title of Gloucester Place. And Gloucester Place it accordingly has been ever since, and is now, because the Duke of Gloucester was spilt there. There are few places with a high sounding name that can give so good a reason for their christening.

Wellingborough church is an extremely handsome structure, principally in the Perpendicular style, though there are portions of Decorated and Norman work. Of the latter character is the inner doorway of the south porch, which has a bold chevron moulding and shafts similarly ornamented. There are parvises over both the porches, and in that over the south doorway are said to be the mouldering remains of old oak chests cut out of the solid wood. The entrances to both these chambers are blocked up. The east window is a noble piece of work, and has a fine effect from the interior. There is some good timber roofing in the interior, especially to a chantry chapel in the south aisle, which is rich with carving, and shields and paintings of angelic figures, and the emblems of the Crucifixion. From this chapel a view of the high altar would be obtained through a squint. On each side of the choir are three very rich and curious old oak stalls with misereres, having grotesque carvings on the under part of the turn-up seats. These seats have a bracket which gives them the effect of a double seat, the bracket affording a rest to the weary ecclesiastic during the long standing part of the service, without giving him the appearance of being seated. The carvings usually found on the under part of this bracket have been the subject of much speculation. Like the grotesque heads of Gurgoyles, and the frequently strange subjects of early corbels, they seem often to be singularly at variance with the sacred character of the edifice to which they belong. Sometimes they seem to be satires on the clergy, sometimes to illustrate the popular literature of their day. Sometimes they are in accordance with what in painting is known by the title of *genre;* and sometimes they are intolerably gross. The inference to be drawn, we think, from all that is known about them is, that they certainly were not intended to symbolize anything; that they were not intended for instruction; that it was the custom, in the lavish adornment of the day, to ornament the seats, and that the sculptor was either left to his own imagination, or was under the direction of the individual ecclesiastic who superintended the works. Sometimes there would probably be a meaning and a direct satire, having reference to events of the day; the mediæval Leech might make them his "Punch" by which to shoot the folly or to satirize the wrong-doing of the time; but there is nothing to lead to the belief that they were treated in any respect systematically, or had any more direct meaning than the subjects on our paper-hangings. Mr. T. Wright concludes an excellent paper in the 4th volume of the Journal of the

Archæological Association on the subject, with the remark that they "form a practical illustration of the kind and degree of scientific and literary information it was thought necessary to place before society at large." This is somewhat, it will be seen, at variance with our own view, and we differ with hesitation from so learned an authority. But some of the illustrations to his paper seem in themselves to support our idea of the absence of any absolute intention. One from Worcester represents a domestic winter scene, where a man who has evidently returned home wet-footed has taken off his boots, and, while he holds his feet to the fire, stirs the great pot which contains his meal. Another from Great Malvern represents a woman in bed attended by a physician, who brings her in two vessels what we may presume to be an effervescing draught, which he is about to mix. In Wellingborough church two of the brackets are of this domestic character. One represents the carver himself cutting the roses which form the side ornaments. He sits with his table before him and his tools spread out upon it. The other is full of genuine humour. The ale-wife is about to fill the goblet for her customer, who stands by in all the felicity of anticipation; with one hand he scratches his head, and with the other rubs his stomach, while his eyes glance sideways watching the process of the "totting out," with delighted satisfaction. The carving of this curious bracket is remarkably spirited and artistic.

A story is told of one of the Incumbents of this Church, the Rev. Aaron Locock, who was instituted in 1718, which is too good not to be repeated in this gossiping notice. In the dusk of the evening he was crossing the long bridge, when he was attacked by a foot-pad. Mr. Locock was tall and athletic; the chancel door was enlarged to enable him to pass through without stooping. Instead, therefore, of yielding up his purse, he collared the foot-pad, and prepared to throw him over the parapet. In doing so he chanced to recognize the man's features, and exclaiming—"If it wasn't more for your soul than your body,

Jack, I would drop you,"—set him at liberty. Mr. Locock was chosen vicar of All Saints, Northampton, in 1731.

In the vestry is a stone to the memory of William Battey, the architect of the Hind Hotel. It has the following couplet:—

All worldly fabricks are but vanity,
To Heavenly buildings for eternity.

Sepult: Novemb. ye 30th 1674 Ætat 80.

A curious relic is kept in the vestry called the Wellingborough lock of hair, which was dug up many years ago in the church yard. It was about a yard in length when it was discovered, but is not above two feet now. It is twisted or plaited, and was evidently the "back hair," of a lady of very remote times. The Anglo-Saxon and Norman ladies wore their hair twisted into long tails, as the fashion was with the Miss Kenwigs of our times some fifteen years ago.

Wellingborough church is much encompassed with buildings, and it was time that burials had ceased there. The access to it is chiefly by lanes—Church Lane and Pebble Lane. At the west corner of the latter, next the church yard, is a miniature house, with the smallest imaginable upper window. The adult head must be small indeed that can project itself through the little opening of the casement. It is of a triangular form, and projects from the building. The house is occupied by the sexton. Pebble Lane was burnt by the great fire, but this little window escaped the general ruin.

On the north side of the churchyard stands the Grammar School, which was built in 1620. It is a respectable, commodious looking structure, with gabled roofs and stone-mullioned windows, after the fashion of the day, and adjoining it, westward, is a house of the same style now occupied by Mr. Hodson, which looks from its situation as if it had at some period been connected either with the church or the school. It has a communication with the churchyard.

Wellingborough has had its fires. Cole gives an extract, probably from the parish register, respecting money "Paid for beer, which poor men had at Wyman's fire, 12s.," in 1663, and in the same year occurs another entry, "Paid for beer at Robert Cox's fire, 10s." Twelve shillings must have represented a very decent quantity of beer two centuries ago. In 1731 another fire, known as "the upper end fire," broke out in the High Street, when about six houses were destroyed. But *the* fire, known as "the great fire," broke out on Friday the 28th of July, 1738, about two o'clock in the afternoon.

The *Northampton Mercury* of July 31, 1738, gives the following account of it:—

"On Friday last, about two o'clock in the afternoon, a sudden and most dreadful fire broke out at the house of Thomas Curtis, a dyer, next the Peacock Inn, in Wellingborough, in this county, which, in the space of six hours, burnt down and consumed near 220 dwelling houses, besides outhouses, barns, stables, &c., amounting in the whole to above 800, mostly in the east and south parts of the town. The fire was so fierce and violent, the wind being very high, and but little water to be had, that in less than an hour it broke out in near twenty places, and the inhabitants were in such distress and confusion that but few of them had time to save any goods, and many of them not more than the clothes on their backs. As it happened chiefly among the trading men and farmers, the loss is very great and heavy upon them; but at present, through the hurry and confusion every poor sufferer is in, it cannot yet be computed.

In the same paper is the following advertisement:—

"This is to give notice to all gentlemen, farmers, bakers, millers, &c., that at the White Hart Inn, in Wellingborough, which hath escaped the dreadful fire, there is good entertainment, with stabling for horses, and store-room for corn, &c."

Cole gives some additional particulars, without, unfortunately, citing his authorities. A lady, named Hannah Sparke, he says, saved a house in the Butchery, by ordering her servants, when water failed, to resort to the beer in the cellar, which they did with such effect as to extinguish the blazing wood-work. Dr. Doddridge referred to this circumstance in a sermon which he preached on the occasion. Mrs. Sparke was at this time 60 years of age. She lived to attain to nearly the age of 107. When she reached her hundredth year she was chaired round the square in which she resided, a testimony to the excellence of her nerves as well as to the enthusiasm and regard of her neighbours.

Wellingborough has a Corn Exchange, commodious also for all those miscellaneous purposes to which Corn Exchanges are usually put. It is a capital place for a concert, for example, or a meeting. Its site is a very good one if it were cleared of the houses next its south front—not those only occupied by Mr. Pendered, but the row forming the south side of the Market Place, and intervening between it and Market Street. Whenever these are cleared away Welling-borough will have one of the finest market-places in the country. The market must have been a considerable one formerly, for Norden says the town was distinguished by the name of "Wellingborowe Forum of the Market theare."

A pleasant walk of about a mile along the Kettering Road brings you to a mill on the left-hand side of the way. Crossing the stile into the mill-field, and following the winding stream which turns the wheel to its source, you reach the once famous Red Well. It is in an arable field, lying between the Kettering and the Hardwick roads—a spot thoroughly secluded and very picturesque. The spring is strong, and the water bubbles up abundantly, leaving a red deposit on the stones and earth over which it flows. Scoop a handful and drink, and you recognise at once the flavour of the "Flat Irons," as immortal Sam Weller says. There is not a vestige of a building about it. Yet there must have been something of the sort in the days of its prosperity, for in 1640, as appears by an account in the old town books, £10 was expended in repairs—a considerable sum in those days. In 1628, Charles I. and his Queen, Henrietta, were at Welling-borough, for the benefit of its waters, under the prescription of the Queen's physicians. We dare say the Red Well offered as good a chalybeate as other waters that have kept their celebrity, and clustered fashionable mansions around their sources. But even so early as Fuller's time it had fallen out of repute. "Now I believe," says that quaint writer, "is it *low water* in its reputation." There is a fashion in physic as well as in dress, and Charles I. was hardly the Sovereign to give permanence to anything. The times that followed were busied with sterner matter than the fostering of watering places, and the merry monarch found wells more convenient at Tunbridge and Epsom.

Wellingborough promises to be more than ever prosperous. It had a reputation as a substantial town always, and although, during the transition days, when railways first came, and coaches and carriers were ousted from their old tracks, it suffered as all other places similarly situated suffered, a good substantial town it has continued. Within the last few years, it has added iron smelting to its other industries. With great perseverance, and in spite of many discouragements, Mr. Butlin has succeeded in establishing works, which may, in course of time, have an important effect upon the character of the district. Iron abounds in its soil. The great question, we presume, is whether it is more profitable to carry the coals to the iron, or the iron to the coals. Mr. Butlin seems, at all events, to have demonstrated that an industry of this peculiar description may be carried on in Northamptonshire, and who shall say that, at some far off time, from this small beginning, Wellingborough may not become another Wolverhampton? We have lived to see changes far more improbable.

The Advent of Spring.

SOMEWHERE past the dismal midnight,
Wakening from a dreary dream,
Storms I heard against the casement
Carrying out the solemn theme.

As old German legends tell us,
Demon troops sweep through the air,—
Skeletons of men and horses
Shrieking maidens Hell-wards bear.

So it seemed I heard the clamour,
And the shrieking and the laughter,
And the frozen bony rattle
Of the death group following after:

Then a pause of breathless horror,
Then a low and sobbing strain,—
Then the soft and welcome South-wind,
With a grateful gush of rain.

Then I knew the fight was over,
And the Winter gone and past,
And I turned and on my pillow
Slept a blissful sleep at last.

Skies are cloudy, ways are miry,
Pleasant yet shall be our way,
For the thawing blood within us
Speaks of Spring-time holiday.

Great Doddington.

ULTIMA Thule. Well, not quite that, perhaps, but, as railroads and the traffic of the world goes on, a little out of the rush and roar. So much the better for those at least who

> "Know the rural feeling, and the charm
> That stillness has for a world-fretted ear."

Pleasant it is to quit the train at these road-side stations that seem to lead to nowhere, though here there is double promise—on one side Castle Ashby, on the other Earl's Barton. Of Castle Ashby, however, or Earl's Barton, we see nothing, and are content. Before us is a mill bestriding the river, and the way thither looks "woody, mossy, and watery." That, therefore, is, for the nonce, our way.

There are two roads—one a good one, fit for travel, and leading, it needs no great shrewdness to infer, to Earl's Barton. Some day our steps shall be thitherward, in due homage to the world-famed Saxon church-tower. Now we choose the right hand and rougher road, which looks as if it had a visit ever and anon from the river. Our mood leads us to the picturesque, and the aspect of the path is promising. A very few steps satisfy us that the promise will be fulfilled. The road continues a reasonable cartway for some distance, but its gravelly character testifies that it is sometimes rather a ford than a road. Trees and tall hedgerows shut it in on the right—to the left is the river. Before long the road becomes a footpath, which diverges, and gives you a choice of winding along by the river-bank, or of crossing meadows which occasionally have little pools even at this season, and which a storm may render impassable. Either way the walk is thoroughly rural and pleasant. With plenty of time at your command, you may go by the river-side all the way—a sedgy track, with here and there a member of the Nene Angling Club, who will hardly fill his creel from water which to-day is glassy as the Rio Verde. If time is an object, you may draw a straight line, and save some distance by going from bend to bend of the stream. It is open country now. Southward the far-stretching meadows are bounded by rising ground, on which you may descry the towers of the churches of Cogenhoe and Grendon, and the tall ever-present spire of Wollaston. Over the river there is rising ground nearer at hand. At length one of the prettiest pictures of its kind breaks upon us. In the foreground is a wooden foot-bridge spanning the river diagonally. Behind it is a mill, just what a water-mill should be. Tennyson's Miller's Daughter inhabited such an one. There is the mill proper, with its arch reflected reversely in the stream; and beside it the dwelling-house, covered with creepers and greenery; and on either side luxuriant trees make the water dark with their rich autumnal hues. The traveller who goes that way in a hurry catches a flash of happy beauty from his hurried glance at it. He who has leisure lingers—own to include the entire scene, footbridge and all, in his study; now to lean over the bridge-rail, and dwell on all the charms of outline and colour in detail, and drink in the picturesqueness and the poetry, and imprint the whole on his memory as "a thing of beauty and a joy for ever."

Great Doddington is not far from the mill. We cross the wooden foot-bridge, and come into an enclosure, where there are ducks and fowls, and we have an uneasy feeling, as if we were on trespass. A short bit of road, and then into fields again, and then we come to the place of our destination.

Great Doddington stands on the northern ridge of the Nene

valley, which it overlooks. It consists mainly of one long-street, and a smaller one on a lower terrace, with house here and there. North-eastward the way is to Wilby; westward to Earl's Barton. The church is on another terrace, the highest of the three. With the exception of some tiles before a row of new cottages, the paving is of that stone which starts into every conceivable variety of shape —more picturesque to the sketcher than practicable to the pedestrian. Altogether it is a pleasant village, with here and there a good old gable, and an inn (the Stag's Head) which is clothed with greenery, and has a covered gallery, from which there is the prettiest and most comprehensive view of the valley—from Wollaston spire to the woods of noble Castle Ashby. It is at the eastern extremity of the village, and its general appearance is very foreign, only instead of a broad lake before it, there is the narrow and sinuous Nene. Near it, on higher ground, is the manor house, a fine old sixteenth century building, with gables and mullioned windows, very comfortable and happy-looking. It is now occupied by the vicar, the Rev. Maze W. Gregory, in whose hands it will lose none of its genial aspect. This, we presume, is the house which in Bridge's time was occupied by Major Ekins, of Weston, who is described as the impropriator of the great tithes, and as having "the largest estate and the best house in the town." There is another house in the village of much the same character, which must have once been of nearly similar importance. On a higher terrace than the manor house is the church, with a background of trees. It has a west-tower, nave, chancel, and north and south aisles. The tower is Early English, with a west door of that period, and a small circular-headed window over it in good preservation. In the inside the splay is very deep. In the upper stage is a window with two circular-headed lights under a circular head, the tympanum of which is not pierced. The tower is buttressed with bold buttresses of three stages. On the south wall are two inscribed stones, which seem to indicate that the tower was once crowned with a spire, unless, indeed, so late as 1737 the Anglc-

Saxon word steeple was used in its original sense for a tower. One of these bears the following words:—"This steeple was pointed, 1688: Jesse Corby, Joseph Pettit, Churchwarns." The other runs as follows:—"This steeple was taken down and leaded at top by Moses Mores and William Pettitt, Churchwardens, July 21, 1737." The first may have referred to the tower itself or to a spire crowning the tower; but the second very much resembles that well-known Hibernicism about General Wade:—

"If you had seen these roads before they were made,
You'd lift up your hands and bless General Wade."

Supposing both inscriptions to refer to the tower, it is curious enough that the re-building should in 1737 have repeated so exactly the earlier work. Bridges, however, writing some fifty years later, makes no mention of a spire. He merely mentions "a ridged tower tiled at the top." A Decorated window at the west end of the south aisle is stopped up, but the remains of it testify to its beauty. It is ogee-headed, and the cuspings were cinquefoil. The inner door-way of the porch has an original Perpendicular oaken door, with much of the tracery and the old iron-work remaining. Some interesting features mark the interior. Four of the stalls in the chancel remain, and the under-part of one of the misereres represents a man carving a rose. The hand is evidently that of the artist who carved the curiously interesting misereres in Wellingborough Church. There is a handsome cinquefoil-headed piscina, and two trefoil-headed sedilia of the same date. Another piscina occurs in the south aisle. The font is a plain bowl on a plain circular base, and may be of almost any date, excepting yesterday. In the north aisle is a slab with an inscription in Lombardic characters, the greater part of which is covered with pews and otherwise defaced, and the remaining fragment would take more time and opportunity to decipher than we had to bestow on it. In the nave is the slab, with the bed of a brass cross fleury and the following inscription:—"Ici gist Willelm de Pattishull qe morust le xvij jour de Septembre, l'an de grace 1359." The founder of the convent at Delapré—Simon, Earl of Northampton, gave the Church of Doddington, with its appendages in frank almoin, to his new foundation.

The lordship of Doddington has had distinguished possessors. In the list of the lands held by the Countess Judith in Domesday Book we find the following entry:—"Ipsa Comitissa tenet iiii. hidas in Dodintone. Terra est viii. carucarum. In dominis ii. carucæ et ii. servi et xii. villani et v. bordarii cum iiii. sochmannis habent vi. carucas. Ibi xii. acræ prati. Valuit et valet iiii. libias. Bondi tenuit"—"The same Countess holds four hides in Dodintone. There is land for eight ploughs. In demesne there are two ploughs and two serfs; and twelve villeins and five bordars, with five sochmen, have six ploughs. There are twelve acres of meadow. It was and is worth four pounds. Bondi held it." This Countess Judith was a daughter of Odo, Earl of Albemarle, by Adeliza, half-sister of William the Conqueror, and the husband of Earl Waltheof, the son of the Saxon Earl Siward. Waltheof, from what cause is not known, fell under the displeasure of William, and, after being long in prison, was beheaded at Winchester. Judith, whether with reason or not, has been suspected of treachery towards her husband. After his death the Conqueror desired her to bestow her hand on Simon de St. Liz, the Norman who is believed to have built the Castle at Northampton. St. Liz, however, was deformed, and the Countess indignantly rejected him. The angry monarch made her pay the penalty of her refusal by seizing upon her possessions, and bestowing them upon her eldest daughter, Matilda, who was willing to accept the bridegroom her mother had rejected. Whether Doddington was included in the Conqueror's seizure we do not know, but in the reign of Henry II., David, King of Scotland, was possessed of the four hides which Judith had held. The lordship has been for some time the property of the Earls of Northampton, and is held by the present Marquis.

The return is not less pleasant than the going. We traverse the same ground, but the points of view are different, and the evening sun throws another light upon the picture. Re-crossing the foot-bridge we turn to look back upon the Mill. The colouring is now intensified: the red roof of the Mill is fired by the setting orb, and it throws a gorgeous reflection on the water, where it glows amidst the dark purple of the shadows. Turning westward again the sky is glorious all the way. The gold and purple dies into grey only as we turn towards the station.

A Legend of Mont du Chat.

THE Lake was bathed in the rosy light
With which dear Italy's skies are bright,
And a beam of which she sometimes sends
As a special grace to her nearest friends.

Azi, Grenier, and Nivolet
Sharply were shadowed in Lake Bourget,
And the triple summit of Mont du Chat
Blended the beauty with something of awe.

The elder of our boatman three
(For our craft was heavy as craft could be)
Paused awhile on his lumbering oar,
And pointed north to the farthest shore—

Pointed to where in the distance dim
The outline rose of a Castle grim,
Blackened with fire and crumbling with time,
Calling up visions of terror and crime.

In days remote 'twas the lordly hold
Of a baron,—wealthy, and wise, and bold,
Yet less renowned for his prowess and gold
Than for two bright daughters of heavenly mould.

It was said he loved them with a love
All that he had on earth above,
Yet wisely he loved them not, if well,
As my story will in its sequence tell;

For he kept them close in that Castle grim,
Never indulging a girlish whim,
Leading them never to ball or Court,
Where gallants and ladies love to resort.

Knights and squires haunted in vain
The precincts of his vast domain,
Hoping a fortune and bride to win;
He let them ride, but he let none in.

All day long they would wheel about,
In and out, in and out,
On chargers taught to curvet and prance,
After the *manége* new from France.

He let them wheel and he let them prance
After the *manége* new from France,
But he never asked them in to dine
Or an after dinner glass of wine.

Once only one well-favoured knight
Got an "invite" to sup one night,
But the ladies both were gone to bed,
As the Baron observed, with an aching head.

That very night when the mid-hour came
The Castle was wrapt in a mighty flame,—
In a mighty flame like a dreadful pall
Covering, clasping, dooming all.

"Water! water! Fly to the Lake!
Fly for our dear young ladies' sake!"
Vassal and tenant off went they;
They might as well have remained away.

The greater the deluge the greater the blaze,
As it's office were not to subdue but to raise,
Oil or spirits of turpentine
Could have made no blaze so fearfully fine.

The Baron rides here, the Baron rides there,
With a madman's shout and a madman's stare,
Over the wide Lake's burning waters
Echoes his shriek for his perishing daughters.

Perishing? No! Behold, behold!
Dash from the Castle two champions bold
On sable coursers, in sable mail,
Gaunt of form and of visage pale.

Before him each in his saddle bears
One of the Baron's lovely heirs,
Closely, closely they clasp them both,
And the ladies scarce seem *very* loth.

There isn't a struggle, there isn't a shriek,
There's a conscious blush upon either cheek,
And I think (though I can't be sure in the haste)
That a white arm circled each gaunt knight's waist.

Yet the coursers black those knights bestrode
Like red-hot furnaces burnt and glowed,
And a fiery blast from their nostrils rolls,
And their eyes gleam like two living coals.

A fiendish yell and a fearful scream,
A splash and a hiss and a column of steam,
And a thunder-clap and a lightning gleam,
And a wailing sound like the song of a dream,—
And the shivering grey of the morning's beam.

The rosy hue from the Lake is fled,
And it frowns in purple and lurid red,
And a keen wind over the surface sweeps,
From crag to crag the lightning leaps,
And the echo, thunder-roused, upleaps,
And shouts to her sister nymph who sleeps.

* * * *

Our boatman bow'd and cross'd his breast,
And again to his oar himself addrest.
" It is ill to tell these tales of awe
In the solemn shadow of Mont Du Chat."

Weston Favell.

QUIET, secluded Weston Favell has had its days of stateliness and glorification. It is mentioned in Domesday Book as Westone, and in the beginning of the eighteenth century there were no fewer than three mansions in the village. The whereabouts of two of them may yet be traced—one north and the other south of the Church. But its greatest ·ity is derived from its sometime minister, the Rev. James ·y, one of the most popular religious writers and preachers of ay. The story of the Herveys goes back to the sixteenth ry. The first of whom we have any record is Stephen ·y, of Cotton, in Hardingstone, who was auditor of the Duchy ncaster. He died in 1606, and was buried at Hardingstone. of his sons, Sir Francis Hervey, was a Justice of Common Others are described in the family pedigree as of Weston l. In 1660-61, Francis Hervey, who was born in 1611, ented Northampton in Parliament. He presented to the s of Weston Favell and Collingtree, his son, the Rev. William y, who was succeeded in 1736-7 by the Rev. William Hervey, ras the father of the celebrated author of the Meditations. Hervey was born at Hardingstone, February 14, 1714, in a which is still standing. At seven years of age he was sent Northampton Free Grammar School, of which the Vicar of pulchre was then the master. Afterwards he was entered at n College, Oxford, where one of his tutors was the famous Wesley. Hervey was one of that knot of fifteen students,

George Whitfield being also one, who met together for religious exercises and studies, and inaugurated the great religious movement known as Methodism. Hervey did not join the connexion, but he retained his friendship for its leaders, and its influence may be traced in his life and writings. He was ordained in 1736, and relinquished on the occasion an exhibition of £20 per annum from his college on the ground that others might stand in greater need of it. At first he assisted his father; for twelve months was curate of Dummer in Hampshire; and afterwards undertook the curacy of Bideford, Devon, with a stipend of £40 a year. Here is the best evidence that he made himself valued and beloved, for of their own accord his congregation added £20 per annum to his pittance, and when in 1742 his rector died they further offered to pay the whole of his salary by voluntary contributions in order to retain him. His rector, however, seems not to have assented to this proposal, and Hervey returned to Weston Favell, and officiated as curate to his father till the death of the latter in 1752. After that event he succeeded to the family livings of Weston Favell and Collingtree, and held them till his death, which occurred on Christmas Day, 1758. He was buried in the Chancel of Weston Favell Church, and the spot is marked by the following inscription:—

— "Here lie the Remains
of the Rev. James Hervey, A.M.
(late Rector of this Parish).
That very pious Man,
And much-admired author,
Who died Dec. 25, 1758,
In the 45th year of his age.
Reader, expect no more to make him known,
Vain the fond elegy and figur'd stone:
A name more lasting shall his writings give;
There view display'd his heavenly soul, and live."

An active parish priest, Hervey was also a diligent author. The works by which he is chiefly known are Theron and Aspasio, and the "Meditations"—the latter especially. They were published in 1746, and became immensely popular. They were suggested by a visit to the village of Kilhampton, in Cornwall. Both the "Meditations among the Tombs" and the "Reflections on a Flower Garden" are, however, rhapsodies rather than either Meditations or Reflections. Reading them, one is impressed with the idea that they should have been in verse. Hervey was not a deep thinker, but he was a great and various reader; paraphrased what he read in his own enjoying way, and communicated much of his enjoyment to his hearers and readers. That he was a man of large heart is evident from the comprehensive circle of his friends, among whom were Whitfield, Romaine, Doddridge, and Ryland. Mr. Ryland published a volume on his character, "as a Man of Genius and a Preacher—as a Philosopher and Christian united—as a Regenerate man—as a man endowed with the dignity and prerogatives of a Christian—as a man of Science and Virtue—as a Divine and a very eminent Master in the Doctrines and Duties of the Christian Religion." It is written in a strain of enthusiastic, not to say rhapsodic, eulogy. One passage will afford an idea of the whole:—

"By the most keen and incessant attention to nature and Scripture he rose to such a pitch of sacred knowledge and devotion as few good men ever attained. It would be invidious to compare him with the eloquent Dr. Bates; the savoury and judicious Dr. Owen; the accurate and copious Charmack; the great John Smith, of Cambridge; and the much greater man, Edward Polhill, Esq.; the masculine John Howe; the correct and nervous Hurrion; the sagacious President Edwards; the florid Dr. Watts; the sprightly and benevolent Dr. Doddridge; and the fervent zealous Whitfield; with the great and judicious Dr. Waterland. But this I may safely say, that Harvey had those peculiar excellencies which distinguish him from all those great men; and even that prince of all divines, Dr. Whitsius, did not excel him in great conceptions, rich imagination, devotional criticism, deep humility, and seraphic fire. Suffer me to make this remark, that through the defective and faulty method of education, almost all the above divines neglected the beauties of creation and the charms of natural philosophy. Through this defect their compositions want that striking brilliance with which Hervey's writings abound."

Hervey made Weston Favell a shrine to which pilgrims, from

America and Scotland chiefly, resort even now. A more modest one it is not easy to conceive; nor, at the same time, one more picturesque. Approaching it from the fields or from the road, its tower is seen set in the trees which surround it with most pleasing relief. It is of the very late Norman or Early English period. Bold buttresses support it on the north and south sides. Two lights, in the upper stage on each face are hooded by a moulding, which runs round the building. In the west front there is a single light directly under the corbel table, and a two-light window under one head in the lower stage, partly blocked up. There are traces also of a doorway. The tower formerly was crowned by a spire, but on Thursday, the 19th day of May, 1725, about noon, it was "split asunder by the violence of a clap of thunder," according to the testimony of the *Northampton Mercury* of that date. The body of the church has been greatly altered. There are no aisles, and the windows are late Gothic under square labels. A south porch is a still later addition, with a wooden beam for a lintel. The chancel has some good Early English windows of three lights, with very deep splays inside, and there is a good doorway, blocked up, of the same period. The pulpit is of James the First's time. Close by it, fixed in the wall, is the iron framework of the hour-glass, by which the length of a sermon, in days when sermons were of a length which would not be tolerated in our degenerate days, used to be regulated. Sometimes the congregation would call upon the preacher to turn the glass for an additional hour. In the south wall of the chancel is a small trefoil-headed piscina, and opposite, in the north wall, a tall aumbry, which has lost its door. Over the Communion Table is a curious piece of worsted and bugle-work, representing the Lord's Supper, inscribed with the words—"Gloria Deo. Weston Favell, Dec., 1698." It was the work of Lady Holman, the wife of Sir John Holman, Bart., whose mansion stood in a field south of the parsonage. North of the parsonage, and forming the eastern boundary to the roadway into the main Wellingborough Road, is a wall which enclosed the grounds about the mansion of the Ekins family, who had been settled in Weston Favell from 1617 till 1814. One of its members —Alexander Ekins—was deputy to James Earl of Northampton, Master of the Leash to Charles the Second. Baker quotes the Earl's warrant, a document curiously illustrative of the royal privileges of the day. It is addressed to "all Justices of Peace, Maiors, Sherriffs, Bayliffs, Constables, and other His Majesty's Officers and Ministers to whom it shall or may appertain," and proceeds as follows:—

"Now know yee that I, the said James Earl of Northampton, master of His said Ma'ties said Leash, have licensed and authorized Alexander Ekins, of Weston Favell, in the county of Northampton, to bee my deputy and assignee during the will and pleasure of mee the sd Earle of Northampton, to take to His Ma'ties use and in His Ma'ties name, within all places within tenne miles any way of Weston Favell aforesaid, as well within franchises and libertyes as without, such and so many greyhounds, both doggs and bitches, in whose custody soever they bee, as the said Alexander Ekins shall thinke meete and convenient for his Ma'ties disport and recreation, and in such and as ample manner and form as I the said Earle of Northampton may or might have done. And likewise I, the said Earle of Northampton doe hereby authorize and depute the said Alexander Ekins, by himself and his serveants, to seize and take away all such greyhounds, beagles, or whippets as may any way be offensive to his Ma'ties game and disport as fully and amply as I myself, by virtue of the said authority may doe; I the said Earle of Northampton ratifying and allowing whatsoever the said Alexander Ekins shall lawfully, by virtue of the said l'res patent and this my deputation or assignment, doe and execute."

Dated 26 Mar., 18 Car. 2 (1665), and signed "NORTHAMPTON."

The Herveys had a mansion in the road leading to Little Billing, of which traces also remain. There are some mullioned windows of the fifteenth century in some cottages facing the church tower. The present rectory was built on the site of the old parsonage, by the Rev. James Hervey, who, however, never occupied it, having died during its erection in a house still standing east of the parsonage.

Weston obtained its affix of Favell from the family of that name, who possessed lands there in the thirteenth century. The male line became extinct by the death of Sir Wm. Favell, without children, in 1316. On the north side of the Wellingborough Road, facing the entrance to the village, is the school-house, a charity endowed by Hervey Ekins and his wife Elizabeth in 1704, and "in pursuance of the pious and charitable inclination" of their youngest daughter, Gertrude Ekins, who died at Oxford after an illness of two days, in that year, aged 16, two small closes in Weston were conveyed to trustees to be called Gertrude Ekins' Charity, the rents to be applied to a premium of £7 for binding a boy apprentice who shall have been educated three years in the school; 16s. to the minister of the parish for preaching a sermon on the 3rd of November, the anniversary of her death, and the residue to be distributed in bread amongst the poor of the parish on that day. In 1707 the endowment was increased, the school-house having been then newly-erected; and in 1717 a rent-charge of £1 was given for the repair of the building. One of the directions of the deed was that the children were to be taught the art of spinning.

Weston Favell is pleasantly situated on the northern ridge of the valley of the Nene, and commands extensive views over that fertile district, while the interval between the village and the county town includes some extremely pretty close scenery. The eastern suburb of Northampton now stretches far into the fields, and town and country, which a few years ago met face to face, must each make a long arm to shake hands. But once clear of the houses the whole way is thoroughly rural: park and dell and swelling ground, and a brook, and trees of all sorts, stately and gnarled, and in the season a glorious show of chestnut blossoms. As you approach Weston, the Church shows its venerable tower among the trees; the School-house, with its front covered with trained trees, looks cheerful and old, and the "Trumpet," one of those inns in which "evening weariness" loves to rest, invites you to test its hospitality. There was a time when it was a bustling and far from unimportant hostelry. Stage coaches pulled up there, and numerous carriers. Times change, and the railway has diverted much of the traffic from the road: the "Trumpet" has been abandoned for the scream of the railway whistle. But the pleasantness of the scene and of the inn has lost nothing by the change.

The Church has lately undergone some repairs and slight alterations. It was intended to add to it a north aisle, and abolish the huge gallery at the west end. The carrying out of that intention for the present remains in abeyance, and the chief alteration effected is the restoring the open roof. The gain by the destruction of the gallery would be the exposure of the tower arch and the Early English window in the west wall of the tower; but the gallery, huge and ugly as it is, hides nothing architecturally remarkable, as galleries usually do. The opening of the roof is of course an advantage in respect of ventilation as well as of appearance. There was a time when our ancestors seem to have considered that a Church ought to be made to look as much as possible like a drawing-room. Of all the disfigurements which that perverted taste occasioned, none were so bad as the plaister ceiling, which brought the vitiated atmosphere down to the congregation to be breathed over and over again. Weston Favell has done wisely to remove what was sanitarily an evil as well as an eye-sore. We should not, we confess, lament the abandonment of the new north aisle. There is nothing in the present north wall particularly worth preserving, and the design of the proposed restoration, we are bound to say, so far as we have seen it, is in good taste, and in accordance with the best parts of the building. But in these days of universal Church-renovation we in a sort cling to anything which tells us of days in any degree historic. By and bye we shall have nothing but nineteenth century work—very good work, much of it, we cordially admit, but necessarily without the sentiment which pervades the old, and telling no story of past times. We would fain be spared something by which to estimate our progress or our decadence.

The Water-Mill.

THERE ;—it may serve perhaps some future day,
Dull though the pencil be, and duller he
Who guides it, to recall to memory
The exquisite beauties of this rural way,
Tempting the hurried traveller to delay :—
The mill down in the dell ; the huge beech-tree
Flinging its great black arms protectingly
Over the useful stream, with one hot ray
From Autumn's cloudless sky touched, like a star ;
The feathery greenery sheltering everywhere ;
The one bright strip of greensward seen afar
Between the mossy trunks.—May never care
Come to the Mill, its clattering glee to mar
Making all foul within, while all around is fair.

Lamport.

THE Lamport Station is one of those pleasant rural places which are apt to make us hard-hearted as regards the case of the station-master. In stations on main lines; at dreadful junctions where lines cross and re-cross each other with the complexity of an elaborate perspective drawing; where trains run in incessantly, thundering over turn-tables, and shrieking whistles make "music of the spears;" where the platform is for ever covered with luggage of all kinds, and with bewildered passengers "claiming" it, tumbling over it, and running frantically to their carriages at the summons of a bell huge enough and noisy enough to "fright the isle from its propriety;"—in such places his must be a hard heart indeed who does not pity the station-master. How he escapes a lunatic asylum as his ultimate destiny, if he escapes it, is difficult to understand. Every day and all day long he has upon him the responsibility of the lives of thousands. The distraction of a moment may bring about a chaos. The master, however, of such stations as the Lamport Station has another destiny. Possibly his life may have its trials too; but to the passenger it speaks of an enviably tranquil existence. Enough of intercourse with the world to prevent the moss from growing over him, or the rust from eating into his spirit: intercourse with all classes and all natures; and no more. His simple business to

"Welcome the coming, speed the parting guest,"

and then he may turn to his garden, to the enjoyment of the quiet a time, at least, secure of solitude and uninterruptedness. Of course this is from the passenger's point of view, whose spectacles, for the nonce, show everything *couleur de rose*. We do not deny that the actual station-master's survey may paint a different picture. Having, however, left our own skeleton at home in our own cupboard, we are not going to search after the station-master's, if he has one, as we hope he has not.

Leaving the station, our way lies along as pretty a country road as our shire can boast. On either side the ground is undulatory; swelling now into something like hills, dipping now into dells with a dark pool in the hollow, over which picturesque and informal trees fling their branches. A little way farther on (our attention is chiefly directed to the left of the road) we catch a pretty glimpse of Lamport Church-tower between trees; then a glimpse of the Rectory, a stately eighteenth-century house; farther on still, the Hall, in the Italian style. These in the background: the sloping ground between is chequered with sunshine, and sheep lying in the shade.

Continuing the road, we come to a blacksmith's shed; then to the Lamport Inn, in old times an important halting-place for stage-coaches between Northampton and Harborough, and droves of cattle going southward. It is a large and pretentious building, with ample out-premises, standing alone and having pleasant looks-out. There is little now to indicate its special character of an inn, and as you open a side-door under a porch, into its passage covered with oil-cloth, you might imagine that you were an intruder, if you had not previously noticed the sign over the door—the Isham crest—a demi-swan, wings displayed, proper. Opposite to the inn is a road at right angles with the main road. It has on the right hand a lofty wall, over which tall trees throw their branches, and on the left a few scattered cottages—comfortable, well-to-do looking places. Following it we come to the church. We saw its tower looking picturesque enough among the neighbouring trees, and, coming nearer, it does not disappoint us. It is of the Early English period, battlemented, with boldly projecting buttresses at the angles. In the upper part of the west face is a window with two lights under a circular hood moulding, the head not being pierced. Beneath is a circular-headed doorway, walled up, and directly over it a single light, of the ordinary small dimensions. In the south face a similar window to that in the upper part, has the head pierced with a quatrefoil. The tower has a low pyramidal roof, and about its base cluster mallows with their pretty striped flowers and geranium-like leaf in great profusion and beauty. The mallow was in classic times planted with the asphodel about graves. These have assuredly nothing to do with the custom, but their profuse presence here reminds us of it. The church-yard stands on rising ground, and north and west the look-out is very rural and beautiful; over undulating ground, well wooded.

North-east of the church stands the Rectory; and south of it, on the right hand of the road, is Lamport Hall. The principal entrance is from the Northampton road, south of the entrance to the village.

"The stately homes of England,
How beautiful they stand,
Amidst their tall ancestral trees,
O'er all the pleasant land."

A verse familiar enough, but too truthful ever to lose the bloom of its beauty. A "stately home" assuredly is Lamport Hall. Entering the park from the main road, a fine sweep of greensward, belted by noble trees, leads up to the mansion, which presents an imposing façade in the Italian style, built, about the close of the seventeenth century, after designs by John Webb, the son-in-law of Inigo Jones. A portion of the earlier hall remained, we believe, till within the last fifty years. The Ishams became possessors of the manor about the first year of Queen Elizabeth's reign, by purchase from John Earl of Oxford. Robert and John Isham, the purchasers, were two of the twenty children of Euseby Isham,

Esq., who held the manor of Pytchley. Robert died in 1564, leaving no issue, and his brother John became possessed of the entire property. There is a characteristic contemporary portrait of this ancestor of the family in the house, and his story is told on the monumental brass to his memory.

"John Isham, one of the twenty children of Euseby Isham, of Pichley, and of Anne, his wife, daughter of Giles Pulton, of Desburgh, esquier; married Elizabeth, daughter of Nicholas Barker, citizen of London, and was once governour of the English merchant adventurers in Flaunders, and thrice warden of the mercers of London, purchased the mannor and parsonage of this parish of Lamport, and was twenty-two years justice of peace, and once sherriff of the shyre of Northton, and died the seventeenth day of March, anno Domini one thousand five hundred ninety five, aged seventy years six months, and the saide Elizabeth died the — day of January, ano Dni 1594, leaving iii sonnes Thomas Henry, and Richard. God make us thankful for them."

South of the house, behind a fence of shrubberies, and enclosed by a broad mound, are the gardens. A blaze of colour greets the eye from the borders and beds, which are devised and kept with the most elaborate taste and care. It is not possible to detect a faulty leaf or flower in the thousands of gorgeous plants that fill them and define with the sharpest outline the fanciful patterns which they describe. Something of the taste which was prevalent in the gardening of a couple of centuries ago may be traced here, and has probably been continued from that time. There is, for example, a long straight walk, secluded with shrubs and flowers on either side, and ending in a small temple or summer-house; and clumps of box and other evergreen trees, which are penetrable, and enclose a spacious room, sufficient for a large assemblage of visitors, and secure, by the denseness of the foliage, against sun or shower. These vary a large grass plot, which is also ornamented with some handsome cedars, planted, we believe, by the hand of the venerable Dowager Lady Isham, some forty years ago. Near the extremity of this long walk are three enormous cages, till very lately occupied by a pair of eagles and a horned owl. The two eagles fell sudden victims, there is reason to fear, to foul play. The owl remains, one of the grandest of his grand species. He is of enormous size. During the day he sits perched in the darkest corner of his den, with half shut eyes, looking at once wise and wicked. If by chance he is aroused, it is fine to see him swell into double his size by the expansion of his beautiful feathers, and open his monstrous eyes, with a really terrible fierceness. At night they must look like a couple of tail lamps to a railway train.

Next the south side of the mansion is a rock-garden, which we take to be almost unique. It is the work, we believe, of Sir Charles Isham himself, who has bestowed upon it endless care and attention. The rock-work rises some twenty or five and twenty feet, and is arranged with a perfectly natural aspect. Myriads of lichens and ferns and other rock-loving plants cover the rockery. Altogether, it is a rare and curious nook—a singular and beautiful variety in a garden of singular and various beauty.

But if last, certainly not least, in respect of the skill and care of the gardener in this very skilfully managed and well-cared-for garden, come the vineries. We do not know that we ever saw grapes in the like profusion and perfection, or graperies in such marvellous order and cleanliness. Grapes, as if bursting with their wine, hang over head, not in scattered bunches here and there, but in rafters of huge clusters. The sunlight comes unstained through the beautiful amber leaves, not one of which is marred with mould or insect.

No lover of books will pass by Lamport Hall without remembering the discovery there, no long time ago, of a copy of an edition of Shakespeare's "Venus and Adonis," of which the bibliomaniac had never dreamed. Other rare works of about the same period were there also. They look like new books, bought as soon as published, not at second-hand, or in the spirit of a collector, but of the book-lover. There was a Sir John Isham, who died in 1651, and who was contemporary with Shakespeare. We are not aware that anything is known to justify the supposition that he was a man of special literary tastes; but he was, no doubt, a man of education, and there have always been many quiet lovers of literature none the less earnest in their love for not making proclamation of it. His son was a Sir Justinian Isham, whom his monument specially commends for his learning:—"Optimis disciplinis atque artibus domi forisq: instructus et excellenti ingenio, eruditione, eloquentia, prudentia, omnique virtute cumulatus." He may have inherited his love of books from his father. Mr. Edmunds, who made the discovery of the precious volume, suggested that it was purchased by Thomas Isham, who was in possession of Lamport Hall in 1599, when the "Venus and Adonis" was published. The guess may be well founded, but Thomas Isham died in 1605, and among the precious books is a copy of Nash's "Have with you to Saffron Walden!" which was published in 1607.

The Tun Unvisited.

OF Heidelberg we oft had read,
And of its many glories;
And often to ourselves we said
These are but idle stories.
But still there is that Tun that holds
Three hundred thousand bottles,
And what a sight that Tun must be
To thirsty travelling throttles.

And so we said, "We'll take the train
Before the one for Basel,
And go and have at Heidelberg
A look at Tun and Castle."
And so we went and took the train
Before the one for Basel,
And did our merry best to get
A glimpse of Tun and Castle.

Along the Linden avenues
We went, admiring greatly
On either side the gardens bright,
The houses new and stately;
Yet this, said we, Love would not choose
His honey-moon to spend in,
And Age would seek a calmer nook
His latter hours to end in.

Still up the winding path we went,
    And down the sun came pouring,
And ever and aye an upward glance
    The ladies turned imploring;
And we, who find there's room to get
    Wiser as we grow older,
The knapsack we had borne in hand
    Strapped fairly to our shoulder.

We clomb the mountain still, still looked
    All vainly for the top on't,
We only saw the shaggy sides,
    The trees, and viny crop on't.
At last said we, the train will be
    Soon coming in for Basel,
And we shall surely lose our day
    If we should gain the Castle.

And after all, although it makes
    A Gasthof keeper's handle,
Can we believe the game can be
    Worth all this waste of candle?*
Be Heidelberg unseen, unknown
    Its Tun and all that's by it.
We have a Meux's of our own,
    Oh why should we deny it?

A Tun is but a Tun, though of
    Three hundred thousand bottles;
And what are they, if none of them
    May trickle down our throttles?

*Le jeu, vaut-il la chandelle?

Besides, a sight is but a sight,
  And disappoints us sometimes,
And Castles made in modern times
  To us seem made in rum times.†

A noble river is the Rhine,
  We have its course unravelled,
And all from Bonn to Bacharach
  Its shores on foot have travelled.
Let's leave a sight in Germany,
  That when we tell beholders
We have not seen it, they may shrug
  With pitying gaze their shoulders.

Sunrise is grand from mountain tops,
  We've seen it from the Righi's,
But then we missed its gorgeous set,
  For we were down at Weggis.
We've hailed the Lake whose shores repeat
  The story of the apple,
And yet we missed—ah woful miss!—
  The glorious William's Chapel.

We take with philosophic mind,
  Like sagest Samuel Weller,
Whatever beverage we find
  Remaining in the cellar.
We eat with grace the doubtful steak,
  And glory in the mustard,
Nor spoil our dinner with a sigh
  For oyster sauce and custard.

†Pendant la guerre du Palatinat en 1689, le géneral Mélan, contrairement convention conclue à cet égard, fit sauter le chateau: en 1693 la devastation renouvelée. Le chateau fut restauré sous Charles Philippe (1716).—BAEDEKER.

Then why should we, who take what sun
    Or shade our pathway mottles,
Lament we missed a Tun that holds
    Three hundred thousand bottles?
Sore words seemed these to folk who came
    Resolved for Tun and Castle:
—We turned about and down we went
    And took the train for Basel.

Newport Pagnell.

NEWPORT PAGNELL has recently opened a railway. It is a pudding-bag railway it is true, but it promises to go on some day to Olney and Wellingborough. At present, however, it is only a pudding-bag and a promise. When you ask Newport Pagnell people when there is to be any more of it they generally answer, curtly and grimly, like 's raven above the chamber door—"Never more." "Only this nothing more." "Never" is a long date, and we, having lived enough to see greater marvels than anything implied in the tinuation of a few miles of railway, have faith that the Newport gnell line will have stations at Olney and Wellingborough some . Have not all railways, and has not the electric telegraph ing into existence within living memory? Do we not remember n canals were the marvels of civil-engineering, and four-horse ges the wonders of travelling? Meantime, even as a pudding- , Newport is benefitting by her railway. Assuredly the good town looks cheerier than it has done since that woe-begone day n it shook hands with the last coachman; and nine-caped coats, long whips, and "ribbons," and ostlers, and horses with not ch more than three legs perhaps, but full of blood and breed, kicking, and corn and "go" were put *hors de combat.* wport is Newport still, a pretty, pleasant town, and to be gnized even through the changes of forty years. There are r houses indeed about it. But there are old places to met with, some of which scarcely seem older than they were in that far-off time, and unspoiled by improvement. The "Swan," for example, is the "Swan" of the coaching days, externally, and, apparently, internally too, and the still older adjoining structure, the Saracen's Head, though an inn no longer, and divided and sub-divided in respect of its ground floor, wears the same aspect in its upper stories, and has the same windows which it probably had when the town was held by the Parliament against King Charles. What we chiefly miss is the bustle of the busy traffic of the coaches, the incessant going and coming, and "the old familiar faces" that greet us no more. Standing opposite the "Swan" we can recall the arrival of the Northampton stage, as it swept round the corner of St. John Street, and drew up before the well-known hotel. The horses were all upon their haunches, for the coachman had a pride to show with what ease they had done their stage, and the horses were sure to put a best foot foremost coming to the close of their work. But the coach is nothing compared with the landlady. Who has forgotten her who ever saw her? She was out at the doorway the moment the coach drew up, dressed "up to the nines," whatever they might be; dressed, at all events, not a little in excess of the prevailing fashion. Gorgeous in silks, gay with streamers, and "washing her hands with invisible soap," she was there to welcome all comers. Endless house-bells and ostlers' bells at her summons set ringing; chambermaids and other maids followed in her wake; ostlers and stable boys sprang from every coigne of vantage; if you wanted anything your fear was that you might have it ten times over; if you wanted nothing you felt ashamed in such a supplying presence that you had no demand to meet it. A model landlady she was. There remains the wainscoted parlour to the right—the commercial room we believe it is—at the door of which she used to stand, still performing the operation of washing her hands, but with a slower movement, as if to give greater emphasis to the bill of fare at your command, as she called it over item by item. Before each was a conjunction in very large type, a kind of flourish of drums and trumpets to introduce it, something after this fashion :—WE have roast beef—AND we have boiled beef;—AND we have loin of mutton ;—AND we have mutton chops ;—AND we have pork chops ;—AND we have pigeon pie ; and so on, heralding the contents of everything in the larder. Not hurried on, but in a slow time, sufficient for the hearer to taste, as it were, preliminarily, each dish in imagination, and with a few bars rest between to give each its independent value. Business is business is her motto. But on drowsy summer afternoons, when the bustle was over, and all things promised a calm, she might be seen sailing down High Street under a parasol, the glass of Fashion, conscious that she had earned a right to her leisure. Other landladies have come and gone since then, each with her special merits doubtless. But this was the typical landlady of the time, living in our memory. Somehow she always reminded us of a song in a farce very popular in our boyhood, in which a traveller halts at an inn kept by a widow. He had the misfortune to be a very ugly man, and the landlady slighted her guest, and the chambermaid laughed at him outright. But the traveller had money, and manifested his wealth ; he paid like a Prince—

———— "gave the widow a smack,
Then flopped on his horse at the door like a sack,
While the landlady, touching the chink,
Cried, 'sir, if you travel this country again,
I heartily hope that the sweetest of men
Will stop at the widow's to drink.' "

We cannot say we ever saw a man ugly or bold enough to give "a smack" to our typical landlady, nor was she a widow when we knew her. Yet so it was. We always thought of the widow in the song, when we saw the landlady of the Swan, and the last three lines insisted on thrusting themselves into our memory, as if she were repeating them.

It has been the fate of Newport Pagnell to have all its entrances made highways in their turn. Less than forty years ago, the London entrance was by St. John's Street. The railway brought the London traffic along the Wolverton road. Now, the new railway debouches at Mr. Hives' wharf, and the way into the town bifurcates, partly at the entrance to the Wolverton road, and partly along Marsh end, which has hitherto been a sort of back street. Already we see some alterations, apparently in consequence. New houses have been built, and there is a general air of traffic which was wanting heretofore. It is a picturesque way upon the whole, with every variety of house in it; charmingly irregular gables next the street, and rambling backways with out-houses and gardens and old trees and tumble down sheds; stately houses with pretensions to respectability; houses with pleasant gardens before them, well cared for; cottages thatched and latticed, well-to-do and ill-to-do; little shops and big shops; and lodgings for travellers. Marsh End debouches into St. John Street, which, narrow as it is, in the part next the High Street, twists and turns, and grows wider and pleasanter towards the old London road, which crosses the Ousel by an iron bridge. Before reaching the bridge, however, we come to St. John's Hospital, a modern Gothic building of no architectural interest, but having inserted into its front the following inscription from an earlier structure:—

AL YOV GOOD CHRISTIANS THAT HERE DOOE PASS
BY GIVE SOMETHING TO THES POORE PEOPLE
THAT IN ST. IOHN'S HOSPITAL DOETH LY ANNO 1615.

Sometimes this Hospital is called Queen Anne's, a curt description calculated to mislead. The original foundation dates as far back as Edward I. It had fallen into decay, however, at what period we do not know, and was re-founded by Anne of Denmark, Queen of James I., for a master, three poor men, and three poor women. With this latter foundation the inscription we have quoted is contemporary.

Crossing the bridge over the Ousel, we come into a wider road, whence, in the coaching days, the traveller from London saw on the right the noble church, charmingly situated. The ground rises rapidly from the Ousel, and the church stands at an angle on the eminence, showing its entire southern side from west to east. Of the church itself presently. It is a pleasant suburb along the London road, including every variety of building. "The Wrestler's Inn," on the east side, is picturesquely primitive and comfortable. It is a long, low, respectable building, thatched, one storied, with dormer windows in the roof, and barge boards. Re-crossing the bridge, we can get to the church by a turning to the right, and winding round the northern side, reach the churchyard through the cemetery, which was attached to it a few years since. The cemetery is healthily situated, and looks over a wide expanse of country to the east and north. The old churchyard and church are to the west. The church is a large and handsome structure, with a tower of the Perpendicular period. The labels of the east windows form a depressed arch, and are curled up at the end. The south aisle is modern. Over the north porch there is a parvise. The south porch is very lovely. The outer archway is boldly and elegantly cusped over an inner arch, also cusped. The inner doorway is of the same character, and the effect is very rich and beautiful. The mouldings are terminated by grotesque descending lions. The inner walls are ornamented with an arcade of sexfoil arches surmounted with a notched double moulding. The original wood roof is in excellent preservation. Cross timbers are carried on four small whole length figures, and a corbel head is at each corner. A central boss is carved with flowers.

On the north side of the churchyard is a row of seven small houses, over which is the inscription "Revis's Almshouses, 1763." They are an endowment by Mr. John Revis for four poor men and three women, with six shillings a week, a chaldron of coals, a coat to each man, and a gown to each woman. Mr. Revis was a linen draper at Charing Cross, the son of an apothecary of Newport Pagnell, where he was born. He acquired a good fortune "with justice and honour," as his epitaph says, and died in 1758, leaving these and other charities to his native town. The name of Revis is still familiar in the neighbourhood, but this good Samaritan was, we believe, the last of his family. The houses consist, apparently, of one lower and one upper room. Looking into the churchyard (where now, we presume, no burials take place), they also look across it towards the river with a row of trees bordering it. A quiet retreat for weary age, not a hermitage quite, nor yet in the stream of active life. Faint sounds of street music reach it on week days, and on Sundays the organ and the church choir must be yet more audible—fittingly so for those who are nearer the close than the commencement of life's journey. At the entrance to the cemetery there is a very neat lodge and chapel for the burial services of those who dissent from the Church. Not far off is a notice that "all visitors are expected *in general* to keep on the gravelled path"—somewhat reminding one of that old translation of Giraldus Cambrensis, in which the "variable and fickle nature of woman" is referred to as the source from which "all evils, *for the most part*, do happen and come." The notice would be better without the qualifying words. What they refer to may be well understood, and should be felt reverently by all. The custom which has come to us of late years from the Continent of decorating the graves with flowers is here largely observed, and is in itself touching. It cannot be maintained permanently, but it is a graceful token of remembrance while it lasts. And this practical world of ours is none the worse for a sentiment of any kind, especially for one so sacred as the keeping alive the memory of the beloved dead.

A stone bridge crosses the Ouse at the north-eastern entrance to the town. Drayton, in his Polyolbion, speaks of the Ouse and Ouselle—

"Invention, as before, thy high-pitched pinions rouse,
Exactly to set down how the far-wand'ring Ouse
Through the Bedfordian fields deliciously doth strain,
As holding on her course by Huntingdon again.
How bravely she herself betwixt her banks doth bear,
Ere Ely she in-isle, a goddess honour'd there;
From Brackley breaking forth through soils most heavenly sweet,

> By Buckingham makes on, and, crossing Watling-street,
> She with her lesser Ouse at Newport next doth twin:
> Which from proud Chiltern near comes easily ambling in.
> The brook which on her bank doth boast that earth alone;
> Which noted of this isle converteth wood to stone,
> That little Aspley's earth we anciently enstyle
> 'Mongst sundry other things a wonder of the isle;
> Of which the lesser Ouse oft boasteth in her way,
> As she herself with flowers doth gorgeously array."

The Ousel is also called the Lovatt and the Willen.

Leaning over the parapet of the Ouse bridge on either side is a pleasant idleness. On one side a well-kept garden sweeps down to the water's edge, and the opposite bank is overhung with trees. On the other side the river is crossed by a mill, and the water comes spitting and dashing through in a mass of white foam. Gardens here, too, of humbler character, but not less gratifying to the sight, come down to the stream. To the north are far-stretching meadows, green with moisture, and reminding one of Cowper. At this end of the town, on the south side of the street, is a good old brick house. One would like to know who lived there a hundred years ago. The opening opposite leads to a way which runs the whole length of the back of the High-street. An almshouse connected with the Independent chapel is in this lane. Of the chapel itself there is an interesting account in the Rev. Josiah Bull's Memorials of his eminent grandfather, the Rev. William Bull, the friend of Newton and of Cowper. Somewhere about the middle of the seventeenth century the living of Newport Pagnell was held by the Rev. John Gibbs. Early in the year 1660, he was ejected from the vicarage for having refused the ordinance of the Lord's Supper to a man of considerable influence in the parish, who was notoriously immoral.

"At this time," says Mr. Bull, "Mr. Gibbs possessed two houses in the High street of Newport; and at the farther end of a long yard, running by the side of them, was a barn which tradition informs us had been once used as a Quakers' Meeting House. Excluded from his pulpit in the church, this good man retreated with a considerable portion of his congregation to this place, and there administered to them the Word of Life. In the persecuting times which soon followed, the situation of this barn was such as to afford great facility of escape to the congregation when they were likely to be disturbed by informers, for not only was the barn at some distance from the High Street, but there was also access from it to a back street. Amongst Mr. Gibbs's devoted followers was a physician in the town, a Dr. Waller. To avoid imprisonment for the crime of obeying his conscience, he concealed himself, it is said, for ten months in some of the out-offices belonging to his house, which being immediately contiguous to the barn in question, at the time of public worship, he left his retreat, and availed himself of these religious opportunities, thus no doubt rendered very precious to him. It may be added that so great was the persecution of Nonconformists in the county, that having filled the common gaol at Aylesbury, the magistrates were compelled to hire two large houses in the town to receive their prisoners. The Toleration Act was passed in the year 1689, and it was probably about this time that the Meeting House at Newport was erected. It joined the barn where the congregation at first worshipped; and eventually the greater part of that humble but hallowed retreat was removed to increase the accommodation of the more permanent building. The barn subsequently became the property of the Rev. William Bull, and what remains of it is still sacredly preserved. Mr. Gibbs now preached the Gospel without fear or hindrance; but in the erection of the new place of worship an opening was left in the wall at the back of the pulpit to afford means of escape should times of persecution again return. This good man continued his labours till 1699, when he died at the age of 72, having been vicar of the parish for twelve years, and for thirty-eight the pastor of the Independent Church. In the year 1769 the Rev. William Bull became the owner of the premises once in the occupation of Mr. Gibbs. Mr. Bull had lived in the house for about fifty years, when in making some repairs he accidentally came upon a small room or closet about four feet square. It was between two walls at the side of a large old chimney, and had evidently been a hiding place, for the only entrance to it was from a trap-door beneath, which was concealed from view in the old-fashioned chimney place. I have now in my possession some buttons of a coat, two tobacco pipes, the bowls of which are exceedingly small, and some silver coins—all of which were found there."

We fear this curious chamber exists no longer. Pity it was not preserved, as an elegant chapter in the history of an intolerance utterly at variance with the Christianity it affects to vindicate. A cheap edition of the volume from which we make this extract has recently been issued. It should be a household book with Nonconformists. In what estimation the Rev. William Bull was held by the good and the learned and the gifted of his time we gather from the eulogies of such men as Cowper and Newton. In a letter to Mr. Unwin, Cowper says of him:—

"You are not acquainted with him; perhaps it is as well for you that you are not. You would regret still more than you do that there are so many miles interposed between us. He spends part of the day with us to-morrow. A Dissenter, but a liberal one; a man of letters and of genius; a master of a fine imagination, or rather not master of it—an imagination which, when he finds himself in the company he loves, and can confide in, runs away into such fields of speculation as amuse and enliven every other imagination that has the happiness to be of the party. At other times he has a tender and delicate sort of melancholy in his disposition, not less agreeable in its way. He can be lively without levity, and pensive without dejection. Such a man is Mr. Bull. But he smokes tobacco! Nothing is perfect. *Nihil est ab omne parte beatum.*"

Cowper, however, became very tolerant of his friend's failing. Apostrophising the nymph of Orinoco he supplicates for pardon for having touched—

"With a satiric wipe
That symbol of thy power, the pipe."

And he concludes:—

"So may thy votaries increase,
And fumigation never cease.
May Newton with renew'd delights
Perform thine odoriferous rites,
While clouds of incense half divine
Involve thy disappearing shrine,
And so may smoke-inhaling Bull,
Be always filling never full."

More poetical still, though the form be prose, is a passage in a letter from the poet to his reverend friend himself:—

"My dear Friend,—My greenhouse, fronted with myrtles, and where I hear nothing but the pattering of a fine shower and the sound of distant thunder, wants only the fumes of your pipe to make it perfectly delightful.

Tobacco was not known in the golden age—so much the worse for the golden age! This age of iron or lead would be insupportable without it, and therefore we may reasonably suppose that the happiness of those better days would have been much improved by the use of it."

About the year 1738 the ground upon which the Chapel stood belonged to a person who became bankrupt, and being seized by his creditors, Dr. Doddridge generously purchased it, and conveyed it to trustees, taking his chance of being reimbursed by a subscription. In 1743 the pastorate was held by the Rev. Humphrey Gainsborough, a brother of the eminent artist.

To talk about Newport Pagnell, and not to say a word about Hudibras would be the proverbial Hamlet, without the Prince of Denmark. In 1645 Sir Samuel Luke was governor of Newport, and held the town for the Parliament. Sir Samuel had a seat at Cople Hoo, near Bedford, and other estates in Bedfordshire and Northamptonshire, and was altogether a man of wealth, of mark and of influence. Butler had been brought up a staunch Royalist, yet he entered the service of Sir Samuel Luke, under what circumstances does not appear, and while there is supposed to have made the observations and collected the materials for his famous poem. It is scarcely possible to resist the evidence that Sir Samuel was the original of Hudibras. There can be no doubt of the name required to fill up the blank in the following verse:—

> " 'Tis sung, there is a valiant Mameluke
> In foreign land yclep'd "—

Rhythm and rhyme alike require the name, Sir Samuel Luke, and it would need the marvellous rhyming dexterity of Butler himself to devise anything which would fit the occasion so thoroughly.

Newport Pagnell derives its second name from the Paganells, whose ancestors held the land at the time of the Norman Conquest. Fulk Paganell, in the reign of William Rufus, founded a cell of Cluniac monks at Tickford. The Paganells had a castle at Newport on the site of the Castle Mead.

To H. P. P.

OF worthy sire the worthy son,
Welcome, Hugh, to Twenty-one;
Mark the day with feast and fun,
Bid the cask and bottle run,
Cares of every colour shun—
Devils blue and black and dun.
June! shine out your gladdest sun!
Hugh to day is twenty-one.

When a man is twenty-one,
Then life's battle is begun.
Farewell lollipop and bun!
Work before us must be done,
Duties to ourselves and others,
To our sisters, fathers, mothers;
Duties not without their guerdon,
Heavy sometimes though the burden,—
Duties that we must fulfil
With a hearty, earnest will,
So we may in joy or sorrow
Fearless face the coming morrow.

Ah! it will be so with you,
Open-hearted, kindly Hugh!
Easily in whom we trace
Father's heart as father's face;

Liberal hand and active mind,
Earnest spirit, tastes refined;
Nothing selfish, nothing sordid,
Shall of either be recorded.

Welcome, then, to twenty-one;
May your path be in the sun;
But, lest shadows chance to fall
(As they will sometimes o'er all),
Cheerfulness within your breast
Keep, an ever cherished guest;
Mindful of what sages say,
Merry hearts go all the day—
All the day unwearied, while
Sad ones tire within the mile.
Hail the day, then—gladder none;
Welcome Hugh to twenty-one.

Weedon Beck.

WE can imagine a time when Weedon, or, what is now distinguished as Lower Weedon, was a very rural, very picturesque group of thoroughly rustic cottage sheltered north and east, and sleeping in the sunshines with a clear brook running through the midst singing a lullaby. But to realize this picture we must go back more than half a century. Within that period civilization has been paying court to it with an assiduity which, as compared with its beneficial results, affords firm ground for an action for breach of promise. No doubt the Grand Military Depôt spends much money there, but hardly, perhaps, in proportion to the magnitude of its pretensions. The Grand Junction Canal also brings, we suppose, something, but in very insignificant proportion to its huge embankment. Lastly, the Railway. That, too, must do something for it, but certainly not sufficient to counterbalance the injury it inflicted by driving the coaches from the road. And woefully have these two latter visitors marred its village-like character and picturesqueness. The traveller looks down with astonishment at that lonely church isolated and banked in an angle of dreary ground, treeless and shrubless. Once the site must have been pleasant enough, just without the village and with a sweep of open country eastward and gradual slopes to the north. The canal was the first innovation, shutting it in on the east with a long embankment 30 feet high. Then came the railway, with a still more formidable fence, cutting it off from the village, and leaving it in a sort of triangular hole. Seen from the rail the edifice has a very unattractive appearance. In 1823 the nave was either rebuilt or so much repaired and altered as to be "as good as new," in the most approved style of churchwarden's architecture. But the tower is not without interest. It retains its Norman arched belfry windows on the north and south sides, and on the latter a Norman loophole. There is rather a curious assortment of corbel heads, two rows of four each, in each front. The west door has a good flat-headed arch, with spandrels under a flat hood moulding. Leland describes the "Paroche chirch" as "meane." It is dedicated to St. Peter. The village, the same venerable antiquary describes as "a praty thorough fare sette on a playne ground, and much celebrated by cariers, bycause it stondeth hard by the famose Way there, communely caullid of the Peeple Wãthelinge Streete. And upon this the tounelet is caullid Wedon on the Streete. The tounelet of itself is meane, and hath no market. And the Paroche Chirch is as meane." Leland's mention of the carriers is very suggestive of a state of things long past away—of a time when goods were transported by long strings of pack-horses, and such conversations took place in early morning as Shakspeare thus records :—

"*An Inn Yard. Enter a carrier with a lantern in his hand.*

"*1st Carrier :* Heigh ho! An't be not four by the day, I'll be hanged; Charles's Wain is over the new chimney, and yet our horse not packed. What, ostler!

"*Ostler (within) :* Anon, anon.

"*1st Carrier :* I pry'thee, Tom, beat Cut's sadddle, put a few flocks in the point; the poor jade is wrung in the withers out of all cess.

"*Enter another Carrier.*

"*2nd Carrier :* Peas and beans are as dank here as a dog, and that is the next way to give poor jades the bots : this house is turned upside down since Robin ostler died.

"*1st Carrier :* Poor fellow! never joyed since the price of oats rose; it was the death of him."

Who that has heard Cowden Clarke deliver this scene does not roar with the very remembrance of that rich and truthful bit of acting? There is a small house, "The Fox and Hounds," just at the entrance to the village, which may have been in its day one of those carrier's halting-places. Standing near this house one seems to see the events of centuries flung in confusion together. The huge railway arch is over-head, and the train flies by with a shriek like that of a fiend on some direful errand; the view is bounded by the lofty canal embankment, along which a worn steed slowly labours with the canal boat; midway stands the church tower, originally and still obviously Norman; on your right is the little hostelrie just mentioned; and as your thoughts go back to poor Robin Ostler, who died because the price of oats rose, you see a smart artilleryman issue from the door. What a chronological jumble it is!

Once upon a time the Mercian Kings had a palace here. One of them, Ethelred, converted it into a nunnery, which he placed under the superintendence of his niece Werburgh. That good lady took the veil in the abbey of Ely, and on her appointment to Weedon the wild geese of the Ely marshes seem to have considered that they had thereby acquired a right to participate in the revenues of the new demesne. Northamptonshire farmers in those days were not exactly what Northamptonshire farmers are now, but they knew how to grow corn of a quality which appears to have been eminently grateful to the geese of Ely, and heavy was the tithe those fearful wild fowl took of it. At last such was the grievance that St. Werburgh forbade them the parish, and they obeyed her, geese as they were, and in Bridges' time, about the commencement of the last century, it was the popular belief that no wild geese were ever seen to settle or graze in Weedon field. Drayton alludes to this legend when, speaking of the course of the Nen, he says:—

> "She falleth in her way with Weedon, where 'tis said
> St. Werburgh princely born, a most religious maid,
> From those peculiar fields by prayer the wild-fowl drove."

St. Werburgh's nunnery was destroyed by the Danes in the ninth century, but so late as the time of Leland there was "a faire chapel" dedicated to the saint, a little from the south side of the church. And in the "Ashe Yards," south of the church, old foundations have from time to time been disturbed, the probable ruins of nunnery and palace.

"The Roman Watling Street," says Baker, "is generally supposed to quit the great Chester road at the lane, or street road, as it is called in Lower Weedon; but the Roman road diverged from the present turnpike road at the bottom of the hill near Stowe, passed along the Hill Land lane, by Ash Yards near the church, over the Nen, leaving the Ordnance Buildings to the right, by Leesborough way towards Mr. Hewitt's, formerly the Globe Inn, and thence into the lane above alluded to, which from this point is identified with the Watling Street, and leaves this county at Dove Bridge."

In Lower Weedon there are traces of sixteenth-century domestic buildings; one on the right, now divided into different tenements, appears originally to have been of some importance.

A Sudden Winter.

YESTERDAY, Autumn. On the slope we stood,
And saw beneath us the umbrageous wood,
Rich with a thousand hues,—crimson and gold
And most luxurious brown. The air was chill
And moist, but the leaves cluster'd thickly still,
Like mantles, which around us closer fold
When mists about us rise; like the warm load
That ever-provident Nature hath bestowed
Upon the patient sheep 'gainst freezing rains.

Yesterday, glowing Autumn; and to-day,
Winter. In one fierce night the yellow plains
Are whitened, and the rivulet's pleasant way
Is stayed; the woods, beneath a double weight,
Are bending to the ground.

Heap high the grate,
And gather round the hearth dear friends, and loves
Domestic; wheel the glad piano round,
So that the hand that o'er the ivory roves
May feel the generous warmth, and livelier bound.
Bring us, too, piles of our beloved books,
That we may read of Summer haunts, where brooks
Are singing in the sun, and Bacchant girls,
With amber vine-leaves twining midst their curls,
Dance onward laughingly, and, merry-eyed,

Dash with white foot the glittering stream aside;
Of moon-lit orange-groves, where virgin ears
Drink love-draughts poured by mantled cavaliers.

And bring us pictures: Titian's glowing hues,
And Claude's immortal sunlights. So diffuse
Summer about us, till by some rude token
Of the rude season the strong charm is broken;
Then, having known the change a little time,
Plunge with renewed delight back to our generous clime.

Barnwell St. Andrew's and Barnwell All Saints'.

EVERY Railway has its secluded Stations—Stations of which you may remain in utter ignorance, though you may have travelled the line for years, till, for some reason, disjointed and out of all ordinary course, you chance to travel by a train by which you never travelled before, and, lo! a swarm of Stations crop up which never blossom'd for you till now, and which you had shot by in bewildered ignorance. Yet they are the prettiest of all. Between first-class Station and first-class Station what is the difference? Simply that between Pompey and Cæsar, who are proverbially "very much alike, 'specially Pompey." There is the same long platform; the same W. H. Smith and Son's bookstall; the same invitation to become the proprietor of a "Sommier Elastique portatif"; or a Brogden or a Wotherspoon's gold chain; or an overcoat from Moses; or to encase yourself in a remarkably unsymmetrical pair of peg-tops (with pockets to thrust your hands in); the same multitude of out-goers and in-comers, the same compound odours of steam, smoke, lamp oil, and railway grease. Give us for our holiday delectation none of these entrance gates to new Babels, but one of those by-way Stations which only the slowest trains discover, and which make you marvel how they ever came to be made.

Such a Station is Barnwell All Saints' on the Northampton and Peterborough line. On a railway though it be; though thousands of busy human beings fleet past it daily, and it would scarcely answer to the ideal of Spenser's "little lowly hermitage," yet on approaching it one can scarcely help breaking into the enthusiastic greeting:—

> "Hail, abode of sacred quiet,
> Deep embosomed in the glen;
> Far removed from pomp and riot,
> And the busy hum of men."

Not far removed from the latter in reality, but rather on the very brink of it, but no more affected by it than by the brief flash of the "lightning in the collied night."

The Station itself modestly befits its condition. It is small, picturesque, and unpretending, with snug, in-door shelter for winter travellers (who must rarely indeed travel there); and pleasant out-door seats for the bright summer-time. There is garden ground attached, carefully tended. The station-master must have, one thinks, a pleasant time of it, working tranquilly at his little plot. Through the loopholes of his retreat he sees the stir, without feeling the crowd. Better be a cyclop in Vulcan's own caverns than a station-master at a first-class Station, where intersecting lines cross each other in bewildering confusion; where all is clamour and noise, the thundering of wheels and the shrieking of whistles, and the ringing of railway bells and the bawling of newspaper boys, and dread of careless switchmen and reckless platelayers, and horrible anticipations of trains running into each other; but here there is quiet and, one imagines, leisure, and time for thought and tranquil enjoyment. One wouldn't object to being a station-master here with one's books and pencils.

But the special attraction of Barnwell is its bowery aspect. Noble chestnuts, glorious in the Spring-time with their pyramidal blossoms, invite you to explore its rural paths. We only wish the Post Office did not stand where it does, or that it were more in keeping with its neighbour cottages, and not a horrid bit of Batty Langley Gothic, that sets one's teeth on edge. It is worth anybody's while to stop for a train or two at Barnwell; it has its peculiar characteristics, natural and artificial. Descending the winding road from the Station, with the Church on your left, and Latham's Alms Houses on your right, the village crosses you at right angles—one long street, with a stream running through its midst, not the gutter of a French town, but a broad, natural piece of water; now rolling with a good volume; sometimes, after a draught, fertile with watercresses and tall grasses, covered with duck-weed and all aquatic plants, and crossed by all kinds of bridges: here, by a one-railed plank; there, by stepping stones; then by a single ivy-clad arch, and here, opposite the Montague Arms, by a bridge of two arches. The houses stand on the bordering slopes—not in continuous rows, but with frequent intervals of vacant closes on either side. This is Barnwell St. Andrew; at its southern extremity lies Barnwell All Saints'—once, evidently, of far greater importance than it now pretends to be. Here the interspaces become more frequent and larger, and in them, occasionally, are traces of old foundations. A path leads to the remains of the Church, now a mortuary chapel merely. The Churchyard is bordered on the north by a row of fine old walnut trees. In Bridges' time the Church was still standing, and the historian tells us that it had a nave, with north and south aisles and chancel. At the upper end of the south aisle was Mountague's aisle, with a porch which bore a spire steeple, in which were four bells. The Manor came into possession of the Mountague family in the 24th year of the reign of Charles II. Nothing but the chancel remains, which serves, as we have said, as a chapel to the burial ground in which it stands. The rest of the building was demolished about forty years ago. The remains, generally, are of Perpendicular style, but the chancel was fitted up by the Mountagues in the style of the day, with oak panelling and black and white marble pavement. Among the monuments, with which the walls are covered, is one in the gorgeous taste of the period, quaint and fanciful enough, yet touching in the sad story which it tells. Beneath a pyramid of alabaster, profusely covered with the armorial bearings of the Mountagues, duly blazoned, is an arch which over-canopies the figure of a child, in the costume of the aristocracy of two centuries and a quarter ago, with the inscription—

"Obiit, proh dolor, immature per aquas 28th Apr. 1625."

And beneath—

"Here under lyeth Interred Henry Mountagne, Esq., the only son of Sr. Sidney Mountague, Kt., one of the Masters of Requests to the Ma'ties. of King James and King Charles and of Dame Paulina his Wife, third daughter of Job. Pepys, of Cottenham, in the County of Cambridge, Esq., a wittie and hopefull child, tender and deere in the sight of his Parents, and much lamented of his friends."

The story is that the poor child, who was but three years old, fell into the moat while reaching at an orange which he had dropped in the water, and was drowned. The moat partly remains—a gloomy ditch, overgrown with trees and rank weeds. The Manor House which it once surrounded has long been demolished. It was probably an ancient structure. Over the chimney, says Bridges, "is a rude representation of Bel and the Dragon, and of King Nabuchodonosor looking on." The foundations of the Parsonage House may be traced, with its terraced walks.

Returning northward, the only building requiring notice is the Boys' School, a small building in the Tudor style, with this inscription over the door :—

"Instruct me O Lord
That I may Keep
Thy Lawes."

Crossing the bridge the visitor will find at the "Montague Arms" a clear and cheerful parlour, good fare, and a civil host and hostess.

The Burial-place of Beethoven.

"As Beethoven was at my visit no longer to be found in the body, I resolved to make a pilgrimage to his tomb. * * * Beethoven resided in one of a row of tall white houses, overlooking the city-walls, on the road to Währinge, the prettiest outlet of Vienna. In the cemetery of this quiet little village, in a corner, against a low wall, from whence an infinite deal of country may be seen, he reposes. * * * And here, among rustic chapels, wooden crucifixes, mounds of earth with flowers growing on them—such are the simple memorials—one might become 'half in love with easeful death.' The place itself might have been in Beethoven's life-time his study, for it was in the green lap of Nature, and among the old trees, that the composer wove his fancies, and not by the flickering of a night-lamp. * * * The Germans have a very pretty appellation for Beethoven; they call him 'Tondichter' (the Poet of Sounds), instead of the ordinary name 'Tonkunstler', (the scientific musician)."—Ramble among the Musicians of Germany.

An Attempt to Versify the Preceding.

A Little from Vienna, as you go
To Währinge, there is a pleasant row
Of white suburban houses—white and tall,
And over-looking the gay city's wall;
Search every outlet, this the prettiest is of all.
Yet for its beauty only love it not;
A charm more lasting consecrates the spot.
Perhaps the time may come when it shall be
Pent in a squalid, close vicinity
Where no sweet summer breeze shall bathe it balmily.
Let it be so, yet still about the place
Itself, there shall endure a kind of grace,

Keeping it lovely in poetic eyes,
What crime or woe soever round it lies;
Enthusiasts from all climes through many a year
Remote shall journey hither. It was here
Beethoven lived;—and died.

Onward a little still your footsteps guide,
Until you reach a quiet burying-ground,
In part by a low wall compassed around.

A lovely haunt it is, with much to charm,
And nought to make the timid dream of harm;
The pleasant country stretching far away
Looks happy thence, warm in the evening ray;
And there the wind that sweeps o'er distant fields
Comes unobstructed and its fragrance yields;
There among rustic chapels, crosses rude
Shaped by affection from the yet green wood,
And grassy mounds of earth with flowers above,
The simple tributes of surviving love,
The Poet of Sounds reposes:—Fitting rest.

Not by the flickering lamp his fancies blest,
'Tis said, were woven; but in the green lap
Of Nature, lingering by the gravelly gap
Whence the clear rivulet trickles;—by old trees
Eloquent with remotest memories
Outnumbering their leaves, and phantasies
Goblin and Faëry;—down the moonlit Rhine
Silently borne, by fort and ruined shrine.
Here too upon the threshold of his home,
Well may we deem that he was wont to come;
And from the music of the wild bee's hum,—
And from the invisible lark's high treble,—from

The thousand sylvan sounds that distance blends
(Harsh separate sounds) into one strain that ends
Upon the ear like music heard at night
O'er wide and tremulous waters,—from the sight
Of the far landscape lapped in misty ease
(For every sense bringeth sweet subtleties
To Genius—sisters true the Muses three,
Music, and Painting dear, and Poesy,
Each ministering to each)—from these, and more
Than the ungifted mind can dream of, store
Of priceless thoughts to hive.

A pleasant creed
It is, nor of the wildest that we read,
That those we loved and honoured upon earth
Not wholly pass from us in their new birth;
But purer, happier essences, still keep
Sweet watch about us when we calmest sleep,
Or wakeful, think of them with moistened eyes,
And hearts inform'd with fitting sympathies.

We'll hold that creed at least in haunts like these.
And hear Beethoven in the plaintive breeze,
Faint echo of remote, and subtlest harmonies.

Northampton.

Bridge Street.

BRIDGE Street is the principal thoroughfare of Northampton, and, like all hardest workers, gets the most kicks. Nobody has a word to say in its favour. It is our *Via Mala.* It has everything that a great thoroughfare ought not to have, and nothing that it should have. It is narrow; has hollows and steeps; is dirty; its paving is always out of order; it is choked with unsavoury smells; is smoky; squalid; full of "courts;" always crowded with brewers' drays and trollies and carts full of the deposits of the pig-sty. Late on a November night, when the fog lies low and undisturbed, you walk through distinct strata of smells—grains, pig-sties, oil cake, tallow-melting. The indictment is not to be gainsaid. All these ills it has, yet something is still to be said in mitigation of the censure. Let us take an impartial walk up it, supposing ourselves just arrived by the train. Of course topography is like biography. In both cases your eyes must see as much as they can of the past as well as of the present, or you will make a sorry and imperfect, if not an unjust, record of it. Eminently unjust and uninteresting the mere present would be in the case of Bridge Street, for, as we have admitted, the name of its *désagremens* is legion. They thrust themselves upon us during its entire transit; while its more interesting qualities may be passed by unobserved.

By the general name of Bridge Street we now understand the entire thoroughfare from the South Bridge to the George corner.

But that was not so within present memory. Bridge Street was probably named, not after the bridge that spans the Nene, but after a Bridge which crossed the moat by which the town in its fortified state was surrounded. The stream ran beneath the chapel of St. Thomas's Hospital, and the South gate of the town was just above it. St. Thomas's Brygge it is named in early documents. The interval southward, between this bridge and the river, was known as the South Quarter, though the distinctive appellation is dying out. We begin our survey—if we may apply so grandiloquent a term to our gossipping walk—at the south end of the South Bridge, and we do so that we may call the reader's attention to the pretty views from the bridge itself, on either hand; on the right, especially, with the poplars and other trees on the river bank, and the island by the lock. The river on summer evenings is gay with pleasure boats, and so far the entrance to our town is cheering enough. The predecessor of the present bridge had six arches, though its span was probably not greater. In the memorable May-flood, which occurred on the 6th of May, 1663, the two chief arches were carried away, and one large one was afterwards substituted for them. The water, says Bridges, flowed up into the town almost to St. John's Hospital. Pepys makes this memorandum of the event in his Diary:—

> "Strange were the effects of the late thunder and lightning about a week since at Northampton, coming with great rain, which caused extraordinary floods in a few hours, bearing away bridges, drowning horses, men, and cattle. Two men passing over a bridge on horseback, the arches before and behind them were borne away, and that left which they were upon; but, however, one of the horses fell over and was drowned. Stacks of faggots carried as high as a steeple, and other dreadful things; which Sir Thomas Crewe showed me letters to him about from Mr. Fremantle and others that it is very true."

While yet the walls were standing which surrounded the town, there were houses down to this point. Speed's map, which is dated 1610, gives nearly a continuous line on each side, with intervals only for bridges, to span streams crossing the street from the western to the eastern bend of the Nen. There were four of these streams between the South Bridge and the St. Thomas's Bridge of which we have already spoken. In that early time it is probable that the houses were small, with the exception of the inns, which were no doubt numerous, with spacious accommodation in the way of stabling and shelter for waggons and merchandize. The "Malt Shovel" is one of these old hostelries, and was certainly existing at the time of Speed's survey. It is, indeed, the oldest house in the street. Its overhanging upper story belongs to an early time, though it has undergone in other respects great and many alterations. With this exception there is no house which is prior to a rather late period in the seventeenth century; but of these there are several. Even within living memory this portion of our southern entrance retained something of a suburban aspect. There was a brewery indeed, but it was of singularly unobtrusive proportions compared with the towering chimney and gigantic structure which has risen on its site. There was, we think, no foundry fifty years ago; at all events it was of very modest pretensions. Entering the town by night on the box seat of the Northampton coach, its small shops, lighted by one or two glimmering candles, looked at least sixty miles from the metropolis. Diversified as its character now is, here huge breweries, there a thatched cottage, here a little shop, there a large private residence, it indicates a town of importance and wide extended business. It is a suburb no longer, and has no suburban characteristics. Tall chimneys wave their black plume of smoke across it; brewers' drays, huge trolleys, railway omnibuses, and carriers' carts choke it with traffic. Country odours find no way up it, but smells antagonistic fight each other, not in the November night fogs only, but every day, and all the day long.

Yet glimpses of country are to be had notwithstanding. At what period of civic history people began to build courts at the rear of their houses we cannot tell; we suspect not much earlier than the beginning of the eighteenth or quite the latter end of the seventeenth century. One's theory about them is something of this sort:—A house in the country had usually a garden behind it —an ample slice of ground with an orchard and ordinary trees, and a paddock included. Between the houses on the east side of the South Quarter, and the common called the Cow Meadow, there is a very broad belt of land. A demand of tenements in the town induced the owners of houses in the main street to build rows of cottages at right angles with their houses; a great sacrifice of comfort to pecuniary advantage, according to our present ideas. Still, when it was country all round about, when the main street was a country highway, when the breath of the field was omnipresent, and the cottages themselves were faced with flower gardens, and their occupants were, in a sense, members of the family circle, the arrangements may not have been so objectionable. Not in Northampton, at least. At Birmingham, the usual form of these courts is a quadrangle, houses looking upon houses. In the South Quarter, the ends of the courts, instead of being blocked up with a tenement, were open to the fields beyond; most of them had a way into the meadow. The cottages, or court-houses, are small enough as a rule,—"cabin'd, cribb'd, confin'd;" but there are classes who live very much out of doors, and, like the birds, want but a roost for the night-time and a nest for the hatching. How much this habit prevails may still be observed at the entrance to these courts in the South Quarter. They are seldom wholly deserted. A mother with a baby in her arms, and a great-grandmother at her elbow, are pretty sure to be found there; later in the day the knot grows larger, and towards evening it is larger still, augmented by the father, or the brother, or the friend, or the sweetheart, who adds a pipe to the enjoyment. The scene is not equal to the poet's sketch of children running to

> "Lisp their sire's return,
> Or climb his knees the envied kiss to share"—

but the children are there too, and share the kisses and the cuffs after the manner of the country. Multitudinous children there are of course, who tumble about the footway, and escape miraculously the perils of the horse road, which they love to defy. He must be a churl who would pass the group without a certain sympathy with their cheap indulgence, though one wishes that there was among them a larger manifestation of attachment to soap and water and combs. It has often struck us as a singular evidence how people overlook the needs as well as the pleasures at their feet to seek for those afar off and obscure, that no mission has ever been instituted for the promotion of the personal cleanliness which these three words imply. A missionary in the shape of a sturdy and strong charwoman would be a real blessing to many householders, morally as well as physically. Too much of our teaching begins at the wrong end, and topples over accordingly. The South Quarter courts were formerly bounded by an open ditch, fed by the stream which ran under St. Thomas's Bridge and Chapel, and there may have been a time when it was a tolerably pure brook, pleasant for the trees to dip in; but it had long since become a sewer and a nuisance, and was rightly covered over. On the site of Mr. John Perry's house formerly stood a house which must have been of considerable antiquity. The wharf adjoining was called Thaves' Wharf. Carter, who etched the Architectural Antiquities, described, in the *Gentleman's Magazine* for 1811, the front of this house as having a basso relievo representing four combatants—two engaged one with a sword, the other with a club; the other two attacking each other—one wielding a two-handed sword, and the other defending himself with a quarter-staff. A drawing of this basso relievo was in the possession of the late Miss Baker, but what has become of it we do not know. Of St. Thomas's Hospital a fragment yet survives, though sorely mutilated. Its front has been modernized in all respects but one, but for which it might be passed by unnoticed. Along the first story runs a band of fifteen stone panels, each having a shield within a quatrefoil. Within the gateway, the original beams are supported by grotesque corbels, somewhat rudely sculptured, and in the right hand wall are recesses, or aumbries, with shelves. One has an ogee head, and probably has been a piscina. The Perpendicular east end window still looks grandly over the ruin beneath it, and is a picturesque object from the Meadow. In the brook, Bridges tells us, "which runs from St. Thomas's Hospital, on the north side of the Cow Meadow," stood, during the wars between Charles I. and the Parliament, a gunpowder mill, which was fed by saltpetre dug out of the old cellars of the town. Fuller, writing of the Natural Commodities of Northamptonshire, says :—

"Now, though this shire shares as largely as any in those profits which are general to England, grass, corn, cattle, &c., yet it is most eminent for saltpetre."

He goes on—

"But why is saltpetre (common to all counties) insisted on in Northamptonshire? Because most thereof is found in dove-houses, and most dove-houses in this great corn county. Yet are not these emblems of innocency guilty in any degree of those destructions which are made by that which is made thereof. All that I will add of saltpetre is this: I have read in a learned writer that saltpetre men, when they have extracted saltpetre out of a floor of earth one year, within three or four years after they find more generated there, and do work it over again."

St. Thomas's Hospital was founded about 1450. Adjoining is the adjunct to it, founded in 1654, by Sir John Langham. Immediately north of St. Thomas's Hospital was the South Gate. It had chambers over it, which were inhabited by poor people. The town walls were embattled, and are said to have been broad enough for six persons to walk abreast. In an inquisition, taken the 6th year of Edward I., it is stated that there were steps at different places within, so that the inhabitants might take the air upon them, as in the record it is alleged that they were accustomed to do. Whoever has been at Chester may form a fair idea of the kind of promenade which the early inhabitants of Northampton possessed in their defences. Invalids and old people frequented them, and looked far over the surrounding country, wilder then, less enclosed, with more wood, and more marsh, and watched the arrival of the strings of pack-horses, and heard the jingling music of their bells as they drew nigh. In winter, according to the same authority, they passed by these means from one part of the town to the other; a scrap of information from which we may infer that walking in the town in the days of Edward the First was not particularly inviting. The streets, we may assume, were unpaved; the rain shot in sheets from the roofs, or in water-spouts from the fantastic gurgoyles; and the mud and slush were equally abundant and unsavoury. The wall was of stone, and drained, and though between the battlements the wind and rain came in bleak blasts, it was better and drier walking than below.

At St. John's Hospital we are within the precincts of the town proper: within the space, that is, that was enclosed within its walls. It is a noble ruin, and its elegant circular window, and spacious inclusive arch and sub-doorway, cannot fail to attract the attention of the passenger. It was founded, in 1137, by Walter, Archdeacon of Northampton, for the benefit of poor and infirm persons and orphans. Bridges says of it:—

> "The hospital consists of a chapel, a hall, or common room, with lodgings for the poor, and two rooms over them for the co-brothers. The master hath a good house and garden. The windows and walls of the hospital are old, but it hath been altered in some parts by modern reparations. The present master hath neatly fitted up the chapel, at his own expense. In the windows are some imperfect coats of arms and broken figures, and in one window the centre portrait of a person, mitred, with a crozier in his hand, and of another in a posture of prayer. In several places of the east window, in small black letters, is 'Honor Deo.'"

This description serves fairly well for its present state. The chapel has a good Decorated window of three lights at the east end, and at the west end a Perpendicular door, with a richly-panelled door beneath. There is a cemetery in the chapel ground. The master's house had long been in a pitiable state of dilapidation, when it was taken down to make way for the new station of the Bedford and Northampton Railway. It was very spacious; truly a princely residence. Portions of it were as early as the reign of King John. Nothing can be conceived more charming than its situation must once have been. It had an enviable outlook, with the woods of Delapré, Hardingstone, and Hunsbury Hill before it. It had a noble garden, with a postern gate opening into the meadow, still traceable. A drawing of it in glypograph, from the very faithful and tasteful pencil of the late Mr. Pretty, is to be found in Wetton's Guide to Northampton. Opposite to St. John's Hospital stood the House of the Friars Augustine, founded in 1322 by Sir John Longueville, of Wolverton. It was surrendered to the crown in the 30th of Henry VIII. We are not aware that any record exists of its demolition.

Between St. John's Hospital and the George corner there is little to call for observation. The Corporation Charity School is about as ugly a bit of nineteenth century architecture as the nineteenth century has produced. The best that can be said for it is that the architect (if by that name we may call him) had the good sense to provide a couple of niches for the reception of the two figures of an earlier time which belonged to some older building. Here and there some odd little old houses may be seen that have had their faces shaped from time to time as much as may be to the shifting fashion of the day, but retain their original proportions. They stand oddly between their aspiring neighbours. A little public-house, with the sign of the Eagle and Child, an old clothes shop, and its neighbour, with the old-fashioned half-door, are the oldest in this part of the street. The Waggon and Horses, on the West side, belongs to the time of Charles II., and till recently retained generally its original character. North of this house there is nothing calling for special notice. Several of the houses are as old, but have been so transformed as to be scarcely recognizable. The George Hotel has some tokens in its basement of an early building, as if, which is probably the case, the present structure was erected upon a very old foundation. But the George Hotel hardly belongs to gossip about Bridge Street, and is not to be talked about when one's "yarn" is well nigh spun.

A wide street, level and long enough to carry its perspective to a point, is an imposing sight, but more picturesque is a street like Bridge Street, irregular, and with a dip at one end and a steep rise at the other. It would be difficult, perhaps, to put into comparison two towns more dissimilar than Northampton and Bath; yet in one respect our town occasionally reminds us of the fair Western City. The valley of the Nene, like the valley of the Avon, is hollow enough for the eye to overleap the intermediate space, and to rest on the opposite hills. The charm of Bath is that the heights of its basin are visible from well nigh every street in it. Rocks and trees terminate every view, and give it cheerfulness and beauty. One's spirit exults unconsciously in those lofty outlooks of Nature as it were benignly smiling over us, "with a fine unconquered wish to bless," and winning us from sordid and petty thoughts and carking cares. No such wealth of scenery have we in Northampton, but the Hardingstone heights give us a glimpse here and there of tree tops, and standing at the top of Bridge Street and looking back southwards, the eye is gladdened with a background of hill and grove that is, in its way, eminently beautiful:—

> "Towers and battlements it sees,
> Bosom'd high in tufted trees;"

only our "towers" are the tall chimneys of the breweries, and our battlements the crested roofs of Messrs. Phipps's new buildings. At that distance they help the picture, and it is something that they recal, too, the poetry of Milton. So Nature triumphs over the busy thoroughfare:—

> "And even where gain huddles its noisiest rout,
> The smiles of her sweet wisdom will break through."

November.

THE dreariest month they say of all the year
   Thou art, November. If they tell us true,
   The Poets should invent them phrases new
Wherein to speak of seasons held most dear.
Young May or ardent June, November sere,
   Runneth the whole vocabulary through;
   Lo here are sunny days of cloudless blue
And lustrous nights. Is *this* November "drear?"

My boyish faith comes back to me again;
   Nature has nothing "dreary;" every moon
Her gladness changeth: but it doth remain
   A gladness still. 'Tis we who, "out of tune,"
Make the sweet music harsh—whose purblind eyes
See not the endless wealth that round us lies.

Northampton.

The Drapery.

IF we desired to impress a stranger with Northampton, we would smuggle him into the town late some Friday night. When he reached our railway station we should desire the weather to be so "dirty," in nautical phraseology, as not only to make the omnibus absolutely necessary, but to preclude the possibility of investigating the route up Bridge Street. The darker the night the better. He should be late enough when he had achieved that *via mala*, and reached the George Hotel, to have no wish to explore the town that night—to desire nothing but his supper, his cigar, and his bed. We would stipulate that next morning he should have his breakfast in one of the front upper rooms. We should even like to go so far as to supplicate Mrs. Higgins to allow us, for that one special occasion, to occupy her own sitting room. Of course we should desire that during the night our bad weather should have spent itself, and that the morning should be one of the brightest and sunniest of summer. When our friend entered the breakfast room, we would take him to the open window, and, pointing to the vista before him, exclaim—"There!" Dull must he be if he did not respond to our enthusiasm. Directly beneath he would have the bright green limes in the churchyard*; beyond, on either side, lines of stalls of all fashions buried in greenery and flowers. Probably he would suppose that some chivalric procession was contemplated, and that

* The Ramble was written before the recent alteration, which deprived the front of the Churchyard of its "bright green limes."

he saw before him the avenue of flowers through which it was to pass. So much for the scene viewed from this vantage ground. Nor when he descended into the street would the beauty of the vision be lost, though it would be changed to something more in conformity with our ordinary work-a-day world. He would find a market, but a sort of Covent Garden Market. Crossing from the George to Mr. Fred. Perkins's corner, he would go up the west side of the Drapery, with a fencing of stalls against the roadway. A motley range is that line of stalls. Mr. Perkins begins at the angle with a cluster of flowers of all hues, then come "sweets" parti-coloured, up-piled peas, mounds of gooseberries, all fruits of the season, and, above all, crowning all, intersecting all, adorning all,—flowers. Flowers everywhere, of every hue and odour; flowers in all forms; flowers in pots; flowers in bouquets. Presently his ear would be saluted with the hoarse crow of a Cochin-China fowl, and looking in the direction of that un-Chanticleer like summons, he would see a miniature menagerie. Cochin-China stands atop, looking as if he had got on a new pair of Dutch inexpressibles much too large for him. Sometimes his heavy proprietorship is superseded by a peacock. In the compartments below are fowls of all kinds, from diminutive bantams to stately Dorkings, pigeons various also, pouters, carriers, doves, rabbits, ordinary and lop-eared, guinea pigs, and magpies. Recrossing the street at the top, where at its eastern corner another Perkins gladdens the eye with a shop full of flowers, you push your way southward again by a third Perkins with more flowers,—as if Perkins was only a synonym for plants—among a motley crowd of loiterers; not idlers, but people who come out to look at the stalls and be tempted, and who move slowly, therefore, and stop the way as of right. Returning towards the churchyard you come upon the fish-stalls. Well, excepting in a Dutch picture, fish stalls may not usually be regarded as particularly pleasant objects. But these fish stalls of ours are pleasant in their reality, and would be singularly pleasant in a picture. Scarlet lobsters intervene with silvery salmon—a brilliant contrast, and, above all, the green lime trees make a cool and most graceful canopy. If our imaginary friend does not go away after this little excursion down the Drapery strongly impressed with the beauty of some at least of our Northampton streets, he is not the man we meant him to be.

It has occurred to us frequently that this Northampton thoroughfare of ours is as unique as it is lovely. Midland town though it be, and thoroughly English, there is yet something about the markets of Northampton that recall certain Continental characteristics. Looking down, for example, upon the tilted stalls of the Market Square, you are reminded of the markets at Rouen or Treves; walking down this Drapery you think of Amsterdam. Of course the differences are enormous. No central canal runs through our thoroughfare, bearing, as at Amsterdam, barge loads of flowers; no double lines of trees border the roadway; nor is it our fashion to go up a flight of steps to our door-way bordered with flower-pots. But for barges we have shallow carts laden with the same odorous burthen, and there is a strong disposition towards window gardening in the Drapery. We jot down our impression of this picture because, for aught we know to the contrary, this may be the last year of its existence. When the cattle market is removed, the flower and fruit and vegetable market will be transferred to the Market Square. Possibly the Drapery may gain by the change. Readier access will be had to the shops, and there will be elbow-room on the foot-way, and free carriage way in the road. But one cannot have advantages in this matter-of-fact world of ours without paying for them. What it will gain commercially it will lose æsthetically. There will be more convenience, but the Saturday glory of the Drapery will have departed.

We cannot but remember, however, that this Drapery splendour is of comparatively modern growth. Forty years ago the Saturday market there was very small and very brief. The vegetable market was on Wednesday, and was held on the Market Square, and was but an inconsiderable matter, By dusk the Drapery was well-nigh deserted. By broad daylight you had no crowding, and nothing to crowd for. The "green-grocery" business was on a very small scale, and the taste for flowers—flowers anywhere except in the gardens—was undeveloped. Then there were no fish stalls. The venerable adage that the Mayor of Northampton opens his oysters with his dagger, to keep them as far as possible from his nose, did not, indeed, then apply. But fish was a sort of special importation, chiefly in the hands of the guard or the coachman of the stage coaches, who brought down from London soles or salmon or oysters by individual order. Nor at that time, indeed, had All Saints' Churchyard the glory of its trees, which make so lovely a termination to the vista.

The Drapery is a very ancient, and must always have been a very important thoroughfare. It is marked in the earliest maps, and is spoken of in the earliest writers. It was, indeed, the main track from the South Gate to the North through the town. The very name speaks its antiquity. It was acquired in those days when trades were congregated together, and had localities specially appointed to each, probably under the rule of Simon St. Liz, for the word is of Norman origin. Formerly it was a street of many inns—inns with vast yards and stabling attached, for the accommodation of long strings of pack horses, and later of heavy stage waggons; later still of post horses and relays for the stage coaches. Swan Yard takes its name from one of these ample inns. We may picture the street before the great fire as being well-built, with houses of wood, with gables in front, and projecting stories, each overhanging the one below it. There was no doubt a good cloth trade carried on here by substantial tradesmen, who necessarily kept large stocks, for supplies were not to be had with the readiness of modern times. The great fire, no doubt, while it destroyed its picturesqueness, gave it certain advantages. The street was more regularly built, and the way skywards was more freely opened. Then, too, the setting back All Saints' Church, which formerly extended to the boundary of the churchyard, was a gain.

Great changes have taken place in the character of the Drapery within living memory. Some of the odd little low shops, with half door-ways, still existed. Well-to-do tradesmen were content to drive a comfortable trade in very small premises half a century ago. Business was transacted and over at a much earlier hour than in our competing days, and over the half door very respectable and substantial tradesmen could enjoy their afternoon leisure with the dignity of a long pipe; content with that unpretending relaxation. We have changed all that. The fashion is extending of separating the domestic establishment from the house of business, and bye-and-bye, possibly, every man, at the close of the day, will lock all his cares up in his warehouse, and go to his home and his family a cheerfuller, if not a wealthier, man for the change. ***Cœlum, non animam, mutant,*** it is true, and we can't always get our old man of the sea off our shoulders by this process, but these should be the exceptions to a rule which probably works, and we hope does work, beneficially upon the whole.

A Poet's Home.

A Poet's home!—a Poet's fitting home!
Look how it lies amidst the embowering trees,
A very nest for song-birds. You might come
A hundred times in its vicinities,
Nor ever think to find such "lap of ease,"—
Such nursery for out-gushing minstrelsies,
Where the green ozier unrestricted shoots,
And mossy boughs bend heavy with their fruits.
There be no trim walks here; no greenhouse, where
The poor exotic pines its life away
In sad degeneracy; but flowers that bear
All weathers bravely, perk their blossoms gay
'Midst knee-deep grass, and "wilding-flowers" less rare,
Yet to the Poet's sense as sweet as they.

[THE SAME SUBJECT CONTINUED.]

All day the air trembled with sylvan music.
At earliest dawn the swallow, from the eaves
Down darting, with a sharp, clear, ringing call;
Then finches of all tribes, by merry hundreds
Pouring a thrilling treble like the rain
Of pearly beauty when a master's hand
With choicest art, yet with most random seeming,
Flies o'er the rapid keys. At glowing noon
Another strain—the cuckoo's measured note,
Full, deep, and rich—issuing from midst the bushes;
The shrill grasshopper, too, of whom Anacreon
Sang an immortal song.

The moon is up,
And we have other minstrels. Hark, that gush
Of sudden notes!—the very utterance
Of passionate love—love passionate, yet pure
And pensive; yet methinks not sorrowful,
Nor mirthful either, but a song which speaks
Of *thoughtful* happiness.

And so with all this flood of melody
Circling our senses, we retire to sleep,
To dream of golden groves of singing birds,
As told in dazzling tales of Araby,
And be again awakened by the swallow.

Northampton.

The Mayorhold and Horsemarket.

AMONG the documents belonging to the Corporation of Northampton is one relating to the paving of various streets of the town, in the 9th year of the reign of Henry VI—1431. It directs that the highways of the town, from the north gate to the bridge called Saint Thomas Brigge in the south, and the way from the west gate to the east gate, and also the streets called Berewardstrete, Seynt Gylestrete, Swynwelstrete, Kyngeswellstrete, Seint Martynstrete, Seint Marystrete, and the way called the Market Place—"et la chemyn appellé le market place"—shall be paved by the owners of messuages or tenements abutting upon these several ways, 30 feet from their frontage. Where Swynwell Street and Saint Martyn Street were there is, so far as we know, no record. There were also in 1275 streets called Salt Street, and Krakeboll Street, all traces of the localities of which has long been lost. The Market Place, however, was not the present Market Square, as may be readily gathered from the description "la chemyn," the Norman-French for highway or thoroughfare, which is not a characteristic of the Market Square. We know, in fact, that the market was held in the Mayorhold prior to 1535, when the Market Square was paved for the purpose, and a market cross erected there. The term Mayorhold is, indeed, supposed to be synonymous with Markethold. In Speed's map (1610) it is called "Marhold." It is easy to understand how Markethold may have become corrupted into Mayorhold when the market had ceased to be held there, and the prefix was no longer supported by the fact. There is a tradition, how far to be accepted we do not know, that the Mayor of Northampton once lived on the west side of the Mayorhold, where a low down-hill gateway leads to an open space, now occupied by some sufficiently squalid buildings. The supposed fact may have grown out of the corrupted name, or the name may really record a fact. It is far from improbable that a house of sufficient quality for the residence of the chief magistrate of the town may have stood there. In remote times the site must have been a very pleasant one; in front a wide open space; behind, gardens and fields and a far-stretching country prospect. At the present day the Mayorhold seems to be inconvenient for a market; but, if we may trust the proportions of Speed's map, it was not so before the great fire. The south gate crossed Bridge Street at the boundary of the town wall, by St. Thomas's Hospital. Apparently the way into Kingswell Street was far more open and direct than at present. Of the two ways Bridge Street is the narrowest. A broad and very direct way continued to Gold Street, crossing which into College Lane a still goodly way led to Silver Street, and so sweeping by an easy curve into the Mayorhold. Whether these streets were really as wide as they appear in Speed we cannot pretend to determine. It is quite possible, however, that they may have been narrowed after the fire. Silver Street had houses only on one side. Whether there was ever a beast market in the Mayorhold we do not know. If there were, it is probable that it had become decayed. Beast, at all events, were not brought to the market in the latter part of the last century. We learn from evidence in the famous Toll-cause that Mr. Nunneley, of Market Harborough, was the first who established the beast market, somewhere about 1805. Till that time beast were brought to fairs only. Markets for cattle were a consequence of better roads and improved facilities of inter-communication generally. Neither do sheep appear to have ever been sold in the general market. In Speed's map the sheep market is placed in Sheep Street, to which it of course gave its name. Our general markets, indeed, up to a comparatively recent date, resembled the Continental markets rather than our own markets at the present day. Markets for the sale of animals were specially so named according to the kind brought to them. Over four hundred years ago, therefore, the Mayorhold was bordered by buildings; the outline, perhaps, resembling the present. Broad Lane was probably a lane then. Sawpit Lane may also have existed in some form, bordering the lands of the Priory of St. Andrew. Sawpit Lane, however, is a comparatively modern name. In Jeffery's map (1746) it is called St. Andrew's Street, though there were but few houses in it. On the west side there were fields all the way. It was the ancient way to the Priory of St. Andrew's. Horsemarket was part of the "chemyn" into Gold Street, as it is now, and was no doubt partly built. But on the west side there was the house of the Black Friars, or Friars Preachers, who were settled there before 1240. The founder was supposed to be one John Dabyngton. The revenues of the house were rated in 1535 at £5 11s. 6d., the relative amount of which may be estimated by a comparison with other houses of Friars in the town at the same period. The Grey Friars had £6 17s. 4d.; the White Friars were valued at £10 10s. There were customary deductions from all these;—the Black Friars paid 3s. 4d. to the Abbot of St. James, and fourpence to the Mayor and Bailiffs of the town. In 1539 it was given up to the Crown by William Dyckyns, the Prior, and seven other Friars. In 1545 the site of it was granted to William Ramesden; it was afterwards possessed by Robert Burgoyne, Esq., and in 1586 it was in the possession of Francis Samwell, Esq., who died in that year, when it passed to his eldest son William. After this we have no record of it, though its history may possibly be traced in title-deeds and muniments to which we have no access.

After the dissolution of the Fraternity of Friars Preachers, it seems probable that the house was demolished. In the Horsemarket, a short distance south of the Mayorhold, is a beerhouse, rejoicing in the name of "The Jolly Bricklayers." The neighbourhood has a penchant for the jovial adjective. Not far off is "The Jolly Smokers." The front of "The Jolly Bricklayers" wears a clean new face, but it is obvious enough that it is not a house of the present generation nor of many a past one. Its present aspect, however, would lead nobody to suppose that in its rear is a house which was, there can be little doubt, erected immediately after the demolition of the religious house. There is no external evidence of an ecclesiastical building. It is a mansion house of the time of Henry VIII.—such as one might expect would be erected by Wm. Ramesden or Robert Burgoyne. Originally it may have consisted of a long building with three projecting gables. One only of these projections remains, and an altered portion of another. The interval was lighted by long mullioned windows, the upper one of which is traceable. The projecting gables were similarly lighted; the lower one has suffered from the many changes and adaptations which the building has undergone; but the upper one is still a window with its four stone mullions perfect and its diamond panes. The eastern projection has lost its gable; it underwent great alterations at various remote periods, and the roof is finished with a hip. The interior has been so changed and divided and sub-divided as to leave none of its original stateliness. But one may recal what it once was. There are the remains of a fire-place under a depressed arch, with sixteenth century mouldings, in the room on the upper floor. The room was of goodly size, lighted from its ample windows in the gable. None of the panelling remains on the walls, but some fragments of it are in another part of the house—the good square oak panelling of the days of the 8th Henry. The window faces due north, but there were probably windows also looking east and west. It probably had a return to the north, giving on the Horsemarket on the east. Everywhere the building speaks of its varied fortunes, and they have been sufficiently severe. Its surroundings partake of its evil days. But one sees through them what it once was. Such a house had assuredly its fitting gardens, and as assuredly there was pleasant open country before it and to the west of it. In the place of tall chimneys and racks of timber-planks, and huddled buildings, and squalid walls and pig-sties, there were tall trees and pleached alleys, and glowing flower-beds. It is difficult to guess what was to the south. There were probably other buildings in the Horsemarket, which would have obstructed the view that way. In summer the mid-day sun was not needed, and the evening was welcome and glorious. At this season the solid walls and the stout panelling would keep out "the winter's flaw," and within, the huge logs on the andirons in the spacious fire place would send a ruddy glow through the Christmas room. Many a silver tankard must have reflected it, many a jovial, many a lovely face must have been glad in its brightness; many a hearty laugh the now sombre walls must have re-echoed. How delightful it would be if one could retrace a few centuries, and drop into one of these gatherings of the old old time, even as a fly on the wall or any other unnoticed entity, instead of going there in these vague imaginings.

A Ballad.

SHE was a haughty creature,
With an eye as black as jet;
But her lip was the loveliest ruby
That ever I gazed on yet.
She looked supremest scorn on me—
You need not ask me why;
She was lady of half a kingdom,
And a homeless wanderer I.

It was the glad Midsummer—
'Twas a night of choicest mirth;
There were bright stars in the heavens—
There were brighter eyes on earth:
We danced on the greensward, chequered
With moonlight through the leaves—
Oh, readily in such moments
Wild dreams the heart conceives.

She was a haughty beauty;
And on the morrow morn
Her gentle smile had vanished,
And her lip was curled with scorn.
The dazzling memory she left
Hath no half-hoping sigh;
She is lady of half a kingdom,
And a homeless wanderer I.

Northampton.

St. Thomas's Hospital.

OLD Northampton is crumbling away. New interests, new exigencies, day after day push down the old glories and the old characteristics, and lay the axe to the root of the evidences of our local history. In a short time one of the relics of the institutions of our forefathers will have fallen before modern wants and modern love of change. The Corporation, under the provisions of the Markets and Fairs Act, will take possession of the old St. Thomas's Hospital, in Bridge-street, in order to make an opening in connexion with Weston-street to the west end of the town. Thirty-seven years ago the inmates of the Hospital were transferred to a new building at the east end of St. Giles's-street, and the old structure is occupied by Mr. Cooper, the cab proprietor. It is a ruin, but not without some points of interest, which it is as well to record before it is entirely swept away. Exteriorly the front in Bridge-street presents, with one or two exceptions, the ordinary features of an old house which has suffered many changes. The roof slopes backward, and is surmounted by the point of a gable, in which, if our memory does not deceive us, there was once a small bell cot. Over the first story is a row of sixteen blank shields in as many quatrefoil panels, and a spacious gateway cuts into the lower half of the front. Within this gateway, on the right-hand wall, are several recesses. The first is a square-headed aumbry or cupboard, divided in the middle by an oaken shelf; the second a similar cupboard, also divided in the middle by an oaken shelf; a smaller square recess is immediately underneath it, the purpose of which is not very obvious; the third is a large and wide recess, under a disfigured arch; the fourth is an upright round-headed opening which has served for a window, the lower half having been closed as if for a seat in the recess; the fifth is simply an upright recess with a square head; the sixth a small square recess; the seventh is an upright recess, with an arch in the inside, perhaps for a window-head; the eighth a large square recess; the ninth an upright square opening, divided by a shelf similarly to number one. All these are beneath a not very lofty flooring, the old oak beams of which are carried on the south side by huge corbels of various grotesque characters. They are all much knocked about, and choked with whitewash. Beyond this portion of the building, which constituted the residence of the alms-women, was a small chapel, which was not divided by an upper story, as in the case of the portion we have been describing, but was open to the roof. Some remains of old woodwork at the east end of this upper story would seem to indicate that there had been at one time something of a screen there, so that inmates who were sick or too infirm to descend into the chapel might witness the services from above. The chapel was lighted by a lofty Perpendicular east window of four lights with cinquefoil heads, and above them eight lesser lights with trefoil heads, the whole under a very depressed arch, with a simple moulding terminating in blocks as if for carving which had never been executed. This window is in a very perfect condition, and, with the gable, is an agreeable object from the meadow walk. Half a century ago it had much of its original stained glass remaining. The chapel was also lighted by a window in the upper part of the south wall, by a three-light Perpendicular window, with cinquefoil heads, which, with its mullions, remain complete, but has its lights stopped up. In the wall beneath, but a little further eastward, is an ogee-headed arch, covering, no doubt, a piscina.

Such is the present aspect of the Hospital, which was founded about 1450. The earliest benefaction we find given to it, says Bridges, is by William Green, who by a deed which is among the archives of the Corporation, dated 9th May, 1460, settled upon the keepers, brothers, and sisters of the fraternity of S. Thomas, and their successors for ever, a tenement, in Gold Street, for the perpetual relief of the poor in the said Hospital.

"William Rowland, by deed bearing date 13th March, 1511, gave to the poor in St. Thomas's house, a close, in West Cotton, for ever. In 1592 Edward Elmor settled upon the Mayor, bailiffs, and burgesses, three messuages in Abington-street, and one messuage in Gold-street, to provide for one poor householder and for the relief of the other poor in this Hospital. In 1599 Thomas Croswell and Roger Higham, pursuant to the intention of Thomas Wastell, gave one tenement in Sheep Street, and John Bryon, in 1630, five acres of meadow in Cotton Marsh, towards the support of the poor in the said house. Mr. Edward Collis gave also by will two tenements in Newland for the relief of the poor in St. Thomas's Hospital for ever. By the original foundation, twelve poor persons were maintained here at an allowance of 1s. 11d. weekly each with clothing, firing, and washing. In 1654 Sir John Langham added six others, with an appointment of 20 pence per week. For this purpose he settled £36 per annum, which is paid by the Corporation; and for which the Cow Meadow, Balmshole, and Midsummer Meadow are security. One other poor woman hath lately been added by the charity of Richard Massingberd."

So far Bridges. We are not writing the history of the charity, but simply some notes concerning the house in which it was for nearly four centuries located. Now, as everybody knows, its funds are administered by trustees. St. Thomas's Hospital was just without the South Gate, by St. Thomas's Bridge, which gave its name to Bridge Street. "The stream," says the late Mr. Pretty in Wetton's Northampton Guide, "which ran in front of the town wall, passed under the Chapel into the Cow Meadow. At many of the crossings of streams we find places dedicated to the memory of St. Thomas à Becket." The stream was traceable within living memory. The South-gate was a short distance to the north, in a direct line—that is with the town-wall which still borders the St. John's Hospital Gardens. In those early days the Hospital had open country both in front and to the rear. Not many years after the establishment of the pious foundation, its aged inmates must have witnessed from its walls the great battle which took place in July, 1460, between the Confederate Earls and Henry the Sixth.

"The King," says Stowe, "lying at the White Friers, Northampton, ordained a strong and mighty field in the meadows beside the Nunry having the river at his back. * * The tenth day of July, at two of the clock afternoone, the Earles March and Warwicke let crie through the field that no man should lay hand upon the King ne on the common people, but on the Lords Knights and Esquires; then both hosts incountred and fought halfe an houre, the Lord Edmund Grey of Rathen that was the King's vaward, brake the field and came to the Earles party, and was a great helpe to them in obtaining the victory; many on the Kings side were slain, and many that fled were drowned in the river, the Duke of Buckingham, the Earle of Shrewsbury, the Lord Beaumont, and the Lord Egremont were slaine by the King's tent with many knights and esquires, the Kings ordinance of guns might not be shot, there was so great raine that day. When the field was done and the Earls had the victory, they came to the King he being in his tent, and said in this wise: Most noble prince, displease you not though it have pleased God of his grace to grant us the victory of our mortall enemies, the which by their venemous malice have untruly stirred and mooved your highness to exile us out of your land, and would have us put to finall shame and confusion, we come not for the intent to unquiet ne grieve your said highnesse but for to please your noble person, desiring tenderly the high welfare and prosperity thereof, and of all your realme, and to be your true liegemen while our lives shall endure. The King with these words was greatly comforted, and anon was led to Northampton, with procession, where he rested three daies."

The army going to battle in all its defiant array probably passed from the White Friars through the South Gate, and by the then new Hospital of St. Thomas. A few hours after the defeated King returned a prisoner, though reverenced still as a King. We realize such things with difficulty. East or west, north or south, the outlook is not so fair as it was in those days. Crowded buildings choke the landscape; the traffic is of drays and waggons and carts, the busy vehicles of prosperous trade, prosaic enough, but indicative of comfortable homes, and well-to-do citizens. 'Tis better as it is. There is, unhappily, a parallel to the old spectacle in many a provincial city on the Continent. We do not desire it to come nearer to us.

The Haven.

"The same pleasant prospect still shineth before me—
The river—the mountain—the valley of green"—

BARRY CORNWALL.

WE will dwell beneath the old oak tree,
In our childhood's happy home;
And beyond its village boundary
We never again will roam.
We have bitterly repented
Our heresy gone by;
And we dream no more that pride or wealth
Can affection's place supply.

We shall see again our youthful haunts,
And wander as of yore,
Down the verdant hill's enamelled side—
By the river's willowy shore;
And the sun shall shine again for us,
As it long has ceased to shine;
And fairy visions once again
Shall haunt the day's decline.

Oh dreams of youth!—there only, where
Ye had first your glorious birth,
Will ye ever rise to gild the dull
Realities of earth.

We may dwell 'midst scenes more splendid,
  We may find a wealthier lot,
But the blissful phantasies of life
  Haunt but one only spot.

In the placid light of a summer's night
  Together we will sit,
Breathing the jasmine's fragrancy
  As the wind sighs over it;
And the songs and strains we used to love
  We will once again awake;
And dearer than ever will they be
  For hallowed memory's sake.

Northampton a Hundred Years ago.

AMONG the curiosities brought together in the Northampton Museum, when it was opened in August, 1866, was a plan of Northampton at the great Election of 1768, when Sir George Osborn and Sir G. B. Rodney, and the Hon. Thomas Howe were the candidates. It is the property of Thomas Scriven, Esq. It is on twenty-eight sheets of foolscap paper, beginning with a general plan of the town, and following with sections, in which every house is marked with the name of the occupant. The first section gives Abington Street, from the fork where the Wellingborough and Kettering Roads meet, westward to the Market Square. We cannot, in all cases, identify the houses with the existing buildings because there have been, of course, innumerable alterations and changes since that day, two or three houses, in some cases, having been converted into one, and as often one into two or three. But of some we can speak with certainty. There was then, as now, a house at the intersection of the Wellingborough and Kettering roads, which was occupied by Tim. Penn. There were no tenements along the Kettering road, and two only a little way up the Wellingborough Road on the left hand, which were occupied by Thomas Thompson and Thomas Pennocks. The Bantam Cock was occupied by one Edward Nicholls. Whether it was an inn then does not appear in the plan. The last house on the north side of Abington Street was the residence of Thomas

Caldicutt, Esq. It is difficult to identify it with any existing house. Was it Mr. Markham's? And did the garden house at the corner, formerly in Dr. Kerr's garden, belong to it? The character of the intermediate buildings do not negative the supposition, but the grounds about the house must, in that case, have been very extensive. A hundred years ago the ditch round the town still existed, and the garden-house looked uninterruptedly over a wide extent of beautiful country—the woods of Delapré, and the meadows all the way to Houghton, with the Nene, an unpolluted stream, winding through them. Wood Street, in 1768, was called Cock lane, though the Inn at the corner, from which it took that name, no longer existed. Between Mr. Caldicutt's house and Cock Lane were fifteen houses, and the eighth from Cock Lane was the residence of Purbeck Langham, Esq., and the ninth of Wm. Gates. Mr. Langham's was probably the houses now occupied by Mr. Evans and Mr. Hall, which were originally a single structure. The house at its western corner, recently occupied by Dr. Faircloth, then belonged to Major Cunningham. Two houses farther westward, and there was a yard, at the extremity of which lived one Wm. Dunkley. Three more houses westward and we come to an entrance described as "The Peacock back gate." Four houses still further westward and another entrance occurs—"The Chequer back gate." Two other houses westward, and the house next the corner is set down as "The Chequer Inn." Part of this inn, probably, still remains at the rear of the house, at the corner of the Market Square, to which it appears to have been subsequently attached. The "Stag's Head" was the "Stag's Head" then also, and was occupied by one James Sutton. The plan does not mention the Stag's Head, but only the name of its occupant, who, we find, by a reference to the *Mercury* of the period, lived at "The Stag's Head," and was a maker of bandages for surgical purposes. The union of surgical instrument maker and innkeeper seems an odd one in these days; but it is possible that Mr. Sutton lived at the sign of the Stag's Head merely, the house not being an inn.

Trades of all sorts had signs in those days. Crossing over to the south side of the street, and going eastward, we find the site of the present Saracen's Head appropriated to "Wm. Dorrell." It was the Saracen's Head Inn then, and included the entire space from the Town Hall to the turning into Dychurch Lane, as indeed, it did within our own memory. The west corner of Fish Lane—Mr. Hewitt's House—was the residence of Mrs. Isted. One Thomas Rigby occupied the opposite corner, now Mr. Dunkley's shop; next door to Rigby lived Robert Bilson, and then came a house occupied by Charlwood Lawton, Esq. We cannot identify with certainty any of the intermediate houses. The last house before St. Giles's Church Lane was occupied by one Wm. Cartwright. The fine old house now occupied by Mr. Kingston was then the residence of "Doctor Blencowe."

Going down St. Giles's Church Lane into St. Giles's Street we find that Thos. Samwell occupied the house at the corner of the "Way to Dearn Gate," on the south side of the street—the house now occupied by the Rev. W. H. Robson. Three houses westward, and then came the County Closes as now. The west corner, now encumbered by the huge factory of Messrs. Homan, is marked "Mr. Clift's shop," Geo. Clift having a residence adjoining. On the northern side opposite the "Closes" lived "Henry Markham;" next to him westward "Wm. Gibson," and then came the Garden Wall as now attached to Mr. Gates's house. "The Playhouse" occupied the site of the new houses facing Castilian Street. It had been a malting, we believe, and had then newly been adapted to the purposes of the children of Thespis. In the *Mercury* of this year there is the following announcement of a performance there:—

"At the NEW THEATRE, in St. Gyles's Street, Northampton, on Monday, the 23rd of May instant, will be presented a Comedy, call'd

THE STRATAGEM

Archer by Mr. M. Durravan; Aimwell by Mr. Carrol, Sullen by Mr. J. Durravan, Sir Charles Freeman by Mr. Jacobs, Foigard by Mr. Jones, Gibbet by Mr. Clifton, Bonniface by Mr. Hardwicke, Hounslow by Mr. Berry, Bagshot by Mr. Norris. And Scrub by Mr. Benson——Mrs. Sullen by Mrs. Roberts, Dorinda by Miss Roberts, Cherry by Miss Hopton, Lady Bountiful by Mrs. Grimes, Gipsey by Mrs. Bakewell.

End of Act the 1st, A Song by Mr. Clifton.
End of Act the 2nd, A Song by Miss Hopton.
End of Act the 3rd, A Song, in character of Diana, by Mrs. Jacobs.
End of Act the 4th, A Dance by Mr. Benson and Miss Hopton.
To which will he added a Musical Entertainment
(Never Perform'd Here) call'd,
The Chaplet.

Damon by Mr. Carrol, Palemon by Mr. Clifton, Shepherds by Mr. Hardwicke, Mr. Durravan, Mr. Benson, Mr. Norris, &c.—Laura by Miss Hopton, Pastora by Miss Roberts.

The Doors to be open'd at Half past Five, and to begin exactly at Half past Six——Boxes 3s Pit 2s Gallery 1s. Tickets to be had of Mr. Lacy and Mrs. Pasham, Booksellers, and at Mr. Dyer's House on the Market-Place. Places for the Boxes to be taken of Mr. Norris opposite the Theatre.—The House will be lighted in the Manner of the London-Theatres.——No Person can be admitted behind the scenes.

☞ The Days of Playing are Mondays, Wednesdays, and Fridays."

Among other plays performed here we find Kane O'Hara's admirable "Burletta of Midas," which we are told had run fifty nights in London; Fielding's "Virgin Unmasked," "The Constant Couple," "The Beggar's Opera," and "The Tempest or the Enchanted Island," among the attractions of which are enumerated, "two entire new Sets of Scenes, proper to the play; with all the Music, both Vocal and Instrumental; Scenes, Machines, Sinkings, Flying, and other necessary decorations; the Ship, Sea, and Artificial Shower of Hail and Fire; and all other incidents proper to the Tempest Scene. The Play to conclude with a beautiful View of a Calm Sea, on which appear Neptune and Amphitrite on a Chariot drawn by Sea Horses," &c., &c.

Coming into St. Giles's Square, we find on the north side (going westward) five houses, occupied by Alderman Plackett, the

Rev. Mr. Graham, Mr. Litchfield, Mr. Kerr, Silvester Ager, and John Swindell. Mr. Litchfield and Mr. Kerr were surgeons. On the opposite side was "the Sessions House," the County Hall as we now call it; next to it, eastward, the house now occupied as the Judges' lodgings, was the residence of Robt. Clavering, Esq.; then came Timothy Rogers, in the space now filled by Mr. Bayly. The Honble. Mr. Hamilton and Wm. Henry Markham appear to have resided in houses which have been removed to make way for the new street leading to the Northampton and Bedford Railway Station. In the fork dividing St. Giles's Street and Dearn Gate, where the Savings Bank now stands, was a house occupied by James Woolston, an attorney and steward to the Earl of Northampton.

In Dearn Gate, the Swan was kept by Thomas Norcutt, and beyond Cow Lane there was but a solitary house, occupied by Thos. Smith. A yard ran down by the side of Smith's house, and there was a small tenement at the bottom. On the north side there were four houses from the corner, and a yard, at the bottom of which also there was a tenement. Then came gardens, and one isolated dwelling belonging to Henry Cox, who is gibbeted as "not polled,"—for what reason the record does not say—whether he held aloof from the fray indignant, like Achilles, at some supposed wrong from his party, or whether he wanted more than the current value of his vote and overstood his market. The ground now occupied as garden ground is called "The Field." St. Thomas's Well was of course there. A windmill, close to Vigo, was then in full sail, and near it lived one "Messenger Ball." With these exceptions, it was country everywhere.

Returning westward to the Sessions House—All Saints' Church was surrounded by a wall—as indeed it was within our own recollection—instead of an iron palisading. At its north-east corner, facing Mercers' Row, were two tenements occupied by John Potter and Sam Swinfen. In Mercers' Row there was another "not polled" man—one Hunt. Drum Lane is written down as Drury

Lane. In George Row, between the Sessions House and the present Telegraph Office, lived Philip Warwick. The Telegraph Office was then the County Hospital. The "George" is not so mentioned. Its apparent site is marked "John Page," who was probably the landlord. It was the St. George Inn a century earlier, when Cosmo the Third, Grand Duke of Tuscany, visited Northampton. Count Magalotti, who chronicled his Highness's travels, describes it as situated near the belfry of the principal church, and the bells being rung to welcome him, the ringing continued the greater part of the night, keeping him miserably awake. At the election in 1768 "The George" was Lord Spencer's house.

On the east side of the Drapery occurs the name of one John Wyatt. On reference to the *Mercury* we find that John Wyatt was a staymaker, who made, as his advertisement stated, "All sorts of women's and children's stays in the best and newest fashion, viz.,—Turn'd stays, half bon'd stays, French stays, pack-thread stays, jumps, slips, robes, &c." "Children's packthread and boned stays ready made." A Benjamin West occupied the Drapery front of the premises now occupied by Mr. Osborn, and the house on the opposite side of the "Passage into Market-hill" was inhabited by John Agutter. At the Post Office, in the Drapery, lived Jno. Lacy, a bookseller. On the west side we find William Marshall, a drugg'st, who advertizes in the *Mercury* inter alia, "Some curious Hissoon Tea, very little inferior in quality to the finest Hyson, at 12s. per pound," a price to make modern tea drinkers stand aghast. In "Drury," or Drum lane, there was a butcher's shop then as now, and the White Hart had a back way into the Lane as it has at this day.

In the Market Square, on the south side, there were five houses between Drury Lane and the passage leading into Mercers' Row. Mr. Becke's offices were then occupied by Wm. Woolstone; the present Stamp Office is named as the residence of Richard Woolley, which, however, is apparently a mistake, for Edward. Richard lived on the west side of the Square. "Edward Woolley and Co." were braziers, who also sold "exceeding fine broad and Dutch white clover, trefoil, and rye grass seeds," and "fine-cured and dry Derbyshire bacon." Mr. Tomalin's office was then occupied by Mr. Hutt, and the two houses, now one, constituting Mr. Smith's establishment were occupied by Brown and (at the corner) Williamson and Staples, one house, as a memorandum on the plan says. The space between the eastern corner of the passage into Mercers' Row and the corner, now all absorbed by the Waterloo House, was then sufficient for three houses, in the occupation of Vores, Clarke, and, at the corner, Medbury. Five and thirty years ago this was a public-house—"The Cook's Arms." Whether or not it was a public-house in Mr. Medbury's time we do not know. Crossing over to the corner of Abington Street the fine old house for very many years the shop of the good old thorough-going Tory magistrate, Mr. Marshall—"Justice John" as he was popularly called—as full of political fervour as an egg is full of meat, yet kind-hearted notwithstanding, shrewd, sensible, and brimming with humour—was a grocer's shop then. Here lived Robert Crabb, a grocer. The Peacock was kept by a Mr. Mills. Mrs. Bamford lived in the house now occupied by Dr. Webster, Mrs. Backwell in that where Mr. Terry lives, and Mr. Cardwell's fine old Elizabethan house was a boarding school. At the corner of the Parade and Newland lived the Rev. Mr. Watts, the space now covered by the premises of Messrs. Mobbs, Snow, and Wood, and Mr. Hall, was occupied by two houses, in which dwelt, in 1768, Joshua Snowden and Mrs. Duke. The Mercury Office was where the Mercury Office now is. It is the single instance all round the Market Square of a property remaining in the same family, and having the same occupation. A Mr. Whitton lived in Mr. Abel's house; a Mr. Wainwright where Mr. Johnson resides, and where Mr. Higgins now lives resided Mr. Breton, who was the Mayor in this stirring year. The ground now occupied by the Bank and Corn Exchange was covered by three houses and the Hind Yard. Next to the

Mayor, westward, lived a person named Hill; next to him a confectioner named Thomas Summerfield; then came the yard, and then the Hind Inn, occupied by one York. Mr. Jeffs' house was occupied by a person named Paine; Mr. Barry's was in the occupation of John Pinkard; and at the corner of Sheep Street and the Parade lived Henry Locock, an ancestor of the eminent living physician, honoured by Royalty itself. On the west side of the Market Square the occupant of every house is traceable. Victoria House was occupied by one Ellstone. Worthy Mr. Swallow, "mine host," of "The Trooper," was preceded in 1768, by one Widow Barker; Mr. Warr's "Lamp depôt" was occupied by a person named Chamberlin—in what line we do not know; a Richard Woolley had the next house, and John Taylor Mr. Bastick's; Edward Revell had the Queen's Arms Inn—not the Queen's Arms Inn then—in living memory it was the Windmill, and owed its present name to the accession of our gracious Queen. Mr. Moore's house was occupied by Sam. Easton; Mr. Bew's by Matt. Tanner; Mr. Emerton's by Thos. Cook; Mr. Rodbard's by John Revell; Mr. Douglas's by Thos. Percival; Mr. Bass's by Michael Dyer; Mr. Lay's by one Satchell; and Mr. Osborn's by Mrs. Greenaway. In Sheep Street, the site of Mr. Buxton's house was occupied by four small houses, which faced a garden wall opposite where Mrs. Horsey's house now stands. South of these four tenements lived Mrs. Thursby. Jeremiah Rudsdell, a surgeon of eminence, occupied the house at the north corner of the Hind yard, where Mrs. Savage now lives. College Street Chapel in those days appears to have stood in the rear of a large house belonging to a Mrs. Richards. The access to it was by a passage, called "Meeting House yard." "The Rev. Mr. Ryland," who was then minister of the chapel, lived at the south corner of St. Mary's Street, in the Horsemarket. Mr. Ryland had then just published "Neatly printed in one Volume, Duodecimo, price, bound, 2s. 6d.—'An easy introduction to mechanics, geometry, plane trigonometry, measuring heights and distances, optics, astronomy. To which is prefixed an essay on the advancement of learning by various modes of recreation, illustrated with twelve copper plates. For the use of schools as well as private gentlemen.' " Lower down in the Horse Market—nearer Mare Fair that is,—on the same side, lived a William Wykes, who was the proprietor of the ordinary means of travelling to and from London. He had a Post Coach, which set out from the George Inn, in Smithfield, at six o'clock every Monday, Wednesday, and Friday morning, and returned from Northampton to London at the same hour every Tuesday, Thursday, and Saturday. This (we presume) was the aristocratic conveyance, akin to the express trains on our railways. For the multitude, Mr. Wykes provided a Stage Coach, which set out on the same days at four in the morning. On the 30th of April there appeared a rival in the field. The "Publics' most obedient humble servants, Thomas Gregory and Thomas Doughty," started a "New Flying Stage Coach with Six Horses in one day, to and from London and Northampton." It does not appear that the public benefitted by the competition in the matter of increased speed, and we may therefore assume that Mr. Wykes accomplished in that respect all that was considered possible. Like the old vehicle, "The New Flying Stage" commenced flying at four in the morning, and going up, stopped at the Saracen's Head, Newport Pagnell, for breakfast, and at the Saracen's Head, St. Albans, for dinner. The fare was fourteen shillings inside, "Children in lap and outside passengers half price, with the allowance of fourteen pounds luggage, the exceedings to pay One Penny per pound." Passengers were taken up at the Red Lion, Peacock, and Angel. This rivalry sorely "riled" Mr. Wykes, who forthwith issued an indignant "Whereas," describing the new machine as being set up in "mere opposition from Election principles," and denouncing the "Performers" Doughty and Gregory, "the last of whom either shamefully deserted or was scandalously seduced from Mr. Wykes's service." Mr. Wykes voted for Howe. In the Horse Market also lived Joseph Young, a chimney-sweeper, who had rivals also, and advertized that "He carries on with Care and Diligence his usual Business of a Chimney Sweeper, and can assure the Publick that Persons advertising last week in this Paper, not having been bred to any Business, boldly assume That of Another, in which he was regularly bred and instructed, and which was derived down to him from his Ancestors." This sweep, with a long pedigree, was also a poet, and vindicated his claims to patronage in the following strains :—

> "In sable Dress I use the Art
> That's black, yet uncorrupt my Heart,
> No other Care disturbs my head
> Than that to earn and get my Bread.
> When Lords and Country Squires command,
> Myself and Imps are strict at hand;
> Smoke condens'd from every Hole I rake.
> Ready Pence for every Job I take,
> When out at Top my head I peep,
> I wake the Maids with "Chimney Sweep;"
> The Cook she brings a friendly Meal,
> The Butler waits with Horn of Ale.
> In every Place I'm welcome made,
> And brisk pursue my Sooty Trade."

There is at least ingenuity in the way in which the hospitable duties of the cook and butler are insinuated. In Mare Fair, the fine old house, lately belonging to Mr. Baker, appears to have been occupied by the Rev. Mr. Rogers, who was master of the Free Grammar School, and chaplain to Earl Spencer, who, in November of the same year, presented him to the Rectory of Brampton Ash, near Harborough. Mr. Woolly had the house belonging to the Free Grammar School, recently demolished. Mr. Woolly had a school opposite, at the corner of Pyke's-lane. In Gold-street, we find "Hill Gudgeon," a name familar in the Corporation Annals as a dealer at the Rose and Crown Inn in all sorts of grass seeds. In Bridge-street, the Angel was kept by Alderman Davis. Charles

Isham, Esq., had the house nearly opposite, where Dr. Francis now lives. John Davis, who was Lord Spencer's apothecary, lived in the second house in Bridge-street. In the South-quarter, the Courts, which are now numbered, were mostly named. The first, going southward from the Fleece, is Glover's Yard, the next Callis's Yard, then comes Taberner's Yard, and Widow Blett's Yard; on the West side is Manning's Yard. Attached to the name of one Edward Watts, in this neighbourhood, occurs the memorandum—"Took away and not polled,"—an incident indicative of the spirit in which the elections were carried on. Those were the days of "Wilkes and Liberty." The Northampton election commenced on the 17th March and ended on April 1. Osborn and Rodney, who were elected, polled each 611, and Howe 538. The total number polled was 1149, although it was estimated that the real electors did not exceed 930, so that no less than 219 persons contrived to vote who did not possess the franchise. The return was disputed, and Mr. Howe was declared to be elected. On the 22nd of February, in the following year, the successful petitioner was conducted into the town, says the *Mercury* of that date, "by the principal part of the inhabitants, with every demonstration of joy which the presence of the man of their choice could inspire. The decency and regularity preserved during the whole evening exceeded everything that could be expected." Mr. Taylor, of Gold-street, has, in connection with this election, a tobacco box with the words "Spencer, Howe, and Liberty" upon it, which every elector who voted for Howe received after the election. Howe was supported by Earl Spencer and Sir James Langham, and the two Sir Georges by Lord Halifax and the Earl of Northampton.

There are in the possession of Mr. Taylor, of Gold-street, some curious documents relating to this election. Some of the papers are the evidence in support of the petition against the return of Sir G. B. Rodney and Sir George Osborne—the two Sir Georges as they are called. Thomas Summerfield, the confectioner on the Parade, describes very graphically how, on a certain day.

there was a dinner at the Red Lyon (the site of which is now occupied by the two houses at the South-west end of Sheep-street), then kept by Martin Lucas, at which Lord Halifax and Lord Northampton were present, with the two Baronets, the Mayor, Bailiffs, and other friends. The company, he says,

> "Were very jolly, and many good healths drunk till about seven o'clock at night it was agreed to march round the town, to shew their friends that they were in high spirits, and to carry with them half a hogshead of ale, drawn upon a truck, in order to drink some healths at the Market Cross, and animate their friends. For this purpose about 200 links or torches were prepared, and lighted, and they all set out (the witness in company), the lords, candidates, and the Mayor at the head of them, with the Militia drums and fifes in full tune and colours flying; they paraded through many of the streets and lanes, and as they passed by the houses of Mr. Hamilton, Mr. Clarke, Captain Atkinson, or any other in the opposite interest, they stopt, howled, hissed, with other demonstrations of contempt and disapprobation of their conduct. This was repeated at the George Inn, where a few of the committee and friends of the opposite party were assembled, and then they went on to the Cross, and the lords, candidates, &c., each drank a mug of ale in a bumper—Success to the Town and Corporation of Northampton."

Returning by the George, a scuffle took place between the two parties, in which a few heads were broken, and the Lords' party had to retreat in confusion to their head-quarters, the Red Lion. Mr. Summerfield did not observe whether the Mayor either gave or received a broken head. At the Red Lion a debate was held (the parties, what with the dinner, the bumpers at the Market Cross, and the broken heads, being in an obviously peculiar condition for deliberation), the question being whether they should put up with the insult or revenge it. The conclusion at which they arrived was exactly what might have been, under the circumstances, anticipated. War was declared for, and everybody was ordered to arm with mop-sticks, brooms, faggots, or whatever they could get, and to put a piece of white paper in their hats to distinguish them. Some cooler head, however, than those of the majority, suggested that the Mayor should first go to the George, as ambassador to ascertain whether it should be peace or war; and the Mayor, accompanied by the Rev. Mr. Watts, went to the George accordingly. On his return he reported that the hostile committee would give no answer to the embassy, so out they sallied, armed as described. At the George they found the best part of one hundred persons of the opposite party standing in the gateway, about the house, and in the street, many of them armed with sticks. The Red Lion party, however, numbered above two hundred, and Mr. Gardiner, Chaplain to Lord Northampton, making a blow at some person (the first the witness observed given), a general engagement ensued. The Spencer party, finding themselves too weak for their opponents, retreated into the George gateway, leaving their antagonists in possession of the field.

"Lord Halifax then made a speech signifying that the town was his patrimony, and he would pitch his standard there. Then the friends of the Lords broke the windows of the George with stones and sticks, but the great gate being shut, they marched down Bridge Street, and then returned to the Red Lion, breaking several windows as they passed."

Mr. Summerfield's brother Joseph, who was a cooper, confirms generally the confectioner's account. "The Lords," he says, "when they got to the Market Cross, declared their intention of building a market cross, and giving £500 to the poor." As they went up Newland-street, at Captain Atkinson's the mob "hissed and howled very violently, and caused the ——'s March to be beat by the Militia drums and fifes." The wounded were taken to the Mayor's house to be dressed. The witness particularly remembered that the Mayor and Bailiffs attended this famous expedition :—

"Next morning," he continues, "a very large mob from the country consisting of the two Lords' tenants, labourers, and other dependants, to the number of 4 or 500 (as he believes), headed by their Lordships' domesticks armed with large clubs, and other offensive weapons, were brought into the town and quartered there, but Lord Spencer coming to town the same day, and finding the whole town in an uproar, went to the balcony of the George, and addressing himself to the populace personally and to his friends, desired they would desist from any acts of violence, and declared he would protect them from any insult, and would give them £1000 to be immediately distributed in bread, coals, and flour if they would go home and behave peaceably. And his Lordship procured a meeting the same day at the County Hospital, with the two Lords and their candidates, in consequence of which the mob were sent out of town immediately, Lord Spencer not leaving the town till he saw they were gone, and from that time there was no further disturbance until the election was over."

The date of these events is fixed by the evidence of Alderman John Davies, Lord Spencer's apothecary, who says the riot occurred on the 20th October, 1767, about eight in the evening. The witness saw it, he says, out of his own house, opposite to the George—the second house in Bridge Street from the corner of Gold Street. The corner house was occupied by Mr. Alderman Lyon, "An old gentleman of 74."

Both the Summerfields were originally partizans of the "Sir Georges," and Thomas, according to Joseph's evidence, furnished a large parcel of the faggot sticks with which the Sir Georges' mob were armed. How they came to change their colours is variously related. Joseph says he intended to serve "the two Georges" originally, "and used his utmost endeavour for that purpose till the beginning of December, when the witness was informed that several tradesmen who had long before that time been employed by the Lords' party and their friends in their several occupations were turned off because they would not vote for the two candidates, which the witness disapproved of, and represented the same to Mr. Litchfield, one of the Lords' agents, telling him that the witness was employed by many of the opposite interest, and if they proceeded in that manner to make removes in business he should be a very great sufferer in his trade, and they persisting in the manner of proceeding the witness left them." Thomas Summerfield states that he had resolved to give one vote for a third man, and on Lord Northampton declaring that he would not regard him as his friend if he did he finally determined to support Mr. Howe. A note with the pen run through it, however, says, "It is said this witness was arrested for £100, and carried to gaol about Christmas, 1767. That the Lords refused to pay the debt, and therefore he went over to the other side, who paid it, and came over to them." The proceedings altogether, indeed, seem to have been marvellously corrupt and violent. One witness had charge of a lot of voters at the Peacock, where three strong gates had been erected to keep them secure. The Mayor and one Alderman Gibson were open and violent partizans. Joseph Clark, a woolstapler, of Abington Street, one, apparently, of the most impartial witnesses, who threw away a small stick which he carried, lest he should be supposed to be a participator in the riot, says—

> "He saw several insults offered on both sides, but happening to be near the Mayor, who was hallooing 'Rodney and Osborn,' and perceiving a rude lad with a torch endeavouring to set fire to his wig, the witness took a great deal of pains to prevent him, and to protect the Mayor's person from insult, upon which Mr. Breton, turning round, and seeing him so near him, as the witness apprehends, mistaking his real intent, with great vehemence and passion thrust his hat in the witness's face, perfectly gnashing his teeth with fury. At the George he found many of his friends washing the blood from their heads, and bathing their bruises with brandy."

Reading these evidences, indeed, one feels that Hogarth's "General Election" was no caricature. There is nothing in the great humorist more extravagant than these incidents of the boy setting fire to his Worship's wig, and the washing and brandying scene at the George.

The Vision of Dry Bones.

"So I prophesied as I was commanded: and as I prophesied there was a noise, and behold a shaking, and the bones came together, bone to his bone.

"And when I beheld, lo, the sinews and the flesh came up upon them, and the skin covered them above: but *there was* no breath in them."

EZEKIEL XXXVII., 7, 8.

THERE was a vale, a lonely vale,
With summer's dainty flowers unstrown,
Where evening's winds made dreary wail
Mid wrecks of nations overthrown.

There was a shaking, and behold!
Dry bones were joined with fellow-bones,
And sinewy band and fleshly fold
Re-clad those dusty skeletons.

And from the south and from the north,
From spicy east and balmy west,
The breath of life, oh Lord, breathed forth,
And Israel lived at Thy behest.

The vision is no more—the type,
My God, hath living import still;
A time we know shall yet be ripe,
Fulfilling Thine Almighty will,

When earth must yield her buried dead,
And scattered dust with dust unite,
And, firm in hope, or shrunk in dread,
Stand in the whiteness of Thy sight.

So may we live that we may gaze
Unharmed upon that awful front,
And feel the scorching of its rays
As life from Love's celestial font.

Canon's Ashby.

The Seat of Sir Henry L. Dryden, Bart.

SPENSER, and Dryden, and Sam Richardson!
What hope of slumber in this haunted place:
The Faëry Queen, with all her Elfin race;
The Red-Cross Knight, Sir Calidore, Guyon,
The lion-hearted Una, harmed by none;
The phantom maiden, and the infernal chase;
The courtly Grandison's unequalled grace;
All these through dreaming memory would run.

'Tis like a holiday deep in the Past;
A backward journey into times gone by;
Life seems in antique moulds to be re-cast;
I hear of centuries dead the quaint, sweet sigh,
Share in their pageants and their revelry,
And doff my cap to Spenser, musing nigh.

Canon's Ashby is situate about thirteen miles S.W. of Northampton. The house was built at different periods. The Dryden arms on the old Hall doors show that they were first put up by Sir John Dryden, between his marriage in 1551 and his death in 1584. He married a daughter of Sir John Cope. The Poet was the eldest son of Erasmus Dryden, who was the third son of Sir Erasmus Dryden, of Canon's Ashby. There is a bust of the Poet in the Hall, which is said to be the model for the bust in Westminster Abbey. Aubrey states that Spenser, the poet, was a frequenter of Canon's Ashby; that there was a room there called Mr. Spenser's chamber; and that Spenser's wife was a kinswoman of Frances, the wife of Sir Erasmus Dryden, and daughter of William Wilkes, of Hodwell. Richardson, the novelist, was a friend of the family, and it is stated that a great part of "Sir Charles Grandison" was written here.

Carisbrook.

IF it had been our destiny
So much of worldly wealth to share,
My Mary, as had left us free
Where fancy willed to shelter there,
I would not seek a lovelier nook
Wherein to dwell than Carisbrook.

I clomb its castled heights to-day—
I looked from off its antique walls,
And golden fields beneath me lay,
And humble cot, and lordly hall;
And clusters of the hoary oak
Luxuriant spread by Carisbrook.

And hills remote, whose bosoms bright
Seemed panting in the noontide ray,
And lofty cliffs of dazzling white,
And ocean stretching far away,
Bounded a scene heart could not look
Unmoved upon. Sweet Carisbrook!

'Twas evening when, in musing mood,
I stood beside thy crystal spring,
And sought a holy solitude,
Through lane romantic wandering :
How calm and sacred didst thou look,
In that chaste twilight, Carisbrook.

And many a cottage home was there,
Embowered in vine and clematis :
Dear haunts, where sorrow's self would wear
Some sacred garb, some touch of bliss.
Had we but one such hallowed nook,
How blest were life in Carisbrook.

I've bade a fond farewell to thee,
Perchance to see thee never more ;
But should a better destiny
Thy wanderer's pathway brighten o'er,
Again, with happier gaze, he'll look
Upon thee, beauteous Carisbrook.

For then another heart than mine
Shall thrill thy loveliness to see,
And lips which are to me divine
Shall breathe their eloquence for thee.
And thou to me shall brighter look,
Companioned thus, sweet Carisbrook.

Forgive me, then, if still my soul,
When gazing on thy loveliest scene,
Avowed and felt one sad control,
And memory dropped her veil between.
Forgive me, if my way I took
Sighless from thee, sweet Carisbrook.

'Twas only love could work this wrong,
All colder cares I could deride;
And thou, when winter howls along
Thy peaceful vale, thy proud hill's side,
Shall find that, in my memory's book,
My heart has writ thee, Carisbrook.

The End.

DICEY, PRINTER, "MERCURY" OFFICE, NORTHAMPTON.